· THE WITCH ·

· THE WITCH ·

BY

HUGH FLEETWOOD

HAMISH HAMILTON
LONDON

HAMISH HAMILTON LTD

Published by the Penguin Group
27 Wrights Lane, London W8 5TZ, England
Viking Penguin Inc, 40 West 23rd Street, New York, New York 10010,
U.S.A.
Penguin Books Australia Ltd, Ringwood, Victoria, Australia
Penguin Books Canada Ltd, 2801 John Street, Markham, Ontario,
Canada L3R 1B4
Penguin Books (N.Z.) Ltd, 182–190 Wairau Road, Auckland 10,
New Zealand

Penguin Books Ltd, Registered Offices: Harmondsworth, Middlesex,
England

First published in Great Britain 1989 by
Hamish Hamilton Ltd

Copyright © Hugh Fleetwood 1989

1 3 5 7 9 10 8 6 4 2

British Library Cataloguing in Publication Data

Fleetwood, Hugh, 1944–
The Witch
I. Title
823′,914 [F]

ISBN 0–241–12700–9

Printed in Great Britain
by Richard Clay Ltd, Bungay, Suffolk

FOR
·ELDA FERRI & ROBERTO FAENZA·

CHAPTER 1

SIMPLICITY, Nora Mellon murmured to herself, as she saw the security guards standing by the door, and looked at the beige plastic posts she would have to pass through, that would sound an alarm if they detected anything unpaid for in her bag. Simplicity, head held high, eyes bright and forward looking, and a firm step. That is all there is to know, and all we need to know. Guard against pretension, listen for those alarm bells that warn of the presence of the stolen, and don't, if you can avoid it, wear make-up.

Three yards, two yards, one yard – and she was through, pushing open the glass doors and stepping out into the crowds of Kensington High Street, unfollowed, unsuspected, undenounced. Not that she had anything to be suspected of, or denounced for. She always expected to be challenged as she was leaving a store, nevertheless; and always felt she had won some sort of victory when she wasn't. A sense of guilt no doubt it was, she told herself as she proceeded along the High Street, a tall striking figure with white hair, clear blue eyes, and unblemished skin, wearing, as she invariably wore, fawn trousers, moccasins, a white shirt, and a dark blue Shetland sweater. A sense of guilt that was shared, moreover, by a great many people; for she had read that it wasn't at all uncommon: the sensation of having something to confess to, something to declare, when one saw a policeman, a customs officer, or a store detective.

In her case, mind you, the situation was complicated

somewhat by the fact that eyes came to rest on her more often than they did on other people. Eyes that seemed to ask: 'Don't I know you from somewhere?' or 'Aren't you what's-her-name, who was in whatever-it-was a few years back?' Now, for example, that Indian woman in her sari, with her two children and her exposed midriff: surely she didn't give everyone such an intense, almost accusing look. And that young Iranian or Egyptian or Iraqi. And those three middle-aged Englishwomen, who seemed to stop in their tracks when they saw her, and mutter amongst themselves. Obviously they could just have been looking at her because they could still detect in the figure and face of this sixty-ish woman traces of the beauty that had been hers when younger. Or because she was so white, so clear, so upstanding; so make-up-less, so simple. As it was possible that despite all her efforts to shake off the beast of vanity, so common in her former profession, it still clung to her with its sharp little claws; and in fact those passers-by were not staring at her with any more interest or frequency than they stared at anyone else. It was more likely however that she was vaguely recognized by a number of people who had once seen her on television, or in the theatre; and because they couldn't quite place her, or couldn't quite give a name to her, they not only gazed at her more insistently than they would, say, at Elizabeth Taylor or Glenda Jackson, but they looked at her as if she were to blame for being known yet, at the same time, unknown. Giving yourself airs and graces, she sometimes felt she was being told. Like to think you *are* someone, don't you? Stuck-up, affected cow. Well don't worry, ducky, we'll get you in the end. We'll teach you to think you're special. We'll teach you, for making us look at you.

There were store detectives and customs officers all round, lurking in the most unlikely places. Waiting to catch one out; waiting to discover just the tiniest packet of phoniness, condescension or dishonesty in the lining of one's bags. It was to stop herself being caught out that Nora had always clung to that faith of hers; and why she repeated, day in, day out, her creed. Simplicity, simplicity, simplicity: head held high, eyes bright, and a firm step.

She could still faintly hear this refrain running through her head some ten minutes later: when, opening the door of the red-brick late-Victorian mansion block in which she lived, she saw an envelope addressed to her propped up on the mantelpiece above the fireplace in the hallway. It must have come with the second post, she reflected, as she picked it up, noted the Italian stamp, and walked down the dark red carpeted corridor and unlocked the door of her ground floor flat.

She put her shopping away and lined her garbage pail with a Marks and Spencer's plastic bag before sitting down at her kitchen table and opening it.'Dearest Nora,' she read, 'how are you? It's been such a long time, and do forgive me for not having written before. However, I hope you will find the wait worthwhile in light of what I have to tell you.

'The other day, I was having lunch with Kostas Evangalides (I think I've spoken of him to you), who is starting a film in New York in a couple of weeks' time. It's got quite a big budget (for a largely Italian-financed film) and it's his first English language film, so understandably he's very nervous. Anyway, I was asking him who's in it, etcetera, and he said that was what was making him particularly nervous. Not only because he's got – or thinks he's got – Bette Davis to play a tiny part in it (just one day), and for the lead a new young stage actor from New York called Michael Toscanini – no relation to the conductor – who apparently is very brilliant and *extremely* difficult. But also because he's got some young rock singer who's never acted before – though according to Kostas is perfect for the part and anyway will bring in the kids – and – and this is the real trouble – because to get the rock singer, whose name is Jimmy X, he had to agree to give a part to Master X's girlfriend. A woman who is slightly older than Jimmy, and who, though an actress, and not a bad one K said, is entirely wrong for the part. In that while she has to play the role of a pathologically shy English girl who writes children's books ("or something," K said) in reality she is a blonde American actress who has only ever appeared in comedies or, once, as a gangster's moll. Also, though again, according to K, she is not nearly so featherbrained as she appears to be, she does not exactly look your bookish type. Apparently it's difficult to imagine her reading, let alone writing; even if she did give K a list of books she thought he should read. (He showed it to me. People like Grace Paley and Joan Didion. "I suppose she did it to impress me," he said. "I've never heard of any of these women.")

' "I'm mad," K told me, stubbing out what must have been his fiftieth cigarette of the lunch and tearing at his moustache. "The dame's going to ruin my film. I mean she's the pivotal character, according to the guy who wrote the screenplay. Some fucking English intellectual. But since I really want Jimmy . . . You should have heard the bums in Hollywood when I said I'd persuaded him to be in it. They were jumping up and down with excitement. So – "

' "What are you going to do?" I asked him.

' "Well, I suppose the only thing to do is find some upper-class English dame who'll sit by Judy the whole time and feed her her lines. And just hope that people don't burst out laughing when she opens her mouth. I mean did you ever see that Christawful film where Jacqueline Bisset and Candice Bergen were playing writers? I mean that was ludicrous. But they were fucking Virginia Woolf or Jane Austen, or someone like that, compared to what bloody Judy's going to be like. 'Oh I know this sounds like a cliché, Kostas,' she told me, 'but really I am a serious actress, and I want a chance to prove it.' Jesus. Jesus Christ. You don't know any upper-class English women who'd be prepared to make a dumb American blonde sound like a British pain in the ass, do you? Bunnie found me a couple of people in

L. A. to give her lessons, but Judy didn't like them – said they patronized her – and said Jimmy could teach her all she needed to know. Jimmy! He can't even speak English, let alone British. I mean he is English, but I must have someone on the set the whole time, to make sure. Because *I* can't hear if people are speaking proper English or not. I mean I can, but there are words and things – "

' "As it happens, Kostas," I told him, "I think I know exactly who you're looking for. She was an actress herself, she gives acting lessons and speech training in London, and her name is . . ."

'So, Nora, what do you think? In fact it isn't quite so entertaining as it sounds, as they're going to be doing all the location work in and around New York, and all the studio work at Cinecittà, in Rome – and this Judy only has dialogue in the studio. So there'd be no New York for you, only two months in Cinecittà in the summer. Which may be a bit grim. But Kostas will pay very well, the dates would be from July 2 to September 7 unless they run over, which they shouldn't, so that shouldn't interfere with your own schedule too much, and though I've no idea what the actors are like, Kostas himself is a real charmer. He's crazy, and unless he stops smoking as much as he does he may not last till July, let alone September. But he's a terrific director, is very intelligent in an intuitive sort of way, and – I think you'll like him. Also, joking apart, and whether with her boyfriend or someone else, apparently Judy has been studying "British" very hard over the past couple of months. So really your work shouldn't be too tough. Just a matter of sitting, listening, and correcting when and if necessary.

'Do give me a call if you're interested – I tried calling you a couple of times, but you were out – and try to come. Apart from anything else, it would be so nice to see you again. You could come up to our new place near Siena for the weekends; and if you prefer to stay in an apartment in Rome, rather than in a hotel, I'm sure there'll be no difficulty in finding you one.

'I hope James is well – is he still living in Canada? – trust the spring in England isn't too cold and wet – I read in the paper that it's been unusually bad – and look forward to seeing you. All my love, Franca.'

The second she put this letter down Nora knew she would accept; even though she didn't really think she should. Also, having accepted, she knew she would spend the next two and a half months, if not the next four and a half months, until the film was finished, regretting her decision. It was however just one of those offers that couldn't be refused, whatever its drawbacks and one's misgivings; and it would be absurd of her, not to mention pretentious, seriously to consider refusing. It was like being offered a plate of some very rare – some unique – food. One might be afraid it wouldn't agree with one; one might be afraid it would be fattening. But, just because it was unique, one had to taste it. Otherwise one was turning one's back on experience, on life itself; and to do that was not only a sin, but would undoubtedly in the long run do one far more harm than ever a plate of food could.

All the same, she told herself as she contemplated writing back to Franca, and then told herself no, she had better phone, she would have liked to refuse. She less and less liked leaving London, or Kensington, or her two-roomed high-ceilinged flat that she had decorated herself, and made most of the fittings for. A flat that was light – despite being on the ground floor, and looking out only over a white-painted brick wall – and easy to live in, and uncluttered. Also, and this she admitted was the more pertinent objection in this case, having given up acting five years ago, she hated to have any real contact with it. She didn't mind giving drama lessons and speech training to aspiring actors; in any case, mind or not, she had to, as she needed the money. But not once since she retired had she been to the theatre, and though she had a television – not owning a television was high on her list of pretensions – she only ever watched news and current affairs programmes, documentaries and nature films. To see people mouthing their way through scripts, be they good or bad, gave her a feeling of vertigo. They also, if she was not feeling absolutely well, and her eyes were not quite as bright and shining as she wished them to be, made her feel sick with anger, and resentment, and a sense of her own – she refused to say failure, but lack of recognition. She had been, still was, she was convinced, one of the foremost actresses of her generation; remarkable, in her opinion, for that very simplicity she prized so highly in her private life. No tricks, no affectations, no putting-it-on; that had always been her rule. And oh how, when she had seen others act, they had always put it on, used this or that little subterfuge to pull the wool over the eyes of their audience, been shameless in their use of masks. Yet those others, or some of them, were critically acclaimed, and had had long and successful careers. Whereas she, the high-priestess of austerity, had only ever been given roles as the stiff English rose type, when she was young, and, when she grew older, as the lonely, sexually repressed, middle-aged, middle-class or upper-class woman, isolated by her nature, her upbringing, and condemned never to achieve pathos – or anything better than the third lead – by her refusal to unbend enough to admit that she was isolated, lonely, sexually repressed or pathetic.

It was so unfair that it brought tears to her eyes when she allowed herself to think of it; which she didn't very often. And what really hurt was the fact that she hadn't been like that when young, yet was afraid she had become so simply by dint of being given, over and over again, such roles.

It would be agony for her, sitting on the set day after day, watching all those clowns going through their paces. Pretending that she was a real professional doing the job she was being paid to do, and that she didn't mind that it wasn't her under the lights being filmed, and that she was off to one side wasting the talents she had been born with.

She talked about sin, about turning one's back on life, and experience. That was the real sin, though: to turn one's back on one's talent; to turn one's back on one's *self*. That was more than a sin; that was a form of suicide. Yet she had done it; and in just two and a half months' time was going to have her nose rubbed in the fact that she had done it. Day after day, week after week. Watching her corpse dangling in the wind; and smiling, and keeping her chin up, and saying, in her light, clear, carrying voice, to whoever would listen: 'If there's one thing I can't stand it's people who aren't professional; who don't do the job they're paid to do, and shut up about the rest.'

Aware that another, less exalted reason for her acceptance of Franca's offer was that still, in her heart of hearts, whenever she met a director or producer she expected him to say, 'But, my God, I saw you in something years ago, you were fantastic, what do you mean you're retired, you're just the person I've been looking for and I've got the part of a lifetime for you,' Nora went to her telephone book, and looked up Franca's number.

CHAPTER 2

'G REAT,' Kostas shouted. 'Fantastic, Michael. Thank you.' He took a fresh cigarette out of his pocket, lit it from the one he was smoking, and dropped the butt onto the grass. 'How was it for you, Gianni?' he said, addressing his cameraman. Gianni, small, fair, and not given to expressing his enthusiasm, nodded.

'You want to do another one, Michael?'

Everyone was still, as the dark-haired young actor stared at Kostas as if he didn't know who he was, then looked down at his hands, to consider the nature of hands, or to reassure himself that they were still there. He appeared to hold his breath for a moment, before gazing at the camera to seek guidance for his answer there.

'No,' he said eventually, and bit his lower lip. 'I think that was okay.'

'Great,' Kostas repeated, as people moved again, unfrozen by the actor's words. 'Terrific. Okay, Marina, print that one, and the one before. The others are no good.'

The blonde, vaguely mole-like Italian script girl wrote something on the pad she was holding.

Kostas went over to his star and put an arm round his shoulder.

'You want to rest for a bit, Michael?' he said. 'The next set-up's going to take some time.'

'Kostas,' a quiet voice called from underneath a bare tree, on the edge of the yard in which they were shooting.

'Derek,' Kostas called to his director of photography, having heard that quiet voice but choosing to ignore it.

'How long do you think we need?'

The tall, huge-bellied Englishman looked around the yard, and out into the leafless wood on the other side of the road.

'Kostas,' the quiet voice called again. 'Kostas.'

'At least an hour and a half,' Derek replied; as a slim, very fair youngish man took off the headset he was wearing, hung it carefully on the side of the table on which his recording equipment was set out, and unhurriedly stood up. He made his way through the small group of people standing around the director – 'Excuse me, I'm sorry' – and positioned himself behind Kostas's left shoulder.

'Kostas,' he said, 'I'm sorry. That wasn't any good for me.'

Once again everyone – or everyone who had heard that murmured message – froze. They knew what was coming. Kostas stood there for a moment or two, as if he himself still hadn't heard. He closed his eyes in an expression of extreme pain. He sucked in so hard on his cigarette he smoked almost half of it in one breath. Then he threw that butt down too, bowed his head and rested his forehead on his clenched fist, and breathed out slowly.

'Fuck,' he said quietly, not looking at the newcomer, who remained still and unflinching behind him. 'Fuck, fuck, fuck you.' He allowed his voice to rise. Then at last he did turn. 'What do you mean?,' he bellowed. 'Why wasn't it any good? Why didn't you say – oh shit, shit, *shit*.'

'The camera noise was too loud,' the fair-haired man murmured, still quite calmly. 'I can't use it.'

'Why didn't you say?' Kostas repeated, almost shrieking now.

'It's usual for the director to ask sound if everything's okay,' the man said, even now managing to keep any rancour or note of reproof out of his voice. 'And I did try to tell you.'

'No,' Kostas suddenly said, starting to pace up and down as the entire crew watched his performance. 'No, I'm sorry,

Stefan, I won't. That was perfect. It'll never go as well again. If we've got any problems we'll just have to loop it afterwards. Jesus. Jesus Christ. If you can't manage to cut out a bit of camera noise – '

'Kostas,' Michael Toscanini interrupted, speaking still more quietly than Stefan, but instantly causing Kostas to stop shouting, 'if Stefan's not happy I'd like to do it again.'

For just one second Kostas considered continuing his explosion. He gave the slight handsome actor the briefest of 'I'll get even with you' looks. Then he sighed, 'All right, let's do it one more time,' and slouched back to his chair, his shoulders sagging under the weight of his knowledge that ultimately that twenty-six-year-old with the pale face, long black hair, and soulfully intense expression had more power on this set than he did.

'And, Kostas,' said Michael – who was also aware of his power, and would not be given 'I'll get even with you' looks by anyone, let alone a Greek director making his first feature in the States, 'please, don't ever tell an actor, "That'll never go as well again." How do you think anyone can give his best, after being told a thing like that?'

He looked down at his hands again; to make it clear he would require at least half an hour before he felt ready to shoot the scene again.

Stefan had behaved perfectly correctly: Kostas should have asked him if the take had been all right for sound, and anyway he had undoubtedly heard him the first time he had called, and known why he was calling. He felt nevertheless that he had behaved in a somewhat brattish way, and was sorry for it. He liked Kostas, liked him enormously, and didn't want to fight with him. But he also knew that if he didn't take a stand now, at the beginning of the film, and while they were still in the States, by the time they got to Italy no notice whatsoever would be taken of him, and his work would be useless. And rather than put up with a situation like that, he would quit the film, get another job, and not go to Italy. Since Al had set his heart on going to Italy, however, and he himself, having never been there, would also like to make the trip, he thought it better to make his point immediately, put up with an hour or two of Kostas's displeasure, and hope that after that things would go smoothly. Not too smoothly, of course; that would have taken the fun and the tension out of things. But smoothly enough for him not to have to cause scenes every day, and thus risk making himself look foolish or disagreeable in Al's, if no one else's eyes; and smoothly enough for him not to incur Al's real anger by announcing that he was sorry, but it was impossible for them to make the trip.

'The fucking Russian,' Kostas called him from then on. Not to his face; but since, when he had his headset on, and Al's microphone was plugged in, Stefan heard more or less every word, every whisper that was spoken on the set, it might just as well have been. To his face, Kostas merely said gloomily, 'Hi, Stefan,' when he arrived in the morning, and thereafter only spoke to him at the end of every take, muttering, or shouting, depending on the day, but always with heavy irony: 'All right, Stefan?' or 'Okay, Stefan?' Or, if he was feeling in a particularly good mood, 'Tell me that was no good, Stefan, and we'll do it again.' Then he would mooch back to his chair, light yet another cigarette, and sigh. 'Jesus. Jesus Christ. Fucking Russian. Fucking sound people. I hate 'em.'

Despite this limited communication between them Stefan remained fond of Kostas – grew fonder of him with every day that passed – and, by the time the first three weeks of shooting were completed, he was looking forward almost unreservedly to the two months he was to spend in

Italy. It wasn't that he felt that Kostas precisely respected him for standing up to him; Kostas wasn't the type for that sort of boy scout morality. Just that he couldn't help feeling that, for all the names Kostas called him, Kostas was fond of *him*; and that, whether he was or not, the Greek director had an energy and a charm that were irresistible. Short, overweight, his long dark straggling hair flecked with grey, he stormed up and down the whole time – when he wasn't flinging down tragically in his chair – announcing that he couldn't go on, that this fucking film was never going to be finished, that the make-up man was a jerk, that Derek the D.P. didn't respect him, and that he should never, never have chosen Jimmy to play the part of a rock singer because, though that was exactly what he was, he couldn't act his way out of a paper bag, and had about as much charisma on screen as a week-old Big Mac or some bum from the slums of Liverpool or Manchester or Birmingham, or wherever it was that English rock stars hailed from.

'Christ Almighty,' he would say about five times a day to the blonde Marina, who was one of the few people on the set he never insulted, or shouted at, or thought was out to get him just because he wasn't an intellectual, 'like all those other bullshit directors'. 'Christ Almighty, will you look at him – ' pointing at the young white-faced stringy-haired Englishman. 'He looks like trash, he sounds like trash, he acts like trash. He's going to make this film a comedy, instead of a tragedy, or whatever the hell it is.'

'Oh fuck off, Kostas,' Jimmy would generally laugh at this; though occasionally he was hurt by Kostas's jibes, and would have to be comforted and cosseted and told it wasn't true, he was great, he was going to be fantastic. 'Just 'cos you're some Greek git who was brought up on the wrong side of the tracks, that doesn't mean that everyone else is shit. You want to be a fucking white man, like Stefan there. But you're not, and you never will be. So just fuck off, and keep your comments to yourself. It's hard enough bloody acting, without you farting away there. " 'Eee loooks like trash.'' Takes trash to recognize trash, Kostas, ya bloody wop. Now put out yer cigarette, and let's do that again.'

Almost the only other person on the set, apart from Marina, whom Kostas never insulted, was his star. Though while he never insulted Marina because she was gentle, sweet, formidably efficient and not least blonde, and he clearly found her more attractive than in the public arena of the set he might have liked to, he never insulted Michael because he was in awe of him, because the young man was extremely reserved or extremely unfriendly, according to one's point of view, and because, above all, he didn't like him.

In private, to Derek or to Jimmy, he would mutter, confident of being overheard by no one except Stefan and Al, 'I can't stand that guy. He thinks he's too good. Jerk. If you ask me, he's not that great.'

One day, soon after Stefan had had his run-in with Kostas, the actor had insisted on re-shooting a scene twenty-six times. He had to come out of a house, walk over to a car, stand by it for a second listening to the radio, and ask the person sitting in the car, 'What did they say?'

For the first ten takes he couldn't decide whether to say, 'What did they say?', 'What did he say?', 'What did that say?', or simply, 'What was that?' For the remaining nineteen, after he had decided that the line was best as written, he couldn't get the inflection he wanted. 'Sorry, Kostas,' he would murmur, as soon as Kostas shouted, 'Cut.' 'That's not it. I mean my life may be in danger. I – I mean I know what happens because I've read the script, but standing here listening *I* don't know yet. And – let's do it again.'

And again, and again, and again. As the crew, on a sunny but cold May day stood around by the water's edge on the end of Long Island, and everyone made a conscious effort not to lose their temper.

'Oh shit,' 'Oh not again,' 'I don't believe it,' ran,

however, like a barely audible but constant chorus being hummed beneath the sound of the waves, the cries of sea-gulls, and the sound of feet being stamped up and down as people tried, in vain, to keep warm.

When, after the twenty-sixth take, Michael declared himself satisfied, said, 'Thank you, everybody,' and gazed not at his hands but at the ground, as if after all that effort he might discover the secret of creation, Kostas stood up, went over to Gianni, the cameraman – who nodded without being asked – and came over to Stefan.

'I think,' Stefan murmured, 'if I told you that was no good you would kill me. So – that was perfect, Kostas. Perfect.'

Kostas put his arm round Stefan's shoulder; he grunted to Marina, 'Print it, Marina. Just that last one;' and the crew applauded.

Aside from the fact that he had never been there and had always wanted to, there was a further reason why, at the end of the first three weeks of filming, Stefan was looking forward almost unreservedly to going to Italy. And that was: Marina. With the exception of the make-up man and the hairdresser – who claimed she was officious and rude, because she had twice reproved them for not being on hand when they should have been and were needed – and to a certain extent Derek the director of photography – who suspected her of suspecting him of indeed not respecting Kostas, and ever so subtly patronizing him – the blonde script girl was universally liked, and for most of the same reasons that Kostas liked her. She was efficient without ever, despite what make-up and hair said, being officious. She was always good-humoured; even if she, like everyone else, sometimes lost her temper. And she was, to men and women alike, attractive, with her longish corn-coloured hair generally pulled back in a rough pony-tail, her nearly but not quite plump figure, and her mole-like air that derived less from her features than from the sense she always gave of having just emerged from some warm dark burrow, and still having the security of the earth about her as she surveyed the world.

If, however, the young Italian woman was almost universally liked, and everyone from the third grip to Kostas and the second assistant electrician was happy to eat his lunch with her, or just chat to her for a minute or two – even Michael Toscanini had been known to stand and talk to her about matters unrelated to work – it was Stefan whom Marina herself seemed to have chosen as her special friend on the set. Stefan, and to a certain inevitable extent, Al: 'my boom man, my right-hand man, my other half' as Stefan had introduced his microphone operator to her on the first day of shooting, with a shy, nervous laugh. It went without saying that after fourteen years in the business – seven in his native Russia, seven here in the States – Stefan knew that one always formed friendships when working on a film. Friendships that in the enclosed environment of the set, and under the pressure of the long hours and frequent tension, flared up with sometimes alarming intensity, and made one certain that this time it was a friendship that was going to last for life. Generally they had died down to barely smouldering ash well before shooting was over; almost never did they endure beyond the last day. Yet, perhaps because once before there had been an exception to this rule, with a part of himself Stefan remained optimistic. And by the beginning of that third week he was telling himself, 'No, this is not just another of those set friendships. For the second time in my life I have found someone who is going to remain a friend. Moreover, I don't feel that our relationship has suddenly burst into flame – into a flame so hot it is bound to burn itself out – rather that from the moment I met Marina we started, as if it were the most natural thing in the world, placing little bricks on the ground. Little bricks of feeling, of understanding, of humour, of kindness, that will eventually, if we are careful and work at it, form a wall around us, and enclose us for the rest of our lives.'

It somehow became natural that the three of them should eat together every night in the hotel where they were staying while on location; and, as the other members of the cast and crew teamed up and formed themselves into cliques and groups, so it became recognized that the sound man, the boom man and the script girl formed a trio.

Quite why Marina had chosen him as her special friend on the set, when she could have chosen practically anyone – including, possibly, the precious Mr. Toscanini – Stefan had no idea. Perhaps it was because they were both Europeans; though both agreed there was nothing worse on an American set than doing 'the European bit', and both hoped sincerely that they didn't. Perhaps it was because Marina felt sorry for him for some reason, and wanted to draw him out. Or perhaps, simply – and this was the most obvious explanation – it was because they did get on well together, did, practically from the moment they met, feel so at ease with one another, and did so immediately feel they understood one another.

Yet if, at the end of three weeks, Stefan was looking forward almost unreservedly to their European transfer, by the beginning of the fourth week, after a weekend spent driving up the New England coast, his reservations had started to grow.

It had been, by and large, a wonderful weekend; one of the best Stefan could remember. As soon as filming had finished on Friday they had driven down to La Guardia and caught the shuttle to Boston, where they had slept. Next morning he and Al had spent a couple of hours showing Marina the city, then they had hired a car and set off north. The weather, after those first unseasonably cold weeks of May, suddenly improved, the thermometer rising in a matter of hours from the upper forties to the lower nineties. The air became dry and clear; and all the trees and bushes, that had been waiting in half-bud apparently uncertain whether to open, and face freezing even at this stage of the year, seemed to be turning green in front of one's eyes.

Al, as always when they were travelling together, drove; and sitting in the back of the car, watching his boom man's neck beneath his thick, smooth black hair, and watching Marina turn to him and say something, and then turn right round and say something to *him*, Stefan felt that if he had been able to he would have cast a spell on this moment, and made it last forever. They would have just driven, the three of them, on and on and on; talking about this and that, laughing, listening to music – rock or folk or jazz for Al, classical for Stefan, 'whatever you like' for Marina – occasionally stopping for meals, and to go for walks along deserted beaches, or through white-painted villages where people were thin and tended to look good-humoured but earnest.

This is what I came to America for, Stefan told himself, knowing he was being absurd and frivolous, yet unable not to think it anyway. To do a job I like, working with people who on the whole are interesting or fun, and then to be able to take off like this, go away and be with people with whom I can relax completely. Oh, Al, Stefan wanted to ask, finding it almost beyond him not to stretch out and touch that neck that he could just glimpse through the glistening black hair that covered it, or the arms that shone white out of the tee-shirt Al was wearing: Oh, Al, aren't you happy? And Marina, whom I really hardly know, yet feel I've known for years, aren't you, too, happy? He didn't ask it, naturally; he didn't need to. He knew the answer. He would have liked to, nevertheless, and then have stopped the car, done a sort of dance with them, embraced them, and then –

As if knowing what he was thinking, and not wanting him, for the moment, to go beyond that 'then', Marina leaned over, stretched out, and squeezed his hand. 'I'm so glad I met you,' she said, glancing at Al to let him know that it was the plural you she was using. 'I'm feeling so happy right at this moment I don't think I'd mind if I died.'

Al, at the wheel, glanced back at Marina, as if to say, I know exactly what you mean, and that's just how I feel; Stefan, unable to resist any longer, allowed himself very briefly to rest a hand on Al's shoulder, and squeeze it; and for just a second, as Stefan exchanged looks with Marina – looks of absolute intimacy that did now exclude Al – he felt that here, in this car, he had touched perfection. The three have become one, he told himself; we have all, all of us, loved, and if I live for another ten, thirty or fifty years, and lose touch with Al and Marina, or even fall out with them, I know, without the slightest doubt, I shall never forget this moment.

They checked into a motel in Rockport that evening; a purple and yellow affair overlooking the beach, only a couple of years old but already dilapidated; and there, in the large bleak restaurant that looked emptier than it was, they told each other the story of their lives. That is: Marina merely recounted how she had started working in films ('My brother was a production manager'), and how she had been briefly married to an Englishman ('Also a production manager'); Al gave a not much longer summary of the twenty-nine years of his on the whole not very eventful existence; and Stefan told the story of *his* life. And told it, while he was about it, at great length.

He told them – or principally Marina, since Al had heard the story many times before – about his parents: his mother a one-time lecturer in English literature at Moscow University, his father a former political correspondent for *Pravda*, and an amateur photographer. He told them about his childhood; about growing up as a member of what in Russia counted as the jeunesse dorée. He told her how, largely as a result of this upbringing and the fact that he had the chance to see things that were barred from the majority of his fellow countrymen, he had conceived a passion for American films; to the extent that by the age of fourteen he had decided that if he had to kill in order to achieve this end, one day, somehow, he was going to go to America and work in films himself. ('Can you imagine? The son of what in Russia would be called a "good family" going on about the colour values of *Gentlemen Prefer Blondes*, about Robert Wise's betrayal of Orson Welles in changing the end of *The Magnificent Ambersons*, about – oh, I don't know, the influence of German expressionism on Douglas Sirk.') And he told them how he had set about putting his decision to leave into practice; even though he knew that his parents, whose only child he was, and who adored him, would insist on following him to the West if and when he managed to get there, despite their having to lose everything, abandon everything they had worked their whole lives for, in order to do so.

'I was young,' he murmured to his plate.

It took the Bischov family seven years to get permission to leave from the time they first declared openly that they wanted to. Seven years during which Stefan's parents did indeed lose everything – and both spent periods in prison as well. During which the son, despite his parents' disgrace, managed to enrol in film school, where he found himself specializing in sound more by accident than design, and starting to work. ('The authorities thought it was my mother and father who had become disaffected. I was looked on as a nice Russian boy who had been led astray. After all, didn't I have the normal tastes of every nice Russian boy? Hitchcock, Howard Hawks, Nicholas Ray . . .') And by the end of which, while the parents had nothing to look forward to in the country to which they were so unwillingly emigrating, the son had already made contact with a dissident producer living in New York, who guaranteed him work almost the second he stepped off the plane.

'You know why I think we did finally get permission to leave? Not because of all the strings we pulled, or because my mother had a cousin in Florida who was prepared to sponsor us or guarantee us or something. Just because eventually the K.G.B. realized the truth. Or anyway realized that my parents were dreading leaving. And so, to punish them, or to spit in the faces of all those thousands of people who would have given their right arm to be able to emigrate to the States – off we were sent.

'My mother teaches Russian now, in Brooklyn,' Stefan concluded. 'And my father takes photographs of weddings and bar mitzvahs. They're still no happier, but – what can you do?'

There were various reasons for Stefan's telling this story at such length. For a start he enjoyed telling it, and felt that every time he did it reminded him of what he owed his parents, and either made him feel less guilty about his having dragged them away from Russia, or, satisfyingly, more guilty. Then: he wanted to deepen his intimacy with Marina, and achieve some sort of physical contact with Al, as he always felt he did when he hauled out his past and exposed it to his boom man. But he told it mostly, tonight, because he wanted to put off for as long as possible the moment when he, Marina and Al had to get up from the table: and go to their rooms, and to bed.

They had taken two rooms, in both of which there were two double beds. When they had arrived, however, they had simply dumped their bags inside one of the rooms, and not thought – or not talked – about who was going to sleep where. The night before, in Boston, the two men had shared a double room in a hotel, and Marina had slept in a room by herself. And, had he been asked about it earlier, Stefan would have said that this would have been the arrangement for tonight, too. As, he was sure, would the others, had they been asked. Only so well had they all got on together today, and so happy had they been, that, now that the moment of decision was at hand, he wasn't certain if this arrangement was still standing.

In one way he didn't mind, in that he felt that, by not sharing a room with Al tonight, he would make it plain to

Marina, in the most obvious yet most discreet fashion, what his relationship with his boom man was. Of course she had almost certainly understood already; as anyone who was remotely interested in him or Al must have understood. But as he liked her so much, and felt that if they were to become true friends it was important that there should not be even the chance of any misunderstanding, he wanted to make quite sure that she did; and to do so without taking her aside and saying, solemnly: 'Now listen Marina, I have to make something clear.'

Somewhat ominously, he saw that Al too wanted to make sure Marina understood without the slightest doubt how matters stood; and that, if it had never occurred to him before to draw attention to the fact that while they were on location they occupied separate rooms, now he was at some pains to. He had, over the course of the afternoon and evening, made two comments upon it. Asking Marina what her room in the motel where they had been staying this last week had been like, and letting slip that Stefan had managed to grab the best room in the place for himself; then announcing that he hoped he would sleep well tonight because last night Stefan had been talking to himself 'over in his bed', and he'd kept him awake much of the time.

'I just can't sleep if someone's making any sort of noise,' he said. 'Thank God this movie's got a reasonable budget. Sometimes we do small independent productions that are trying to cut costs, and have to sleep in the same room for up to a week at a time. Jesus, it drives me crazy. It drives him crazy, too,' he said, gesturing towards Stefan. 'It's his Russian soul. Needs solitude. He generally makes sure he gets it, what's more.'

This insistence of Al's on drawing attention to something that he normally didn't consider worth mentioning had much to do with why, if in one way Stefan didn't mind the uncertainty over the sleeping arrangements, in another way he minded a great deal.

Stefan had met Al within six months of his arrival in the

States, and had, he supposed, though he hated saying this to himself, 'fallen in love' with him almost from the moment he saw him. Fallen in love with his looks: his long black hair, his stocky physique, his air of having just stepped off the side of a Greek vase. Fallen in love with what he saw as his essential good sense and unfailing good taste: to him Al was incapable of vulgarity of thought or feeling, just as he was incapable of true stupidity, for all his lack of formal education and culture. He had fallen in love with him above all, though, for his profound kindness and gentleness. Qualities that according to him had nothing to do with weakness – Al was as capable as the next man of acts that required physical courage, or a show of strength – but had a great deal to do with his understanding of the world, and of the position and condition of people in this world. Al knew about fear, disappointment and loss; and knew, however they were disguised, that they were part of the baggage of every creature on earth.

Yet despite his having so fallen under Al's spell, and against all the odds remained so, Stefan had never once entertained the thought of him and Al becoming lovers. The idea was preposterous. Al had his girl-friends, and in particular Su; a Chinese American art director with whom he had had a daughter; Stefan made other arrangements. That was how matters stood between them, and it would have been an unforgivable lack of taste on his part if he had ever questioned this. He felt faint sometimes, and almost physically sick with the desire to touch Al, or take him in his arms. But never once did the thought that someone else might be doing just that, or even the sight at times of someone else doing just that, trouble him, make him jealous, or make him wish that things were not as they were. Their friendship, or aspects of it, might have been unusual; but it was a friendship that suited him, and satisfied him – made him, taken in conjunction with his work, think he couldn't have been more satisfied – and was one that he wouldn't have changed a single detail of even if

· 23 ·

he could have.

Why then, as it became apparent to him over the course of that afternoon and evening that Al was becoming seriously attracted to Marina, did he feel disturbed? He should have been delighted; and, now that dinner was over, have said that he was tired and was going to sleep, but why didn't they take a walk? He could have gone to the room where they had left their bags, taken what belonged to him, and then gone into the other room; thus allowing Al and Marina to make what arrangements they liked. If they wanted, they could stay together; if not, Al could say 'see you in the morning' and go to sleep in the other bed in Stefan's room. The person he was closest to in the world; going with, possibly forming a relation with, a person who had struck him, from the moment he had met her, as being amongst the nicest people he had met in a very long time. It was ideal.

Or it would have been: had it not become equally apparent over the course of that afternoon and evening that Marina was not seriously attracted to Al – viewing him only as an extension of the sound department off the set as well as on – but was, on the contrary, starting to view him, Stefan, as a very special friend indeed. As special a special friend as he looked on Al as being . . . Of course it was absurd to worry about such matters, and almost certainly Al was well aware of Marina's feelings. So that, while he might wish things had been ordered otherwise, he would hardly consider the little triangle as anything other than the comic affair it was. And yet, and yet, Stefan couldn't help telling himself – as a waitress brought the check and he said no, please, tonight was on him – from such foolish beginnings do tragedies spring; and, should by any chance Al *not* be aware of Marina's feelings, he might be so hurt when he did discover the truth that a little pile of earth might appear on the ground between him and the man he looked on as being not merely a friend, but a kind of brother and father too. A pile of earth that with time might become a range too

· 24 ·

high to cross. And if that happened . . .

Just the thought made Stefan feel cold; and feel, as he almost never did, a certain homesickness for Russia. What was more, he went on, looking out of the large curtainless windows towards the dark, invisible sea, if the molehill did start threatening to develop into a mountain, he could see no way that was not ridiculous, or evil, to stop it doing so. Ridiculous it would be were he to announce to Al that they were quitting this film and going off to work on another; evil, were he to start pretending to Marina that he didn't like her, and wanted nothing more to do with her. Not only ridiculous and evil: counter-productive as well. Because, if Al's failure to realize how Marina felt might cause damage to their friendship, how much greater damage would be caused by a gesture that in Al's eyes would have been made only to keep him and Marina apart. Oh, the whole thing was impossible, Stefan told himself, and maybe the best thing to do would be –

He could think of no best thing to do, and merely smiled and said yes, he was feeling fine, he'd just been miles away for a moment, when Marina asked him if he was all right.

In fact the problem as to who was going to sleep where was solved without any problem: as soon as they opened the door of the room where they had left their bags, Marina picked up hers, took the key of the room next door from the shelf where Al had left it, and said that she was going to take a shower, brush her teeth and change into her night-dress – and then, if they didn't mind, would come back to their room and watch the television with them. All of which she did; and thus was able to note, if she cared to, that by the time she came back Stefan and Al had retired to their separate beds, in one of which Al was intent on writing a postcard to his daughter. Nevertheless, and despite the fact that the following day was still more sunny and glorious than the Saturday had been, and the three of them, perhaps because they had all been thinking about their relationship, felt still closer and at one, Stefan wasn't able to rid himself of the fears that had come to him. Indeed, he became more afraid than ever that some sort of trouble might lie ahead; and by the time they got back to the motel in Southampton that night, to join the rest of the crew, he had such an attack of 'Russianness' that he had to call his parents, just so that he could talk his native language, and they could all, if unspokenly, commiserate with each other on their exile.

It was also because Stefan had this grain of doubt chafing away inside him that he wasn't, from then on, able to look forward with unreserved pleasure to their transfer to Italy. What if things do go wrong, he found himself thinking occasionally; and, instead of evenings spent eating outside in welcoming restaurants, and weekends spent going to places I've always wanted to go to, everything does turn to ashes? And what if days I have been thinking of as likely to be among the best in my life turn out to be the worst?

Still, reservations or no, on the whole Stefan continued to look forward to going to Italy; and with the distractions and problems of work managed to confine his Russian moments to just the odd minute, or half-hour, a day. Most of the time, between that week in New England, and the day they all left for Rome, he felt himself only, as he had in the car driving up to Rockport, the luckiest of men. To have not just a job he loved, in a country he loved; but to be able to do his job with a person he loved, and to meet people through his job who came to love him.

How, he asked himself, could he not have counted himself lucky? It would have been a sin.

CHAPTER 3

'H ALLO, I am Stefan.'
'ʼAllo, Stefan, I am Mauro. And this is my friend
Bruno, and that fat guy over there with the moustache is
Sergio, who doesn't understand English.'

'Hi, Bruno.'

'Hi, Stefan, pleased to meet you.'

'Hallo, Sergio.'

'Buongiorno, Mr Stefan. Come va?'

'He says how are you? How are things?'

'Fine. Very good. Thank you. Grazie.'

'Bene,' Sergio beamed, bowing from the waist. 'Parla
italiano?'

'No, no,' Stefan blushed, and smiled. 'I'm sorry.'

'That's okay,' Bruno said, and explained to Sergio how
Mauro had described him.

'Non e' un gentleman,' Sergio pronounced gravely.
'Come lei, signor Stefan.'

He smiled, bowed again, and resumed hammering a
sheet of plywood to the floor.

It was the first day in Rome; and, as always on the first
day on a new set, Stefan felt it was like starting at a new
school. Or perhaps, in this case, since some of the people
on the set were Italian, and some had come over from the
States, like starting a new term at an old school, after a
break in which a number of the pupils had left, and a
number of others had joined. Stefan had lost count of the
films he had worked on; it must have been getting on for
twenty since he'd arrived in America. But, every time he

started a new one, the first day gave him a rush of energy, and a sense of wonder. There were new people to be met, new problems to deal with, new stories to be heard; and there was above all that sense of becoming, for better or worse, a member of a team, or of a family. Everybody had their job to do; some people working almost constantly while others worked in bursts and then were obliged to sit around doing nothing, sometimes for hours on end. But they were all moving forward towards one goal, everyone, however small his role, however humble her task, had a job that was in some way essential, and all knew that if they didn't carry out that job correctly, they could hold up the entire making of the film, costing the producers a great deal of money – something they didn't, on the whole, care about – and, what did tend to worry them more, rendering useless the efforts of forty, sixty, possibly hundreds of other people.

Moreover today, since this was the first time he had worked in Italy, he was feeling particularly excited. He hadn't known how things would be, how he would be treated; and whereas Al, who spoke Portuguese, Spanish, and a smattering of Italian, always managed to get on with everyone, he knew that sometimes people found him reserved, even stand-offish, and didn't know what to make of him as he sat, pale and blond, always away to one side.

So far, however, he had to admit he had met nothing but friendliness; and it struck him, as it had struck him when he had first started working in the States, that essentially film crews the world over were the same. All right, large dark moustachioed Sergio, who must have been getting on for sixty, bespectacled young Bruno, who spoke such good English and would clearly 'go far', and small elf-like curly-haired Mauro, who was obviously the self-appointed court jester, were unmistakably Italian in appearance. But apart from that they could have been scene-shifters, carpenters or electricians – grips and gaffers – anywhere. As could the make-up men, the hairdressers, the prop man, the set-dresser, and everyone else whom Stefan hadn't seen before.

He checked one final time to make sure that all his equipment was in order; looked over at Marina, who was sitting on a sofa in the middle of the vast set, talking with Kostas; and noted that Al was talking to the new cameraman and his focus-puller as if he had known them for years. (Gianni, the Italian cameraman in New York, didn't like working in his native country, and had at the last minute refused to make the trip home.) Then he glanced at his watch – it was eight-thirty – took a candy from his pocket, and wondered who else he had to meet, and hadn't said hello to yet. Not many people, he thought; which was a relief. Not because he didn't like to meet people, or because he cared whether there were fifty or a hundred people on the crew. Just that he wanted to be sure he hadn't failed to say hello to anyone, and thus be thought of as a snob. He had heard that in France everyone shook hands with everyone else every morning; and not to do so was considered bad form. A story he had his doubts about, and thought preposterous if true. Nevertheless, it was important, particularly on one's first morning, not to put people's backs up; and, if one was going to live in an extended family for a couple of months, one had, initially at least, to treat all the members of that family as equals. Of course some were more equal than others: it was essential to say good morning to Kostas, to the director of photography, to the leading actors; it was merely polite to say good morning to everyone else. Since, however, he was a great believer in good manners and in being correct, Stefan tried to exclude no one from his greetings, and thought that if he did, as he inevitably would, find some people on the crew less pleasant than others, it would not be he who initiated hostilities.

'Hi, Stefan, how you doing?'

Stefan turned to see the young American still photographer, who had also been on the film in the States, putting down his camera case, and looking round the set.

'Hi, Alan,' he said. 'Did you have a good flight?'

'Sure.' Alan frowned. 'It's a great set, isn't it?'

Stefan nodded. 'Yes, I guess. But if we're just going to be on this one set for five or six weeks, we're going to get pretty bored with it.'

'Oh, I don't know. There are all those side chapels, vestries, pulpits and things.' Alan shrugged. 'How d'you like the hotel?'

Stefan nodded again, and wondered why Alan made him slightly nervous. Possibly because like Michael Toscanini – though he was very different physically – he was just a little too good-looking. There was something cold, complete-in-itself about him; about his golden hair, blue eyes, sun-tanned skin, perfect features. He gave off, as it were, no light; or, being so good-looking, didn't need the approving eyes of the world to make him so. It wasn't that he was conceited; far from it. He was hard-working, modest about his undoubted talent as a photographer, and still more unfailingly polite and smiling than Stefan himself. It was just, Stefan thought, that there was no suggestion of fallibility about him. Looking at Al, one could already see autumn in him; disillusion, running to seed, putting on weight. Hence the sadness in his eyes, the gentleness deriving from the knowledge that what would happen to him would happen to most men. To most men – but not to Alan Miller. He, moulded by an ideal hand, would never run to seed; nor, should he live to be ninety, would there ever be weakness in him. Morally, physically lean, he would get through life without ever compromising; and would be as daunting as an old man as he was when young. Whether he would always be as charming remained to be seen; if, under that smooth and perfect exterior, he was in fact charming now. Charm, however, was not a quality required of the cold; nor did they need it to get by. It was the Als of this world who needed that, and the Marinas; and probably, Stefan thought, the Stefans. All

· 30 ·

those people who, without it, might have brought condemnation and rejection upon themselves: for being, simply, human.

'It looks like it's going to be a while before we start,' Stefan murmured. 'Judy isn't even down yet.'

'Have you seen her?'

'No, not this morning. Not since I arrived. Have you?'

'Yeah,' Alan said. 'I just went to her dressing room to say hello. She's sort of nervous now she's really got to start acting. You realize for the next two weeks it's almost all just her. All the heavy stuff. She's scared people are going to say she only got the job because of Jimmy.'

'She did.'

'Yeah, I know. But she's been acting for years. It's just that she's never acted British before. I mean, not just, but – she's afraid she'll sound ridiculous. I said don't worry, lots of British people do too. I don't think that went down too well. Also Kostas doesn't have much faith in her.'

'Kostas doesn't have much faith in himself.'

'I know, but he lets her see he doesn't. It doesn't help matters. The trouble is *he's* nervous about her British accent, because he can't really hear whether it's right himself.'

'She's got a dialogue coach, hasn't she?'

'Sure. Two. One to help her with the dramatic stuff, the other just to keep tabs on her accent. Some English woman. I haven't seen her yet. According to Kostas she's very grand. I don't think he likes her. He just met her yesterday apparently. Actually I sort of gathered,' Alan smiled, a gleam of pleasure coming into his clear blue eyes, 'Judy doesn't like her either. I think she feels intimidated by her. They all had lunch together at Judy's hotel, and Judy said she made her nervous she was holding her knife and fork in the wrong way.' He smiled again. 'Don't you love it, Stefan? There'll be blood on the sand before the week's out. I hope so, anyway. There's nothing more dreary than a set where everyone behaves well and no one falls out.' He looked around. 'I must go say hello to Al. Do you think it's okay if I leave my stuff here? I don't really like to, but – '

'I'll keep an eye on it,' Stefan said. 'I'm not going to move from here.'

'Thanks,' Alan nodded. 'I'd appreciate that. I mean I'm sure it would be okay, but I got ten thousand dollars' worth of cameras here. And you never know, do you? I mean you only need one amongst this crowd of merry men to be light-fingered, and bye-bye ten thousand bucks. But I won't be long and, if you need to go somewhere, just give me a shout.'

'I shall,' Stefan said. 'But I won't, if you see what I mean.'

So Alan went off to talk to Al; so a small bright dark-haired girl came up to Stefan and introduced herself as Rita, the wardrobe assistant; so the time passed and everyone waited for Kostas to call Judy, and for filming to start.

They were still waiting twenty-five minutes later; though Kostas was by now shouting, and pacing up and down, and running his hands through his hair, and complaining that time was being wasted, and generally making it seem likely that at any second he would call Judy. Al meanwhile was trying to talk to Marina, though this was difficult since she had to follow Kostas up and down and take note of anything he might say, and Stefan was talking to the focus-puller.

It was this cameraman's assistant, a tall plump young man with thinning curly blond hair and shrewd slightly bulbous eyes, who drew Stefan's attention to the figure of a clear-skinned, handsome, white-haired woman dressed in beige cotton trousers, moccasins, and a white shirt, who had come to the door at one end of the set and, after a few seconds' hesitation, walked briskly yet at the same time self-effacingly over to Kostas.

It was also this cameraman's assistant, whose name was Riccardo, who said, 'Jesus, who's that? The star?'

'No,' Stefan smiled. 'I don't think so. I've no idea who she is.'

· 32 ·

All the same, though he smiled, he knew exactly what Riccardo meant. There was something so no-nonsense, so 'I'm just here to do a job and not worthy of the slightest note' about the woman, that she managed to achieve the very opposite effect. She was unobtrusive, she was simple; she was ostentatious in her simplicity, in her lack of frills both literal and figurative. Yet by the time she had reached Kostas, and had held out her hand to him, if all eyes on the set weren't on her, the great majority were; and even those that weren't were conscious of someone new, someone remarkable having made an appearance. What was more, Stefan was convinced, the woman knew the impression she was making, and was making it on purpose; and had she come in banging cymbals, and tossing her arms in the air and crying, 'Hallo, darlings, here I am,' she could hardly have been less discreet.

'She certainly acts like the star,' Stefan murmured. 'My God, I've never seen such an entrance. I wonder whether she practised it, or it just came naturally?'

Riccardo shrugged. 'I dunno. But she looks like trouble to me. If people act the diva when they're not the diva – Jesus, I remember when I was working on a film in Canada – '

'I guess,' Stefan interrupted, 'she's Judy's British coach. That's what she looks like, anyway. I'm sorry,' he added after a moment, 'you were saying – '

'No, it's okay,' said Riccardo. 'Doesn't matter. It was just I was making this movie somewhere near Montreal and – '

Once again Riccardo stopped. 'And there,' he said, indicating a slim blonde woman standing in a rather drab flowery cotton summer dress, '*is* the star.'

'Yes,' Stefan nodded, looking where Riccardo pointed. 'That one is. But you see,' he said, 'no one's really noticed her. While that other one – '

Later, Stefan would tell himself he had had a premonition of disaster when he had first seen Nora. Though there he was being over-dramatic, and was reviewing the past in the light of the present. At the time, all he had done was think that what Riccardo had said was true: this woman looks like trouble. And realize, though he was aware it was unjust of him, that without the slightest reason he disliked her.

How can I dislike her? he asked himself as he stared at her; and watched her point out to Kostas that his leading actress was approaching. I don't know her, I've never spoken to her, I know nothing about her. And who was thinking just a few minutes ago that he wouldn't initiate hostilities? Yet he couldn't help it. Partly, he guessed, because the woman's 'Oh, don't look at me I'm *nobody*' act was itself hostile, like a declaration of war against every single person on the set. And partly, though this was less understandable, or justifiable, because he disliked as a breed people of that sort, and distrusted them. The smooth, absolutely professional, there's just the job and nothing else matters type of person generally turned out in the long run to be the least professional, and the most difficult; whereas those who had bits of their personality, their humanity, hanging out, like a badly tucked-in shirt, or a lock of unruly hair, were generally aware of their short-comings, knew how to compensate for them, and on the whole did their job far better than the whole of the perfectly pressed and coiffed brigade put together. Riccardo, for example, the focus-puller: just looking at him, overweight, dishevelled, already losing that curly blond down on his head, one knew he was good, and would end up one day being a remarkable cameraman at least, though more prob-ably a director of photography. And Derek, the D.P. himself, with his great belly, and his bluff, hearty, I'm just one of the boys manner that didn't quite conceal that faint contempt he felt for Kostas: one could see, from the way he moved, the very ease and familiarity he had with the set, the lights, the camera, that he was a master of his craft, or art. Oh sure, he had a touch of arrogance about him, and he wasn't and never would be a person whom he, Stefan, could feel close to. Just as what he supposed was his own brand of hanging-out shirt, or gone-astray lock of hair – his reserve, his pale Russian way of always keeping himself slightly apart – would make it impossible for Derek ever to feel close to him. Nevertheless he respected the man, they respected each other; and he knew that they could have worked on a hundred films, and never really fallen out. Whereas that woman there, now standing ever so demurely in the background, yet not quite out of sight, as Kostas kissed Judy, and told her she was looking great, and said they'd be ready in about ten minutes for her and she hadn't had to come down quite yet but he was happy to see her of course and he'd be with her in just one moment if she'd excuse him he had to finish one last thing – she, he knew, he couldn't have worked with on one film without losing his patience, and becoming so exasperated that he would want to throw something at her. Nor was he going to, he realized; because even now, before this one film – or this part of it – had so much as started, he wanted to throw something at her, or wanted to send her a message saying she shouldn't bother to introduce herself to him, he really didn't want to meet her.

It wasn't only unjust, his dislike of the newcomer – who was now busying herself finding Judy's chair for her, and asking her if she wanted a coffee, and one way and another making herself indispensable, putting herself *entirely* at Judy's 'because you're the *star*' disposal – it was unfair. Undoubtedly the woman was nervous; the first-time student at the school in which others had already put in a term; the new cousin trying to include herself in the family circle without disturbing that circle, or stirring up resentment, or asking for special favours just because she was new. New, yet not young, nor, obviously, a source of fun and laughter.

But he couldn't help it; any more, he guessed, than could Riccardo. Who, after a moment or two continuing to stand by Stefan's side watching Judy and her coach, gave a sort of snort, muttered, 'Well, just as long as she stays out of my way,' and drifted off; tossing, over his shoulder, 'I guess I better go do some work, see you later, Stefan.' And, what made it worse, he was afraid that, as she was there to check on Judy's accent, she was almost a member of the sound department; or at any rate would have dealings with him, and would want to listen to tapes to see if what had been said really was 'British', or whether one could detect just the faintest trace of American.

Oh well, he thought, maybe working in Italy isn't going to be quite so much fun as I imagined. But what can you do – and at least she won't be able to ruin my evenings, and weekends.

Not realizing that these might constitute famous last words, Stefan glanced back at Marina, who was still talking to Kostas, and then allowed his eyes to rest, for a little while, on Al.

Good old Al, he told himself, I wonder what will become of him.

Once they had started, the morning's work went reasonably smoothly. Judy was playing the part of Elizabeth, a pathologically shy English girl who writes children's stories. Confined to a psychiatric hospital, she tells her stories to Billy, a severely autistic boy of fourteen: a child who will never look at anyone, nor speak, but seems happier in Elizabeth's company than in anyone else's. So much so that when she is telling him her stories he once or twice seems about to look up and meet her eye. This boy is the brother of a famous rock singer, foul-mouthed but essentially good-hearted, who comes to visit him at least once a week when he is in England; driving up to the hospital in a great black limousine with darkened windows, in the company of a secretary and bodyguard; who remain however in the car while Jimmy spends his time with Billy. Jimmy has become fond of Elizabeth, and is grateful to her for what she does for his brother; and when the girl tells him that she is being released from the home because according to the psychiatrists she is now well enough to face the outside world – though she confesses she is terrified at the prospect, and doesn't know what to do – he offers her refuge in the huge house he owns in London: a vast semi-converted Victorian church, part recording studio, part home. She can have her own room there, he tells her – a sound-proofed room that was formerly a side chapel – and can stay for just as long as she pleases. His only condition: that she continues writing her stories, and goes at least once a week to visit Billy and read him what she has written.

Elizabeth is happy in this place, though she retreats to her room, or to the old belfry, whenever Jimmy has friends over; none of these friends knowing of her existence. They would be surprised, if not shocked, to learn that foul-mouthed Jimmy is harbouring such an apparently delicate flower under his roof. In fact the only people who do know of Elizabeth's existence – and of Billy's existence – are the secretary and the bodyguard; both of whom Elizabeth is frightened of, and distrusts – particularly the secretary, a sly, smarmy young man who always wears a well-cut dark suit and dark glasses, and who according to her is not only cheating Jimmy, but would like to have some real hold over him, so he can milk him dry and eventually destroy him. His knowledge of Billy is a minor hold; he is constantly on the look-out for the great chance.

After Elizabeth has been in the church for some time, Jimmy, who by now is very attached to her, announces that he has to go to the States for some concerts and recordings. He suggests that she come with him. She can stay in his New York apartment, he says, or travel round with him, whichever she prefers. After much hesitation Elizabeth agrees, and the two, accompanied by secretary and body-guard, set off. Elizabeth isn't aware of Jimmy's feelings for her, because with an uncharacteristic timidity, almost equal to her own, he has never confessed them.

She wanders round New York in a state of amazement, stunned and excited by all she sees. At the beginning she is accompanied by the bodyguard, though they never exchange a word; after a while, finding his presence more disturbing than the idea of being alone, she tells Jimmy she doesn't need protection any longer. Jimmy is nervous about her wandering around by herself – also, he likes keeping her under control: his caged bird – but he agrees. The following day Elizabeth slowly becomes aware that she is being shadowed by someone. Initially she thinks it is another bodyguard whom Jimmy has hired to keep an eye on her; but, when she questions him that night, he denies it. Why? he asks. No reason, Elizabeth tells him. The day after she tries to elude her pursuer, a dark-haired very handsome young man; but is unable to shake him off. In terror she runs into the subway, goes all over town; until exhausted she runs into a coffee shop, on the verge of collapse. The young man follows her in and sits at her table, apologizing for having scared her. For a while Elizabeth is too agitated to listen to him; then she gathers that he is a journalist trying to write a serious article about Jimmy, and slowly, under the influence of his looks, and his quiet voice, and kindness, she relaxes. He wants to write something that stresses the human side of Jimmy, he tells her; something that reveals the man beneath the uncouth, often disgusting image presented to the world. Having seen her coming out of Jimmy's apartment, and no one seeming to know anything about her, he feels that in her he has found the key he has been looking for. Relaxing still further on hearing her benefactor spoken of so well by this stranger, and feeling that, if he understands Jimmy he will probably also understand her, Elizabeth agrees to meet the man, who introduces himself as Robert, the following day. 'Where?' he asks her; 'here,' she tells him. She feels secure here . . .

They meet the following day; and it is clear now that they are attracted to one another. Elizabeth tells Robert about the stories she writes, and shyly shows him one. He reads it there in the coffee shop, and tells her, 'It's great. You should publish it. I'll show it to someone I know who publishes children's stories.' Very agitated, Elizabeth snatches the story out of his hands. 'Never,' she tells him. These stories are only for herself – and for someone else.

As the two sit in the coffee shop they are unaware that they are being watched by Jimmy's evil secretary. But, when Robert tells Elizabeth he has to go, and arranges to meet her again the next day – and then leaves her in the coffee shop – the man comes over to Elizabeth's table and says, 'Who was that?'

Elizabeth, horrified, asks what he is doing there; the secretary tells her that Jimmy had asked him to tail her to make sure she is all right, since she seemed so flustered the other day. Elizabeth doesn't believe him – she thinks he has been tailing her for his own ends – but begs him not to tell Jimmy what she has been doing.

The secretary does tell Jimmy however; and Jimmy, jealous and hurt, loses his temper. He tells Elizabeth that the man is only after her so he can get some material for his article; that she is being used; that all journalists and reporters are liars and scum; that he doesn't want her to see the man again; and that, if she does, she must get out of his apartment, and leave the church in London. Seeing how hurt he is, and realizing now the reason for his outburst – and deeply grateful to him for his kindness, and not wishing to hurt him more – Elizabeth tells him that she will return to London tomorrow, and won't ever see Robert again.

The secretary, feeling that he has possibly discovered the chink in Jimmy's armour he has been looking for, calls Robert after Elizabeth's departure and tells him that Jimmy has obliged her to leave, but if he can help him in any way with his article . . . He cannot meet him in person, and of course no one must ever know . . .

'I would be very grateful,' Robert tells him; though he is

disturbed and made apprehensive by this message.

Jimmy meanwhile has told his bodyguard to discover everything he can about Robert; and Robert finds himself being followed by the man wherever he goes: to his apartment; to the magazine he works for; to his parents' secluded house in a wood on the end of Long Island. It is when staying in this house by himself for the weekend, trying to finish his article about Jimmy so he can follow Elizabeth to London, that he comes to feel that his life may be in danger. Everything seems to remind him of Jimmy – every newspaper he opens has an article about him, every radio or television he listens to seems to mention his name, and though he tries to convince himself he is being paranoid – and his friends try to convince him – he can't shake off his fear.

He is right to be afraid, too. The secretary has suggested to the bodyguard that really Jimmy would like to have Robert 'gotten rid of'; and though the bodyguard can't quite bring himself to act on this advice, not altogether trusting the secretary himself, he is tempted to take action; and does go so far as to beat Robert up.

Robert forces his way into Jimmy's presence to confront the singer with his injuries; Jimmy denies it's anything to do with him, and yells at his bodyguard in front of Robert – so convincingly that Robert accepts his denial of responsibility. All the same, Jimmy can't help but be glad that Robert, so much better-looking than him, so much better-educated, so much more secure than him, despite his fame and wealth, has been hurt.

Back in London, Elizabeth is missing Robert, though she feels guilty about doing so, and tells Billy, when she goes to visit him, that she wishes she could feel for Jimmy what she feels for Robert. She cannot disguise her joy when Robert turns up, however, nor her indignation at the injuries he has suffered. She too denies that Jimmy could have had anything to do with it, and puts all the blame on the secretary.

There follows an idyllic period in which Robert comes to Jimmy's converted church every day, spending all his time with Elizabeth; talking to her, listening to music with her, reading her stories – which he insists must be published. No, no, Elizabeth continues to tell him.

This period comes to an end when Robert, one night, starts to make love to Elizabeth. At first she encourages him, because, she tells him, she loves him. Then she panics; and what has started with tenderness becomes, in the end, a virtual rape. Robert apologizes; but Elizabeth, hysterical, sends him away. She is so upset that she calls Jimmy in California, and tells him what has happened. I will be right home, he says.

The day after, Elizabeth is horrified at what she has done, and tells Robert when he calls to apologize again that he must leave town immediately. She is sorry – both for having been hysterical last night, and for having called Jimmy – and she still loves him – she loves him more than ever. But he must go. Jimmy and I are the same, she tells him. We are both wounded, damaged – and both, poten- tially, violent. I was first sent away to the psychiatric hospital for attacking my father, after he tried to rape me . . . .

I don't believe you, Robert says; you're making up stories. And in any case, even if you're telling the truth – I'm not going. If I leave you will be a prisoner in this church forever, cut off from the world. You must have the courage to step out of your cage. You must have the courage to publish.

That's all you really care about, isn't it? My stories!

No! I care about you . . .

Robert comes round to the church, but Elizabeth, in tears, won't let him in. Go away, she implores him. Forget me!

When Jimmy returns he is both touched by the welcome that Elizabeth gives him, and angrier than ever about Robert's treatment of her. He sees that, despite the violence

Robert has done her, it is still Robert whom Elizabeth loves. The journalist, the would-be publisher, Robert; instead of, as he puts it to her, trying to sound ironic, a fellow artist – a fellow cripple – him.

'I'll go get him for you,' the secretary purrs; and Jimmy is unable to say no. Though he does force himself to say, 'I don't want you to do anything to him – just bring him here.'

The secretary smiles.

Robert knows that something is liable to happen, and tries to take precautions. He changes hotels; he calls the London office of his magazine and tells them he is leaving town. But he has to talk to Elizabeth; make one last attempt to persuade her to leave Jimmy, come away with him – and publish. Unable to reach her on the phone he eventually goes round to the church itself; and there, as he is trying to get in unnoticed, he is leapt upon by the secretary and the bodyguard, who drag him into Jimmy's presence.

'You can do what you like with him,' the secretary murmurs. 'You're powerful, you're famous. If you like, we'll make him disappear for ever.'

Jimmy knows that if this happens he will put himself totally in the secretary's hands, and will never get away. On the other hand he hates Robert so much, and is, as the secretary says, so famous, so powerful . . .

Unable to give the word, he is also unable to say no when the secretary takes a knife, and is on the point of slitting Robert's throat. Robert manages to break free for a second, however, and tear off the gag that the bodyguard has put over his mouth.

'Elizabeth!' he yells.

Elizabeth, as always when the secretary is around, is in her room; the room that Jimmy has had sound-proofed for her so she will not be disturbed by the sound of his music. But the door isn't completely closed, and she hears Robert's voice. She rushes out, sees what is happening, and in a blind rage grabs the first thing she sees – a baseball bat – and attacks the secretary with a ferocity that makes it seem her story about her father was not an invention. Jimmy and the bodyguard drag the man away from her, and she stands there panting, wild-eyed, desperate.

'Elizabeth,' Robert tells her, speaking very deliberately and calmly, 'put that down and come away with me. This is your last chance. You must come away with me. You must step out into the world.'

'Elizabeth,' Jimmy tells her, 'stay here. We belong together. You and I and Billy. If you go away with him you'll never write any more stories. You'll just become his wife, the mother of his children maybe. Or not even that, because he'll drop you in six months' time when he discovers you can't write any more in the outside world. Okay, maybe you are like a caged bird here – or more like a butterfly. But, if you are, you're a unique butterfly, a wonderful butterfly. You step out this door, and you'll become a moth. A moth that either gets burned by the light of the world, or a moth who will soon get squashed, when this guy gets sick of your flutterings. Stay here,' Jimmy begs her. 'Stay with me. I love you . . . '

Elizabeth, still clearly distraught, and still clutching the baseball bat, listens to the two men. And then, very slowly, she walks towards Robert . . .

At which point the story had two different endings. In the first, the one Michael and the producers wanted, Elizabeth/Judy takes Robert/Michael's hand and leads him out of the church. In the second, the one Judy, Jimmy and the writer wanted, Elizabeth smashes the baseball bat down on Robert's head, then collapses, hysterical, into Jimmy's arms.

'Don't worry,' the secretary murmurs, nodding at Michael's body. 'I'll take care of this, Jimmy.'

Kostas, inevitably, wasn't sure which ending he wanted; though he tended to prefer the one which Michael objected to.

And the solution?

Both endings were going to be shot; sneak previews

would be held; and whichever ending the public preferred would be it.

For the moment, however, and on this first morning in Rome, Judy/Elizabeth was by herself in the church, writing one of her stories, when the phone rings. It is Robert, telling her he has followed her to London . . .

She did the scene well, Stefan thought; her British accent to his ear both convincing and appealing. Whether she was entirely credible as a refugee from the world he wasn't so sure; despite her dowdy dress, apparently self-cut hair, and waif-like air, he occasionally got the impression that, though this little butterfly acted so forlorn, given just half a chance she would flutter gaudily up into the sunlight, and be off. But credibility was something one would only really be able to judge when one looked at the dailies; and, even if there was something irrepressibly lively or humorous about her, she knew her business, and would not, whatever she did, spoil the show.

As seemed to be the opinion of everyone on the set except Kostas, who said nothing to Judy at the end of her various takes, but merely grunted to Marina, after the eighth, 'Print four, five and the last one.' Then he sighed, stared at Judy as if he couldn't imagine why she was dressed as Cinderella, and turned to the production manager. 'What's next, Filippo?' he asked.

But Kostas was always like that – he was sure everything he did was doomed – and by now the actors were more or less used to him. Even if, back in New York, Michael Toscanini had insisted on doing scenes over and over until he did get some sort of acknowledgement; and even if, today, being Judy's first day with any real lines, the general opinion was that Kostas might have been a little more encouraging, and that he really hadn't behaved very well.

'Poor girl,' Al whispered down the mike to Stefan. 'She's doing her best.'

'Kostas,' Derek muttered to Stefan, as he marched out – to get a coffee, he claimed, but probably to stop himself protesting to the director – 'can be a real bastard.'

Still, for all her look of understandable hurt, and her own obvious effort not to say anything, Judy didn't allow herself to be too upset by this one voice missing from the chorus of praise, and consoled herself with the 'that was great Judy' Derek pointedly gave her before going off to get his coffee; and with the 'yes, very good' that Stefan murmured to her when she came over to him, said, 'Hallo, Stefan darling, how are you?', kissed him, and muttered, pulling a face, 'How did that sound, okay?'

She even looked quite pleased with the 'that was excellent Judy, really' that the Englishwoman, who had followed her over to Stefan's corner, slipped modestly in, uncertain as to whether such a meagre gift, offered to so great a star, would prove acceptable. Perhaps she should – and would of course in future if Judy preferred – wait to be asked before she spoke. Indeed, Judy looked so pleased that, becoming aware of that hovering, smiling, self-effacing presence, she turned to her, said, 'Thank you, Nora,' and added, 'Have you met, Stefan? Nora, Stefan, Stefan, Nora.'

The two of them shook hands, Nora said 'Hello, Stefan, where are you from?', and Judy said – to Stefan – 'Excuse me, darling, I must go and look at my lines.'

'Oh, do you want some help?' Nora tossed in quickly, before Stefan could answer her.

'No thank you, Nora. Maybe in five minutes or so. I just want to make sure I know them. So Kostas will be as impressed next time as he was this. Bastard.'

'That was really disgraceful,' Nora volunteered, outraged on Judy's behalf. 'I mean that's unprofessional.'

'Fucking Greek,' Judy said cheerfully. 'I wish I didn't like him. I'll call you if I need you, Nora. 'Bye, darling – ' this, naturally, to Stefan ' – see you later.'

'From Russia,' Stefan said, as if there had been no interruption. 'But I've lived in the States for the last seven years. And you?' he said. 'You're from London?'

'Yes,' Nora said. 'I mean that's where I live now.' She paused. 'How did that sound to you?'

'Sounded fine to me,' Stefan said. 'Technically. I can't judge the accent. And to you?'

'I *think* it was fine. But I would like to hear it again. Would that be possible?'

'Sure,' Stefan said, winding the tape back and thinking that, not only were his fears of Nora's attaching herself to him already being realized, but that now he had been introduced to her – as of course it had been inevitable he would be – he more than ever wanted to throw something at her, and have no dealings with her. 'What do you want? Four, five and eight?'

'Yes please,' Nora said. 'If those are the ones they're using. Though personally I thought the second one was best. There seemed to me just the suggestion of an American O in the others. It's really the most difficult sound, I always find. Americans tend to put an "ar" in it somewhere. Maybe Judy didn't. Maybe I was just trying to hear it. But, if she didn't, I felt possibly she was trying a little too much not to, if you see what I mean. She was putting on an accent, rather than simply speaking with one as you or I do. And I'm afraid that on screen – film is the most merciless of mediums. It exposes the bogus, the put-on, like nothing else. In the theatre you can fake an emotion if you have to. On film you can't. It sticks out like a sore thumb. Or like,' she said, as Stefan thought he would scream if she didn't shut up, and handed her a head-set so she would, 'an American O.'

It wasn't only her show of being a professional who was unwilling to indulge in small talk that he objected to, Stefan told himself as Nora squatted down on a wooden box beside him. It was her air of having, or even being, a thin crust that covered the surface of a marsh. A crust on which one trod at one's peril, and through which one might at any moment slip. Into a marsh that wasn't just disagreeable, but downright dangerous; composed as it was of poisonous gases, and matter that had been rotting away for so long that it was no longer possible to tell what it had originally been.

He was, obviously, being still more unfair than before; and the extremity of his reaction to the poor woman no doubt said more about him than it did about her. Nevertheless he did feel he should be cautious as he advanced, as it were, over her surface; and he couldn't help thinking that something unpleasant would be revealed should that surface ever crack. A lake of bitterness and tears, so salty it could sustain no life. Or a dry dusty sandy place, from which all moisture had long ago drained.

Nora, with a rapt expression on her face, sat and listened to the recordings – not just of the three takes that Kostas had chosen, but of all eight – for a good ten minutes. And though after that she announced that really the second *was* the best, and she frankly didn't see how Kostas with his faulty English – and faulty manners? – was in a position to judge, Stefan suspected she would have sat there for some time longer, had she not been summoned by an imperious 'Nora!' from the other side of the set. Then, hearing that call, she fairly scuttled away; with such an awareness of her own humiliation, and such a delight in it, that Stefan could hardly now keep from shivering. Far from being unfair, perhaps I have been underestimating the horrors that would be revealed should her surface ever crack, he told himself as he watched her progress across the set; a progress made more abject yet by the very stiffness of her bearing. And, if it cracks over the next two months, I only hope I'm not standing anywhere near her. Let alone, so to speak, on her.

The canteen at Cinecittà was a long low building with windows down one side and a counter down the other; at which frequently long lines of people waited to be given frequently bad food by invariably bad-tempered staff. Lit by neon lights, shiny with vinyl and plastic, it was not an inviting place. Yet most people who were working at the studio took their lunch there, if only because it was cheap and gave them the opportunity of sitting down; for many of them their only opportunity of the day. Those that didn't went to the bar and ate a sandwich, went to some restaurant nearby, or, as was the case with most of the directors and leading actors, had food brought to them in their dressing rooms.

Stefan and Al ate there with Marina, Alan and Rita the wardrobe assistant on the first two days of shooting; on the third day, just before the set broke for lunch, Judy asked Stefan if she could join him and Al and the others.

'I feel lonely sitting up in my dressing room by myself,' she said. 'I want to be down with the boys.'

'Besides,' she added a few minutes later, as she walked the fifty or so yards from the side door of 'Teatro 5' to the canteen, 'I want to be evil about someone.'

'I wonder who,' Stefan smiled; as, at the door of the canteen, Judy suddenly grasped his arm and said, 'Wait a second, there she is.'

None of them had to look at the crowd milling around the cash desk, at which one fought to buy a ticket before joining the line at the counter, to know who she was talking about. They all simply stepped back and waited outside in the hot sun, listening to the crickets in the umbrella pines, until they could be sure that that gleaming white head was far enough ahead in the queue for there to be no danger of it turning, smiling bravely, and saying, 'Oh hello, can I join you?'

The actress hadn't fallen out with her British coach since that other morning, and she still managed to look grateful when Nora, at the end of every take, seemed to think it her duty to say what Kostas would never say: 'That was excellent Judy,' or a murmured, 'Good, Judy,' or merely a nod of the head and a 'yes'. Which remarks were generally accompanied by a look of great sincerity, that conveyed the idea: 'And that's from one pro to another; that's from someone who really understands.' All the same, it was fairly clear to everyone by now that Judy didn't like the Englishwoman any more than Riccardo or practically anyone on the set liked her, with the apparent exception of the hairdressers and the wardrobe supervisor. It was also clear to most people that, if she was still able to smile and play the student, happy to be complimented by her far more experienced teacher, this submissive act would not be continued indefinitely; and that in a week or two, if not sooner, there was going to be some sort of blow-up; or blood on the sand, as Alan had put it. One could see it in the very way that Judy played the wide-eyed ingénue who was so prepared to admit that compared to her infinitely wiser and more talented instructor she knew nothing; and in the way she invariably fluffed her lines after Nora had followed one of her knowing nods of approval with a 'Just watch that "t" there, there's just the slightest tendency to turn it into a "d",' or a mouthed, round-lipped, 'Wo – oh – oh – n't, not waarnt.'

'I think our Judy isn't too keen on Mrs. Mellon,' Bruno the grip told Stefan on the second afternoon.

And: 'There's going to be a boxing match, ha-ha-ha,' said Mauro the electrician, after the first take on Wednesday morning.

'She hasn't actually done anything,' Judy told her lunch companions, as they all looked furtively across the canteen to where Nora was sitting eating with one of the hairdressers, even here amidst this crowd of technicians and extras managing so to radiate self-effacement that she would have drawn less attention to herself had she stripped naked. 'She's kind, she's helpful, she minds her own business, she's – she's good. At her job. But – oh, I don't know. It's something physical. She just gets near me and I start to cringe. Everything about her – her skin that's so clear, her eyes that are so bright, her hair that's so white –

yaaa, it makes me shiver. The trouble is, I can't go to Kostas and have her kicked off the set. She hasn't *done* anything. I mean I could. But that'd make me feel bad, and – oh shit. Why does there always have to be someone who no one likes? And why – Jesus, there was a guy on my last movie. An assistant director. Yaaa! He makes poor Nora look like a saint. I mean he was a real creep. Do you know – '

So they moved on to other subjects, each of them adding his or her own stories about disagreeable people they had encountered on the various films they had worked on; and soon the lunch hour passed.

Having thus let off steam, Stefan, Al and Marina agreed that evening that Judy would probably now feel slightly better about Nora; and that, while it remained inevitable that the two of them would eventually fall out openly, as long as the actress knew that she was not alone in her antipathy towards her coach, she would probably never go to the lengths of demanding Nora's head, as it were. She might continue to want to go to Kostas and insist upon the woman's dismissal; but, unless something extreme happened, her desire not to feel bad would stop her from actually doing it.

This optimism was misplaced, however; for the very next day insist upon Nora's dismissal Judy did. Her wish wasn't granted, and, since no more than three or four people knew what she had done, the scene she made with Kostas didn't cause that much of a stir. Nevertheless, either it, or the fact that Nora had somehow heard what was being said about her in the canteen the day before, caused enough of a stir for just a hair-line crack to open in the Englishwoman's surface, and for it therefore to become more likely that the surface would give altogether before the end of the film. Also, and from Stefan's point of view more worryingly, just as he had prayed it wouldn't, it caused that hair-line crack to appear in his presence; and therefore made it equally likely that if and when Nora broke altogether, at least some of the effluent would cover him.

Oh well, he told himself with possibly unjustified fatalism, he wasn't really surprised. Just to think something might happen in this world invariably makes it more likely that it will . . .

What made Judy take this unexpected step? Well, the trio concluded on Thursday, as they once again sat in the canteen eating their lunch, there were two principal explanations. The first was that, having found that her opinion of Nora was shared by everyone, Judy had decided she might just as well strike sooner rather than later. Both to get rid of someone she didn't like before she got to dislike her more, and also to feel bad for a day or two rather than, possibly, worse if she let things ride and got to know Nora better.

The other explanation for her misguided attempt was, undoubtedly, the arrival of her boyfriend.

Jimmy had, for most of the time they had been shooting in New York, behaved like an angel. Largely, Stefan suspected, because, very much like the Jimmy he was playing in the film, underneath his grubby foul-mouthed exterior he *was* an angel; an angel who was stung by Kostas's constant sniping at him, and who despite the director's criticism was doing his best to give a good performance, and not make a fool of himself either professionally or personally in front of his more experienced colleagues. The only time he did not behave like an angel was when Kostas pushed him too far – though even then Stefan thought that his response was, under the circumstances, fairly mild – or when his girlfriend or his various hangers-on were around. Then, feeling the need to play the rock star instead of the actor playing his first major role, he became, quite frequently, obnoxious; and made everyone feel that possibly his angel act was only an act, and that underneath he was, on the contrary, the sleazy bullying show-off he appeared to be. Fear, Stefan and the others supposed, was the explanation for these sudden lurches into cheapness and behaviour that was unworthy of him; a feeling that at least this way he was on firm, if foul, ground, and that, even if the film, or his performance in it, were a disaster, he would still have a place in the world. A very comfortable place, too, out there in the spotlight; and, if he had to share it with people who, in his heart of hearts, he despised, that wasn't such a terrible fate. At least they were all at his beck and call, and could be summoned or dismissed at will; and at least, even if he never made another record in his life, he would be a thousand times richer than all of them put together.

That he did, in his heart of hearts, despise the sycophants, hangers-on and so-called friends who clustered around him and cheered at his antics and encouraged him with their laughter and their fawning to act like a pig, Stefan had no doubt. It was what made his behaviour still more unforgivable: he was too good to play to such a worthless gallery and, however fearful he felt, he should never have accepted or welcomed the applause of people whose applause he didn't in the final analysis value. What Stefan was not so clear about was what Jimmy felt for Judy; whether he despised her too, or whether his relations with her, and his reasons for frequently behaving like a pig when she was around, were rather more complicated. Sometimes he thought the former was true: that Judy herself was just a part of that court that surrounded Jimmy, in which he could act the vile tyrant, and was in fact practically obliged to do so by the very position in which his courtiers put him, and themselves. A decorative part, maybe, and a part that was closer to him than any other. Nevertheless, still only a part; and a part that would, eventually, be hoist by the very petard she had helped to construct. But, other times, he felt that Judy knew that, if she was going to save him from one day slipping into his sleazy bully role forever, she was going to have to risk her own soul. It would be no use standing outside the court, making an appeal to the tyrant's better nature: he would acknowledge the truth of what she said, but dismiss her as a prig, or as someone who didn't have the guts to come into the snake pit and haul out the person she professed to love. Yes, she had to laugh and flatter along with the best – or the worst – of them; and she had to do it despite the fact that he felt only contempt for her doing it. But she also had to understand that he loved her for her bravery; and that, if she was steadfast, she would eventually be able to edge him out of the door towards which even now she was very gently leading him. Away from his court, away from his role as tyrant, back to safety, peace, and what was, if not entirely, his 'real' self.

About half the time Stefan favoured his first theory; and half the time his second.

If, however, Jimmy's comportment made Stefan feel unsure as to the true state of the couple's relations, Judy's behaviour, when she was in the spotlight, and Jimmy was merely a watcher, mystified him still further. For on those days in the States when Judy had been filming, and Jimmy had turned up to see how she was doing, the reversal of roles had been so complete as to make him think that perhaps he had misunderstood everything. Judy, normally so pleasant, and easy-going, and fun, had become tough, and shallow, and vulgar, and disagreeable; and Jimmy, normally either an angel or a pig, had become a meek little boy, an insignificant poodle whose only apparent function was to yap with pleasure when his mistress behaved more like an animal than he did.

Standing behind the camera, he had had the look of a poor badly-nourished English boy from a deprived home, who was impressed to see an actress of the stature of Judy Nason.

One day, shooting on the streets of New York – a scene in which Judy/Elizabeth was wandering along looking stunned by the crowds outside the World Trade Center, as she was followed at a distance by Michael/Robert – a passer-by had come up to Jimmy, who was standing by Stefan at that moment, and aked what the movie was, and who the director was, and who the actress was. To all of which questions Jimmy had given immediate, softly-spoken answers, and then had excused himself, and slipped away.

'Who was that guy?' the passer-by – a youth of around eighteen – had asked Stefan. 'One of the sound crew?'

'No,' Stefan had replied. 'He's one of our stars. Only he isn't working today. He just came along to watch his girl-friend.'

'*That* was one of your stars?' the youth had said, disbelievingly. 'Who is he?'

'He's a rock singer,' Stefan told the youth. 'Called Jimmy X.'

'Oh my God,' the youth had breathed. 'Oh my *God*. That was Jimmy X? *That* was Jimmy X?' He turned, and stared in Jimmy's direction. 'Oh my God, I just spoke to Jimmy X, and I didn't even *recognize* him. Oh my God, I don't believe this. I don't *believe* it.' He turned a complete circle, as if performing some little dance of atonement. 'I – I – *shit*,' he said. '*Shiiiit*. How could I – Oh my God, no one's ever going to believe this. I just – *shit!*' He laughed. 'Well thanks, and next time – ' he raised his hand in a half-wave, and walked away; shaking his head, and still muttering to himself, 'Shit, shit, shit. I swear to God – '

That had been in New York. There, however, the Nason/ X duo had had no scenes to play together; Judy having to do no more than drift around the streets of Manhattan either accompanied by the bodyguard, or followed by Michael/ Robert and the secretary.

Now, in Rome, they were going to have to work a great deal together; and, even when they weren't actually in the same scene, they would both be on call practically every day. The first three days had been exceptional, Jimmy having no scenes scheduled, and Judy either working by herself or doing some of those scenes where she is alone in the church with the secretary and bodyguard.

'Jesus Christ,' Al whispered down the line to Stefan when, within half an hour of their starting work that

Thursday morning, Judy had already told Kostas – without any of the charm Jimmy managed to lay on when saying more or less the same things – that he was a fucking little Greek and she wasn't going to put up with any more of his crap and if in future he had anything to say to her would he kindly do it via his assistant director. 'Jesus Christ. If she's like this now when Jimmy's just watching her, what's she going to be like later today? Are they *both* going to carry on like this?'

The answer to that was: no. Jimmy reverted to his angel role, listening carefully and quietly to Kostas's directions; while Judy became more ill-tempered and odious than ever.

'No, I do not want to have lunch with your –' she paused, clearly considered adding 'fucking', then, realizing this would have been going too far, contented herself with snarling 'wife'; when Kostas, alarmed by her behaviour, told her that his wife was coming to the set that day and suggested that maybe she – and Jimmy – would like to eat with them.

'I don't want to have lunch with anyone,' she shouted at the director's back as he walked, offended, away from her. Then she did an imitation of Kostas's wife, who was tall and English and walked in a shy, awkward fashion, and turned to Jimmy to receive his smile of approval.

'See how well I've learned your lessons,' her pale, pretty, yet just at the moment quite frighteningly ugly face seemed to be saying to her lover. 'Aren't you proud of me?'

Or perhaps: 'That's how you've got to do it, boyo; take a tip from me. That's how you've got to stop 'em trampling on you in this world. Trample yourself, first.'

Whatever Judy's face was saying to Jimmy, the rock singer ignored her, refusing today to play his part as the adoring disciple. He gazed at her with his white face devoid of all expression; then turned away and called across the set, ''Allo, Marina? Is it me now?'

'Yes,' Marina called back; as Judy stared after her lover as if she could have killed him.

Indeed, it was probably that blank expression of Jimmy's – an expression that could have been one of disdain, or hatred, or pity, but was in any case not one of encouragement – that was the deciding factor in Judy's determination to ask for Nora's head now rather than later. Goddam it, Stefan felt she was really saying – to Jimmy – as she went over to Kostas and muttered an apology for having refused his invitation so rudely, and then launched into a tirade against the Englishwoman, blaming her for her fragile nerves. Goddam it, you will look at me, you will support me as I have always supported you. It isn't fair that only I have to play the toady. Especially here, where we're on equal ground. You're not the great rock star here. You're just another actor, like me – though possibly not so talented. And if you won't applaud when I show you how to get some respect in this world, to make the performing dogs leap through your hoops – well, what do you say to this? The bleeding, severed head of an Englishwoman.

But if it was Jimmy's blank look that made Judy play, somewhat recklessly, what she hoped would be her winning card, it was her earlier rudeness to Kostas that ensured she would lose this hand, too; and her attempt to make Nora accept the responsibility for that rudeness only made Kostas more determined not to give in, or offer Judy so much as a hair of that white and shining head.

He listened to her, off in a corner overheard by no one but Stefan and Al, as she made her ill-natured speech; twisting his moustache with his left hand and holding his cigarette in his mouth with his right. And, when she eventually came to a halt, having repeated, 'I'm sorry, really I am, Kostas, but that woman just drives me mad, she pretends to be so humble and helpful, but really she just wants me to make a fool of myself, and despises me, so in the end I'm just standing there worrying about whether I'm sounding like an Englishwoman, instead of concentrating on what I should be doing, acting,' all he said to her was: 'Well, I'm sorry, Judy, but I can't and won't fire her. I think she's doing an excellent job, and I just don't think you're being honest. I think you're blaming her for your own sense of insecurity. And if I fired everyone who made actors feel insecure . . . You'll get used to her,' he concluded, starting to move away, back to the middle of the set. 'Bloody bitch,' he added, muttering to himself and, possibly, to Stefan and Al, who he must have known could pick up practically his every word on their headsets. 'Bloody actresses.'

It was soon after this that Stefan, Al and Marina went off to have their lunch; to discuss what had happened, and to come to their conclusions as to why Judy had suddenly turned so nasty.

'Though I'm sure she isn't really,' Marina said with a suggestion of wistfulness. 'I mean deep down I think she's a nice person. She generally is. Really. I suppose it's just that she shouldn't be married or whatever to who she's married to.'

'And he,' Al muttered, 'shouldn't be married to her.'

Yet, while they spent at least the first ten minutes of their lunch hour talking about the events of the morning, today at the table there were just the three of them; so no one else heard what they were saying. Moreover Nora herself, who yesterday had been so prominent in the canteen, with her antennae quivering as she hoped and tried to pick up every word that was said, today was almost equally conspicuous by her absence.

'God, it's a shame she isn't an actress herself,' Al said. 'If she can make her presence felt even when she isn't here, imagine what she must be like on stage.'

'On stage,' Stefan murmured, 'she probably couldn't do it. That's her tragedy.'

If, however, they were alone, and Nora was nowhere to be seen, why was it that Stefan felt so sure, when he returned to the set, that the Englishwoman was aware of what Judy had said to Kostas this morning? Or, at the very outside, that she had indeed managed to pick up

· 57 ·

something yesterday? He didn't know; but he guessed that, in the long run, her being aware, or her having somehow overheard them, was the only explanation for her behaviour.

After half of the lunch break, Al and Marina, who both liked riding, said they wanted to go out to one of the back lots to see some horses they had been told were being trained for some future production.

'You going to come, Stefan?' Al said.

'No, I don't think so,' Stefan told him. 'It's too hot. Anyway, I want to check something on the tapes.'

A statement, this, that wasn't actually true. But apart from the fact that it was true that it was hot today – very hot, and overcast, with a wind that seemed still hotter than the sun – and Stefan had no particular desire to stand in the dust watching a lot of horses being put through their paces, he thought Al might appreciate half an hour alone with Marina. Poor thing, he had hardly seen her at all by himself, away from the set, since that weekend they had spent together in New England. Three days after they had returned from their short trip, the film had moved back to New York, to shoot the scenes of Judy wandering around the city, of Jimmy performing, and of Michael following Judy and being in turn followed by the secretary and bodyguard, who finally beat him up in Central Park. (After he has bumped into his grandmother – a part that in the event Bette Davis didn't play; 'You must be joking!' Alan Miller said – and the old lady has warned him about his ambition and fascination with the famous.) And, in New York, Al had had other commitments. Not only with Su and his daughter, but also with a film editor called Christine, with whom he had been involved ever since Su had made it plain that having fathered a child he had served his purpose and she didn't have much further use for him. Not that that had stopped him, on a couple of occasions when he had been able to get away and the three of them had gone out together, from making a half-hearted attempt

· 58 ·

to take Marina to bed; having offered to accompany her back to her hotel. But they had only been half-hearted attempts, and because of his other problems he hadn't really pressed his case; preferring, Stefan saw, to put Marina on hold until they all got to Italy and he had the coast clear. For the moment, his attitude had seemed to be, no harm can come to your spending your evenings with Stefan, having dinner or going back to his place to watch the T. V.

Little did he know that once or twice, sitting in his small neat apartment on West 22nd Street, Stefan had come very near to asking Marina if she wanted to spend the night there, with him; and would have done if he had been sure how one asked a woman to stay the night. He supposed in the same way as one asked a man – in other words, one didn't really ask, it was just something that either happened naturally or didn't happen at all. But somehow, with Marina, he had been afraid of striking the wrong note. And with an ear as finely tuned as his, he was also afraid that, had he done that, he might have ruined everything. He wouldn't, of course; at most Marina would have been embarrassed for thirty seconds. Still, for his own peace of mind, it had been better not to risk it; and to reflect that, even if he had managed to get his words out without either going flat or becoming sharp, the night might anyway have ended in disaster; in humiliation, awkwardness, and tears.

Stefan was still thinking about Al, and telling himself 'poor thing', when he stepped into the stone-flagged corridor that ran down the middle of the great shabby structure housing Studios 5 and 6, and their related dressing rooms, production offices, workshops, store rooms, and lavatories. A corridor that normally, during the day, was crowded with extras milling around waiting to be called, or people going back and forth between all the various side rooms and the sets. Today, however, either because both productions had broken for lunch at the same time, or because the production that was based in Studio 6 was working on location, or was suspended for some reason, it was almost unnaturally deserted. No chatter or clicking footsteps broke the silence; nor were there any of those loud buzzes that announced either that a take had just started, and therefore one could not enter the studio, or, if there were two buzzes, that a take had just finished, and one could come and go as one pleased.

It was so silent indeed, the very quiet seeming cool after the hot grey day outside, that, as Stefan pushed open the heavy sound-proofed outer door of the studio, closed it behind him, and then opened the inner door, he moved as noiselessly as he could – as noiselessly as if a take had been in progress – and advanced into the positively chilly air-conditioned space between the door and the set itself with all the furtiveness of a thief intent on robbery. To some extent he acted like this for an absurd reason; he felt that if he managed not to make a sound, he would be able to leave outside every trace of the heat and the oppressive, oven-like wind, and could step into the high roofed now darkened studio uncontaminated by the so-called real world. He could step into a cool, shadowy fantasy; where for twenty minutes or so, until the others returned, he could be quite at peace . . . The other reason for his furtiveness was less absurd; and was that while most members of the cast and crew went out to eat something, whether at the canteen, the bar, the local restaurants, or their dressing rooms, a few – Derek the D.P., moustachioed Zapata-like Sergio, and one or two others of the electricians and carpenters – preferred to do without a midday meal, and find some quiet angle – a sofa, a bench, or simply a carpet – where they could stretch out, rest, or sleep through the break. Stefan had discovered this on Monday, when he had returned to the set slightly earlier than the others, and had come across five or six men lying around the great red-brick converted church with its stained-glass windows, breathing peacefully or, in Sergio's case, snoring loudly. In a way, he had thought, those sleeping figures made the set look more realistic than it did when filming was in progress, and the place was bright with lights. A gloomy Victorian pile, that had miraculously been transported from London to Rome, to provide refuge for the weary.

It was largely then to avoid disturbing these weary souls that Stefan trod so quietly on the boards that lay between the studio entrance and the towering flaps that had been painted to look like church walls. A backstage area occupied by a large table on which the carpenters and technicians worked during the day, and by a number of canvas chairs dotted around in which people sat when they weren't needed. As well as by a smaller table on which a coffee dispenser was set; by a large freezer in which bottles of mineral water and coca-cola were stored; and by all sorts of odds and ends that had no apparent relation to this film, but looked as if they had been lying around so long that no one liked to throw them away, in case they did serve some purpose that would only become apparent after they had disappeared.

What is more, had Nora Mellon asked Stefan why he was creeping about the back of the set, and then edging down the side of it, so he could enter by a side door the chapel where he had set up his recording equipment this morning, he would have given her his reasons; or the second of them, suspecting that someone like Nora would not be too impressed by whimsical notions about leaving the heat outside. But Nora was so startled to see him slipping in through that little wooden door with its wrought iron Victorian handle, and he was so startled to see her in his chapel, that she didn't think to ask for an explanation, and he didn't think to offer one. The only explanation that either felt was needed, and was in fact almost instantly forthcoming, concerned what Nora was doing there, behind the wrought iron screen that separated the chapel – or one of the rock-singer's guest bedrooms, as it had become – from the main body of the church.

For when Stefan did push open that wooden door, which swung back more silently than any church door, the Englishwoman was bent over and peering at the floor, intent on picking up a long nail, and adding it to the already large collection of nails and screws of various lengths that she was holding in her right hand.

'It's a mania of mine,' she practically blurted out, as Stefan stared at her, for a moment feeling too surprised and almost guilty to be able to say anything at all. 'Always has been,' she went on more calmly now, collecting herself and recovering her poise. 'Whenever I've worked in the theatre or on a film. There are always so many nails and screws all over the floor. And I can't bear it. Not because they're being wasted – for heaven's sake, what are a few nails and screws when one thinks of the cost of a film? Just because – oh, I don't know. I suppose because I can't stand mess. It's not even as if I ever stepped on one once, and got blood poisoning or tetanus or anything like that. No,' she said, suddenly depositing her collection in a chalice on the side altar that also served as a dressing table. 'It's simply a little phobia of mine and, anyway, it helps me resist the temptation of going off and having lunch. I mean I did yesterday, but I really can't eat twice a day every day. Otherwise by the time the film's over I'll be so fat I won't be able to move. I put on weight so easily.' She stopped; and then, possibly because Stefan himself didn't own up to some similarly harmless phobia, she added, 'I could certainly use some of these nails, mind you. A friend of mine has a house in the country in England, where I spend most of my weekends. And it's my task to play the odd-job man. I make shelves, repair the roof, mend fences – where do you live, Stefan, in New York?'

For all his surprise, and for all that Nora's behaviour required a more immediate explanation than his own, he should, nevertheless, have told her why he had crept up so quietly, Stefan was to reflect later. Not because he thought she would be particularly interested; just that in the absence of any explanation, and in part due to that guilt he had felt at catching her in the act, he was convinced that Nora would believe that he had crept up on her on purpose, in order to catch her in the act; and would, subconsciously or otherwise, blame him for it, and seek to get her own back.

To catch her in the act of what, though? That was what Stefan asked himself as he sat in his chair in the silent side chapel. Stealing a few old nails and screws was the obvious answer; since he didn't for a moment believe that story about Nora's having a phobia about mess on film sets, and in theatres. Clearly she had been intending to put them in her pocket, and take them home. Why she should want to put them in her pocket was, however, another matter. Not because she needed them for some friend's house in England, that was equally obvious. No, he told himself, wishing that he hadn't surprised her like that, and feeling he had unwittingly seen more of Nora than was either decent or, really, safe: the only possible explanation he could think of was that of Nora having either somehow picked up what they were saying about her yesterday in the canteen, or of her having overheard, although she had been on the other side of the studio, Judy's demands for her dismissal. Hurts, or blows to her pride, that she was trying to soothe with one of the oldest remedies known to man: taking something that did not belong to her. Blocking the holes that had been knocked in her defences with other people's property; stealing the love that had been denied her.

Furthermore, he couldn't help feeling, since he had caught her in the act, and been afforded a more profound glimpse into her than he had wanted to have, Nora would probably think of him as one of those people who had knocked a hole in her defences, and denied him love. She might even think of him as one of her enemies; if not her number one enemy . . .

Although, there, he might be going too far.

CHAPTER 4

S HE HAD known she shouldn't come. She had told herself
she shouldn't come. And now, sitting in the small, hot,
overfurnished hotel room that had been reserved for her,
she told herself she should call someone in the production
office and announce she was very sorry, she was leaving.

Oh God, why had she done it? Being 'discovered' at her
age! Being told that she was just the person A, B or C was
looking for! It was grotesque. It was too pathetic even to be
funny. You stupid, stupid woman, she wanted to scream at
herself. And the idea that this was 'life', and that one
shouldn't refuse experience. For God's sake! This, life?
Hanging around a film set, being at the beck and call of a
second-rate American actress who was only working
because of who she was living with? There was more life to
be seen on a cold winter's day in Kensington Gardens, with
not a soul around, the trees leafless, and even the squirrels
in hiding. Nora, Nora, what are you *up* to? And why, even
now, won't you call the production office and tell them
you're leaving?

Well, Nora answered her unavoidable reflection in the
mirror over the dressing table at the end of her bed, that's
quite simple. Rightly or wrongly, you feel that here, in this
tiny hotel room with its dim lights, its brownish gold
wallpaper, its dingy green velvet bedspread, its massive
walnut wardrobe, and that hideous dressing table covered
with what looks like an altar cloth – or, if not here, on that
oppressive film set that has been built to look like an
English church and makes one more than ever wish one

were back in England – you've been pushed into a corner. And if you don't fight back, but simply attempt to wriggle away, you will either be crushed, or you will spend the rest of your life crippled by regret. Even if you do fight back you may well be crushed; by those forces of crassness, commercialism, dishonesty and cruelty that are pitted against you. But at least it will be a fairly honourable defeat, and you will go down with some of, if not all, your colours flying. And at least this way you might be able to take one or two people with you as you go down. That spiteful, common *bitch*. That stupid posturing Greek. That pale, listening Russian . . .

Oh yes, Nora told herself as she recalled Stefan's expression as he saw her collecting her nails – an expression that had plainly said to her 'Thief' – I may be humiliated, made fun of, despised. But you've picked the wrong woman if you think I can be hired and fired just like that, without a second thought. I am too old now, have too little to lose to let you simply walk over me. Besides, if I did commit a sin by turning my back on my talent, and if my sitting on that set day after day is a form of self-punishment for that sin, I'll be damned if I'll be the only one to suffer. After all, it was you stupid, cheap, sneering people who failed to recognize my talent, who made me commit my sin. So I don't see why I alone should have to bear the cross. Oh no: here I am and here I stay; and, if that cruel commercial world that shut its ears to my truth doesn't like it, to hell with it, and to hell with all of you.

Aware, even in her hurt and anger, that this little scene she was playing out in the bedroom of her hotel at the top of the Spanish Steps was the typical hysterical outburst of a lonely unhappy person – but telling herself that, though it was, she didn't care, she *would* get her own back on all those who had rejected her – Nora contemplated taking a walk before going to bed. She was afraid however that if she did she would see people staring at her, managing to detect pathos in her as clearly as if she had an internal battery that was making her glow. And she couldn't take any more stares, any more commiseration, compassion or contempt for one day. She had had enough of the eyes of the false world, that detected only wickedness, hatred, and folly, and failed to recognize truth.

Instead, she would read her Shakespeare, and in particular one of her favourite roles, that of Constance in *King John*; and here, in the privacy of her room, raise up her own hymn to goodness and life; and call down her own curses upon evil and death.

'*I am not mad: I would to heaven I were!*'

Bloody little bitch.

Damned Russian queer.

'Hi, Nora.'

'Hello, Judy, how are you this morning?'

'Oh, fine. Much better. I was feeling terrible yesterday. I don't know why.'

'Oh, we all get these days. It's the weather, or the air pressure, or something like that.'

'It's incompetent directors,' Judy smiled, 'who don't know their jobs.'

'Is Jimmy coming today?' Nora asked with a smile of her own, to make it clear that, whatever her opinion of Kostas, she was not one to indulge in below-stairs gossip.

'No,' Judy said, her early-morning sunniness already starting to lose its warmth. 'Not today. Not till Monday, in fact. Then it's every day.'

So from Monday, was the message Judy's tone conveyed, you'd better watch out. Because, if you thought yesterday was rough, that was just a foretaste of what it's going to be like the whole time from now on. You had your chance to back off; you refused it. But, having refused it, don't expect any mercy from me. If it's a fight you want, that's fine by me. Remember, though: it'll be a fight without rules, without quarter; and I'm telling you now, when I fight, I fight dirty.

'Want me to hear your lines?' Nora said, nodding at the script Judy was holding in her hand. 'Or do you want to have another look at them first?'

Judy hesitated; her eyes narrowed very slightly. Then, once again, she smiled. 'No, I think I know 'em.' She looked around. 'Yes, let's go through 'em. "Once upon a time," ' she quoted, assuming now a parodied English accent, and pretending to be speaking into a tape-recorder, as she would have to in the first scene that was to be shot this morning, ' "there was a little American girl who had to learn to speak English." ' She gave Nora a would-be little girl flutter of the eyelids; and Nora thought: I may have been hysterical and slightly carried away last night. But by God, you bitch, I will fix you before this film is over. It is positively my duty to fix you. You are everything I despise in the world, everything that is vile and corrupt and hateful. And, if I don't fix you, I will be acquiescing in my own failure, my own defeat, and saying to the world, 'You were right not to recognize me.' And that, my dear little Judy, I will never do. So yes indeed – till Monday. And may the best woman win, you – you –

Stopping herself from using a word she hated to hear, let alone say herself, Nora followed Judy across the set, and realized that, determined as she was to fight the young woman, if necessary to the death, she couldn't help with a small part of herself admiring her. She was hard, cold, and represented everything that was detestable; but she had chosen her position, she had accepted all its limitations, and now she was going to do whatever she had to to defend it.

Nora spent the weekend in the country with her friend Franca. Franca was a small, rather elegant, conservatively dressed woman whose invariable little black dress, pearls, and neatly set hair did not make her look like the efficient and generally well-regarded agent that she was and had been for the last forty years. Italian by birth, American by upbringing, the ex-wife of an Italian producer, she presided like a tiny unassuming duchess over a coterie of some of the strangest, occasionally funniest, but on the whole nastiest people in the Roman film world. Apparently unaware of the bizarreness and essential unpleasantness of her friends, she managed to neutralize them, and make them not only seem unexceptionable, but even reasonably decent and amusing. Which talent Nora both admired, and was faintly suspicious of; in that it made her wonder on the one hand if Franca suffered from some sort of moral myopia that was so pronounced as to amount almost to blindness and, on the other, if she was one of Franca's lame ducks herself. Naturally she didn't think she was; but sitting in Franca's garden, looking down over a Tuscan valley with, around her, a diminutive high-voiced anti-semitic fellow agent, a drunken pock-marked overbearing actor, who told constant stories of his sexual conquests, and a fey elderly American actress who could afford to be choosy about her roles in that her family apparently owned half the state of Ohio or Minnesota or Nora wasn't quite sure where, she couldn't help asking herself if a stiff-backed Englishwoman in her early sixties who was constantly fantasizing about 'fixing' people didn't fit in with this company rather better than she might have wished. Franca's little horror group, she thought, as she told the American woman that no, she was not related in any way to *the* Mellon family, and bit her tongue to stop herself asking, 'Are you?', Franca's collection of freaks.

Yet though she could think such things, and look with a reasonably detached eye upon her companions and herself, that didn't stop her doing what she mocked herself for doing: fantasizing about 'fixing' people. She didn't have any definite plans, she realized, as she sat under a tree on this Sunday morning, sipping a tomato juice and feeling about as out of place here amidst the splendour of nature as it was possible to feel. Nevertheless, even given the loveliness of the scene – a loveliness that should perhaps have soothed her, and caused her to reject whatever it was in her that did make her a soul mate of Franca's other guests – she didn't doubt for a moment that come tomorrow she would be ready for anything, and had the feeling that, if in fact the beauty around her served any purpose, it was to strengthen her resolve to do battle. Maybe, she thought, taking in the view, the sound of the birds singing, the scarlet flowers blazing in the great earthenware pots dotted around the garden, everything is curdling inside me, going off, going bad. Maybe here I should feel myself in touch with God; instead of preparing myself for a treaty with the devil. But I don't mind. For ultimately my battle is a battle on God's behalf; and, though I may have to rely on the devil's help to win it, God will understand.

'Won't He?' Nora asked herself as she went to help Franca prepare lunch, and told herself, 'Oh shut up, woman, what are you talking about? Really, you're cracking up.'

Won't He?

What a relief it was! What a comfort! To have that sound-proofed door close behind one; to be back in artificial light; to be back on the set!

It was like returning to reality after a brief period spent dreaming. How far away Franca and the country now seemed, how insubstantial. And oh, Nora thought, how good to be back amongst one's own kind. She had only been working on the film for a week; yet already she was starting to think of all these people hammering away, changing lights, arranging props, as her family. Such good people they were, most of them, such hard-working friendly people; and really, acclimatized now to Rome, and relaxed after her weekend, how lucky she was to be with them.

'Buongiorno, Marina!' she cried as she sailed down the nave, towards Jimmy, Judy and Kostas, who were standing together and talking by the choir stalls. 'Buongiorno, Bruno, Sergio, Annamaria, Rita, Marcello, Luciano, *every*one.'

What was more, she perceived, as she picked her way over cables, and dodged ladders, although last week she had been viewed by all these people as an interloper, the new girl in town, now, on this second Monday morning, for better or worse she had been accepted by them as one of the family. Did they like her? They didn't know, it didn't matter. She was there; she was working; so she belonged. And if she had turned her back on her talent, if she was rubbing her nose in her own disappointment, what did that matter? Everyone here had his or her own disappointments to bear. The important thing was to do one's work; to do it with as little fuss as possible; and to get on as best one could, both for their sake and one's own, with one's fellow workers.

Be professional! One couldn't tell oneself that often enough. Be professional, be professional, be professional!

'Buongiorno, Nora,' the men all called out as she passed. 'Hai passato un buon weekend?'

'Ah si, si, yes,' Nora told them, 'thank you, grazie, a wonderful weekend!'

She stopped a discreet three yards from the director and his actors; and waited for a pause in the conversation to say: 'Good morning, Kostas. Good morning, Jimmy. Good morning, Judy.'

Jimmy was the only one to reply. ''Allo, Nora,' he smiled. ''Ow are you?'

'Very well thank you, Jimmy. And you?'

'Yeah,' Jimmy said. He nodded at his girlfriend and Kostas. 'We're 'aving an artistic discussion 'ere.'

'Oh, I'm so sorry,' Nora murmured, stepping back to show that she knew her place. 'I'll be over there – ' this to Judy '– if you need me.'

Kostas merely grunted in Nora's general direction, sighed, and lit another cigarette. Judy didn't even grunt; she just gave the most baleful stare she had in her repertoire; made it plain she wasn't going to say a word until Nora withdrew; and made it equally plain she hoped this would be as soon as possible.

'Listen, Kostas,' Nora heard her say as, having taken that symbolic step back, she turned and walked away, 'I don't give a fuck what you think. *I'm* the actress, *I* have to play the part, and I'm telling you that Elizabeth would not, could not, behave like that. What do you know about English girls? I mean, for Chrissake. *You* probably think a girl's shy if she doesn't hit you back.'

'Hello, Al,' Nora said to the handsome young American boom man. 'Hello, Stefan. Hello again, Marina.'

'Hi, Nora,' the trio said. 'How you doing?' 'How are you?' 'Did you have a good weekend?'

'Fine, thank you,' Nora said, in reply to all three questions. 'And you?'

'Yeah, great,' said Al. 'We drove down to Amalfi.'

'Oh, it's beautiful,' Nora said, 'isn't it?' She went on, before the others could do more than mutter 'Yes', 'Fantastic', 'Wonderful': 'What's *wrong* with Judy? Some days she couldn't be nicer, other days she's impossible. And today – ' She shook her head in wonderment. 'I mean I know she feels insecure when Jimmy's around. But really. A real actress *uses* her insecurity. Makes allowances for it. Knows how to dominate it, make it work for her. But Judy – no one should talk to her director as she does. All right, in the heat of the moment, if one has a fight. But just like that, first thing on a Monday morning – I feel so sorry for Kostas, really. And Jimmy himself is such a sweet boy. I don't know what she's trying to prove. If she's simply trying to make the point that she's her own woman, and not just Jimmy's girlfriend – she's going about it in the wrong way. Instead of respecting her, he's going to end up despising her. Really. Poor girl. If only I could talk to her. Tell her.'

'I don't think that would be a very good idea,' Marina smiled.

'If I were you I'd have as little to do with her as possible,' Al said.

'Yes, but I have to do something with her,' Nora said. 'That's my job. Otherwise why am I here? Also, you can be sure if I did just disappear she'd be the first to complain about that, too. No, really. I'm so sorry. I feel sorry for her.'

She did, too, Nora told herself; this wasn't just an act, so much gush she was putting on for the benefit of the pretty threesome, as she suddenly thought of them. Poor, stupid Judy. Poor, cheap – trash.

'You're a sight for sore eyes on a Monday morning, you three,' she said, her words following her train of thought. 'The best-looking people on the set.'

Giving them a disarming smile to show they shouldn't be embarrassed by her apparent change of subject – she was doing no more than tell the truth – Nora walked away; to find herself a pew to sit on, where she could read her book until, in an hour or two, Judy decided she had better, after all, run through her lines.

If, however, as far as Judy was concerned, the morning had started badly, it got rapidly worse. She did her scenes, and did them, Nora had to admit, rather well. Somewhat better, indeed, than Jimmy did his; the rock singer, so easy and bright when he wasn't acting, becoming oddly wooden when the camera was turned on him, and managing always very slightly to misread his lines; putting the stress on the wrong word, getting the rhythm wrong. But the better Judy acted, the more wretchedly she behaved: grabbing the lipstick out of the make-up man's hand and deliberately smearing it all over her mouth, screaming at the grips that they mustn't watch her when the camera was rolling, telling the camera crew for Chrissake to make sure they didn't run out of film again she couldn't stand fucking incompetence, and repeating her earlier complaint to Kostas that he wouldn't recognize shyness if it came up and punched him on the nose, so would he kindly keep his comments to himself. With the result that, by the time the lunch break was called, the entire crew had lost the good humour they had come in with, and were disgruntled, surly, and muttering amongst themselves that if *she*, meaning Judy, didn't pull herself together, sooner or later someone was going to hit her.

'And then,' Al murmured to Nora, 'all hell'll break out.'

It was because she too had lost her relatively high spirits that Nora decided that today she wouldn't even go to the bar to have a cold tea, but would instead stretch out on one of the pews in a side chapel, and try to have a nap. She wasn't feeling quite as bruised and angry as she had the previous week, since she realized that, if she did have a fight with Judy, she would not, now, be without her supporters. But she was feeling bruised and angry enough: having been told, 'Please *shut up*, Nora,' when she had tried to correct Judy's accent; having had Judy turn to Kostas and say, in front of everyone, 'Kostas, will you please tell Nora not to interfere with my performance, she is here *exclusively* to listen to my accent and I will *not* have her make comments about my acting. I am the actress, she is here to help me, and I wish you'd make that plain to her.' And having overheard, and been meant to overhear, the following: 'Jimmy, will you get that bitch off my back. I don't care what you have to do. I don't want her around.'

'Oh, fuck off,' Jimmy had said. 'She's only doing her job. It's you 'oo's being difficult.'

Just four hours ago, Nora told herself, as she went in to one of the side chapels and found a pew with some cushions on it, I was glad to be back, and had captured that feeling one generally gets on a set, of being a member of a family. Now, although it's only Monday lunchtime, I'm already looking forward to next weekend, and wondering how on earth I'm going to stand another four and a half days here.

Poor Judy, she told herself, as she lay down, and the lights in the studio were turned off, and she heard the other members of the crew either going off to have their lunch or looking for pews of their own on which to take a nap: poor, wretched creature.

It must have been half an hour later that Nora was woken by voices talking softly very near her, and she realized that people had come into the chapel and didn't know that anyone was there. For a second she thought she should make her presence known, so as not to make it look as if she were deliberately eavesdropping. But she was so comfortable on her high-backed heavy wooden bench, and so wrapped around with sleep, that she remained still, and told herself after all why should she move, it was she who had come in here first.

Besides, what was she likely to overhear? Probably no more than gossip about the film. Or at most stories about girl-friends, husbands, food, politics, or union matters. In Italian, to boot.

When she realized that the voices were speaking in English, and that they belonged to Stefan and Al, she was once again tempted to make her presence known. Now, however, she admitted to herself, she remained still not least because she was curious to hear what they would talk about. She wondered what their relations were. She wondered whether Al too was homosexual – as she was certain Stefan was. And she wondered, though not with any great curiosity, how Marina the script girl fitted in with the set-up. She certainly spent enough time with 'the boys'; and seemed, whatever their sexual inclinations, very fond of them.

It was of Marina that the two men were talking; as they sat, from the sound of it, on the pew two behind hers.

'Oh, don't be silly,' Stefan was saying in a quiet, only very slightly accented voice. 'Of course she does.'

'How d'you know? It's amazing how many women don't. Some of them are married to gay men for years without realizing their husbands are gay.'

'I know. But I know she does. She – I can just feel it.'

Al smiled, audibly.

'So you don't mind – I mean – it'd be okay if I asked her out by herself. Some evening. I mean – you wouldn't mind?'

'Oh, for God's sake,' Stefan murmured. 'You're asking me? Come on, Al. I'd be delighted. I mean – ' he stopped, and gave a shy, nervous laugh. 'I'd be happy if you married Marina. Or someone like Marina. Someone who – you know, I really liked. That way – ' he didn't finish his sentence; but, Nora thought, he didn't need to. It was obvious what he had been going to say: 'That way I could be with you both all my life.'

'Well, I'll see what I can do,' Al said cheerfully. 'Though I still reckon,' he added after a moment, 'that it's you she'd prefer to marry.'

'Oh, for God's sake,' Stefan repeated. 'I mean, even if it is, she's not going to. But anyway – really, you're being ridiculous. Sure, she likes me. I like her. But – maybe she's trying to make you jealous,' he said with another shy laugh. 'Maybe she wants you to ask her out.' He paused, and then went on very softly. 'I mean you must know, Al. I have never been jealous of you. Ever. And I hope I never will be. I am just happy if you are happy, and now – ' a final laugh, 'why don't you go get a coffee, or something. I'm embarrassed. But seriously,' he added, as Nora heard Al stand up. 'Why don't you marry Marina? *You'd* be very happy, never mind about me.'

'What about Marina? How'd she feel about marrying me?'

'Oh, Marina,' Stefan said. 'She'd love to. You see. I mean maybe give it a bit of time, but – weren't you happy this weekend?'

'Yeah. Sure I was, but – ' it sounded as if he had slapped

himself on the forehead. 'It must be serious. Here am I asking you if I can take a girl out. Jesus!'

'Well, as I say, I hope it's serious,' Stefan said. 'I'll see you in ten minutes. I just want to close my eyes for a moment. And then tonight – you can start planning the wedding.'

If only Stefan had lain down on the pew where he and Al had been sitting, he might never have discovered her. But, like her, he apparently wanted somewhere darker, further away from the nave, which was very soon going to start filling up with people drifting back from lunch. Thus it was that he saw her lying there on her back, clearly awake; and thus it was that for the second time he gave her a look that was both accusatory and guilty; as if he felt bad at having caught her doing something base.

'I really wasn't eavesdropping,' Nora said. 'I suppose I should have made my presence known. But I was asleep, and I was so comfortable – '

'That's all right,' Stefan said, staring down at her. 'I'm sorry if we woke you. We didn't realize anyone was here. I'm sorry,' he said again. 'I'll leave you in peace now.'

He turned, and walked away.

For a moment or two Nora wanted to get up and run after him and not just apologize again, but beg for his forgiveness. 'I won't tell anyone,' she wanted to reassure him. 'I won't say a word to anyone.' Then, realizing that there was nothing to tell anyone, and Stefan probably wouldn't mind if she said all sorts of words, she told herself not to be stupid, and lay back again, and closed her eyes.

All the same, she did wish that what had happened hadn't happened; and she did wish that once again Stefan had not apparently detected a flaw in her. She wondered whether he would try to exploit it; slip his fingers into the crack, so to speak, and try to wrench her apart.

CHAPTER 5

A N ELECTRIC screw-driver was missing.
'I put it down here before lunch,' Bruno the grip said. 'And now it's not here.'

Everyone who had heard him looked round.

'Are you sure?' Al said; as the young man was asked the same question in Italian by at least half a dozen other people. 'You didn't put it down somewhere else?'

'No, no, no,' Bruno said, and stuck his hands in his pockets. 'I put it exactly there, and someone's stolen it.'

People muttered that it wasn't possible, that there was always someone on the door, that Bruno must have made a mistake, that – that they didn't know what to make of the case of the missing screw-driver. Then, for the most part, they went back to their various jobs, only Bruno and a couple of the other grips standing around and continuing to complain that there was a thief on the set, that they couldn't do their job without the screw-driver, and that if they now had to be doing all their screwing and unscrewing by hand there would be delays and time would be wasted and it wouldn't be their fault and the production should not and could not complain.

'There obviously wasn't anyone on the door during the lunch break,' Bruno muttered to Al. 'Otherwise how could someone have come in here and pinched it?'

'Unless,' Al shrugged, 'it was someone here.'

'But who?' Bruno said. 'And anyway, even if it was – I mean – if it was, they must still have it with them, in a bag or something.'

'So all you have to do is look.'

Bruno shook his head. 'You can't do that. Search everyone's bags and belongings before they leave the set? There'd be a revolt. Anyway, whoever it was might already have taken it out to their car, or given it to someone else. No, when something like this happens, it's gone for good. But it really spoils the atmosphere on a set. 'Cos after something like this you don't feel you can leave anything around, or trust anyone.'

'That's the last time I leave my cameras on the set during the lunch break,' said Alan, the still photographer. 'I was just saying to Stefan last week – '

'The Case of the Missing Screw-driver' had a dual effect on the proceedings in Teatro 5 at Cinecittà – besides introducing a note of suspicion into the already less than harmonious atmosphere. On the one hand, it stopped people muttering about Judy, complaining of her behaviour and generally analyzing her, diagnozing what was wrong, and suggesting remedies. (A good slap remained the most popular idea.) On the other, it seemed to calm Judy herself down somewhat, making her realize that she couldn't go on as she had that morning, and causing her to discover in herself a sense of solidarity with everyone else on the set that hitherto had not exactly been notable.

It was of course possible that Jimmy had spoken to her during the lunch hour, and told her that if she didn't pull herself together he would have her thrown off the film; which he would have been capable of doing, despite their relationship, and the fact that it was becoming clear that, whatever Judy's shortcomings as a person, she was a better actor than her lover. As it was possible that either Kostas or the producers had spoken to her and threatened her with dismissal; or simply that she had reflected on her behaviour and accepted that she had gone too far, and that if she didn't start acting like one of a team she would be replaced, cost what it would the producers to reshoot all her material.

(And, if she was replaced, she would never work again, whoever she was living with or married to. Not to mention that Jimmy might very well leave her, concluding that she was bad for his career as well as her own.) All the same, Al couldn't help feeling, as he held the microphone above her head in the first take of the afternoon, there was just something about her newly submissive air that was a result of her anger and upset concerning the missing screwdriver. And angry and upset she was when she heard about it; almost unreasonably so. Possibly, there again, because she thought that by siding with Bruno, and so sharing his sense of grievance, she would endear herself to the crew, and make them forgive her for her bad behaviour. Yet, aside from some element of calculation in her reaction, she did genuinely seem to feel that this in itself not particularly terrible occurrence had introduced a splinter under the skin of *The Storyteller*, as the film was provisionally called. A splinter that might well cause some sort of infection, and do far more damage than any blemish her carrying-on might raise.

'I don't know,' Al heard her saying to Stefan, her contrite little girl act being almost overdone now. 'I mean it's a ridiculous incident. I could buy Bruno fifty electric screwdrivers if he wanted them. Fifty? I could buy him fifty thousand.' A brief laugh, to show she wasn't boasting, but that her remark was to be understood as self-deprecating. 'But that's not the point, is it? It's just that it suddenly makes you look round at everyone, makes you feel there's an enemy in the camp. And, if that happens, the whole, I don't know, weave of a movie can unravel. You can lose the spell, if everyone's not caught up in it. And if that happens – goodbye, movie. God knows it's hard enough already here, with bloody Kostas who just doesn't *feel* the story, and can't decide whether he's making a movie about a shy girl trying to come to terms with the world and find some sort of place in it, or whether he's making a heavy metal rock thriller that's got some sort of bullshit plot slowing down the action. That's how he described it to me the other day, you know: "All that bullshit about you writing stories." The only thing he's interested in is having the bad guys chasing Michael, and making the scene where Michael makes love to me as much like a no-holds-barred rape as he can without everyone protesting. But even that, having a director who isn't clear about what he wants, isn't insurmountable. As long as everyone else knows. And Jimmy and Michael both agree that essentially it's *my* story, and it's what I do at the end that's the crucial scene in the movie. The moment you start introducing – oh, I don't know, *foreign* elements onto a set – and a thief is a foreign element, it's like something intruding from the outside world, isn't it? – there's no hope at all. Okay, I know I can be difficult. I can be a bitch, if you like. But that's all part of the score, isn't it? And I'm not a bitch just for the hell of it. It really is because Kostas doesn't know what he wants that I get nervous. Stealing, though – oh, I don't know,' she repeated. 'That is extraneous. That's not part of anything, is it? That's – as I say – foreign. And it makes you wonder what's going to happen next. Do you know those lines of W. H. Auden?' she said, the tone of her voice changing ever so slightly; so slightly, Al thought, that perhaps only a sound man could have detected the trace of affectation, of striking a pose, that had crept into it. ' "The crack in the tea cup opens the lane to the land of the dead." Well, that's something like this. The crack in the tea cup. And – ' there was silence then, and, glancing round, Al saw Judy shrug her shoulders. 'What are you doing tonight, Stefan? Would you like to have dinner with Jimmy and me? And Al too, if he'd like.' She suddenly leaned forward, and spoke into Stefan's recorder. 'Al darling, would you like to have dinner with Jimmy and me tonight?'

'Sure,' Al murmured down his mike and, looking across the set again at Judy and Stefan, waved. 'Yeah,' he mouthed. 'Great.'

And so, no doubt, it will go on, Al thought; with Judy

behaving badly, and then trying to get herself forgiven by inviting us and other people out to dinner. Until eventually she either behaves too badly or, more likely, the film, somehow, gets finished.

And so, no doubt, it would have gone on; if, over dinner that night, the case of the missing screw-driver hadn't surfaced again.

They went out, the four of them, to a small restaurant near where Jimmy and Judy were staying; and it was Judy who seemed unable to leave the subject alone. 'God, I wish that drill or whatever it was hadn't been stolen today,' she shivered in a lull in the conversation. 'I can't stop thinking about it. It's like a kind of omen.'

'Bloody 'ell,' Jimmy said. 'It's only a fuckin' screw-driver. I don't know why you're making such a big deal about it. Christ, when I think of what people've pinched from me.'

'Yes, I know,' Judy said, and repeated almost word for word what she had said to Stefan earlier. The only slight difference was that she didn't assert that Jimmy – or Michael – agreed that essentially the film was about her.

'All right, so there's a crack in the fuckin' tea cup,' Jimmy said when she had finished. 'Now can we please 'ave some more wine and forget about bloody screw-drivers. Jesus. Anyone'd think that someone'd nicked yer bloody virginity.'

'Well, that's how I feel,' Judy said indignantly; whereupon Jimmy raised his hands in the air, rolled his eyes in mock dismay, and moaned, 'Oh bloody 'ell, I can't stand it. Christ,' he said to Stefan and Al, 'she wouldn't even *notice* if someone nicked 'er virginity. I mean I don't suppose she did notice.'

Judy was clearly torn between the desire to smile and the desire to wax more indignant yet. Indignation won.

'Stop that,' she snapped, her face flushing. 'I don't like that sort of talk.'

'Oh fuck,' Jimmy said, waving at a waiter and calling, 'Can we 'ave some more vino please. Yeah. Rosso. Bianco.

Anything. Old Saint Judy's making one of 'er appearances.'

'It's nothing to do with being a saint. I just don't – oh, forget it,' she said. 'Okay, so maybe I'm overreacting – '

'Maybe!'

'But I still wish it hadn't happened. I like Bruno, I don't like that sort of sneaky underhand dishonesty, and – I bet that Nora took it.'

'Oh Gawd, here we go on Nora now. Can't we talk abut fuckin' art, or something? Or sex. Or politics. She's only got two subjects,' Jimmy said to his guests. 'Screw-drivers, and Nora.' He sighed. 'All right, Jude, let's 'ear your latest Nora story.'

'It's not a story,' Judy said, starting to feel uncomfortable in her indignant role, and wanting to get back to light-heartedness. 'It's just that – '

'You know when we were talking together after lunch?' Stefan said to Al, as Judy paused. 'Nora was lying on the next pew, listening to us.'

'There in the chapel?' Al said.

'Yes.' Stefan turned to Jimmy and Judy. 'We were discussing our private lives,' he said with what Al thought of as one of his Russian smiles. 'And Nora just lay there, without saying a word.'

'Yuk,' said Judy; though Jimmy said, 'What you expect 'er to do? She was probably enjoying it. I'd 'ave listened if I'd been there.'

'Yes, I know,' Stefan said. 'I mean I don't think – I mean I know she wasn't doing it on purpose. We did just walk in and sit down. Anyone could have been there. Just that – I don't know. There's something disturbing about her.'

'You've got a partner,' Jimmy said to Judy.

'Stefan's right. There is something disturbing about her.'

'Also last Friday, or Thursday, whenever it was. I came back after lunch and found her picking up a whole lot of nails.'

'*Nails?*'

'Yes. You know. Nails, screws. Not finger-nails.'

'Ah.'

'Well, I'm sure she wasn't going to do anything with them. I mean I'm sure she wasn't stealing them. But – I just wish I hadn't caught her. She made me feel – '

'I told you!' Judy cried.

'What?'

'It was her who stole the screw-driver.'

'Oh, I didn't mean that,' Stefan said, looking embarrassed. 'I wasn't associating the one with the other. Only – '

Only he had said it, Al reflected later. And, though he had flushed and denied he had mentioned the nails because of the screw-driver, having done so he had not only confirmed in Judy's mind her theory that Nora was a thief, but had introduced into everyone else's mind – including his own – the idea that that was what Nora was.

Had he done it by mistake? Or had he, Al wondered, done it partly because he felt, however slightly, upset or threatened by what he had revealed to Nora that afternoon? It was impossible to say, though he guessed there might have been a subconscious element of getting his own back in that story of the nails. What was beyond doubt was that he had made them all believe that Nora was responsible for the loss of Bruno's screw-driver – had made even Jimmy believe it, though he was really quite fond of Nora, Al suspected – and that from now on not only would they view the Englishwoman with a degree of suspicion, but, since Judy was unlikely to keep her suspicions to herself, everyone else would, too. Which development made Al feel suddenly sorry for Nora; and wish, at the same time, that Marina had been included in the invitation tonight. She, Al felt, would have come up with some defence of Nora; or would at least have waxed as indignant as Judy at this attempt to cast doubts upon the honesty of someone who wasn't there to defend herself. Or even, Al told himself, he wished that he had refused Judy's invitation, and had tonight asked Marina to eat with him, as he had more or less asked Stefan's permission to do that afternoon. Just the two of them. Away from Judy; away from Jimmy; away even from Stefan.

Al wasn't sure what he thought of Stefan. He guessed in a way he loved him, not least for the very love that Stefan had always felt for him. He certainly believed him to be a good, honest, kind and intelligent person, and hoped they would remain friends always. Nevertheless, there were times when he wanted to be away from him, when he wanted to be not so much *by* himself as *with* himself, leading his own life, seeing his own friends, having his own emotions. Alpha, his daughter, was his main source of joy outside Stefan's sphere of influence; as Su had been something private, something his, when he had been with her. And now he wanted Marina to fulfil that role; as a provider of solace, of happiness, to him and him alone; and to be someone whom Stefan, however friendly he was with her, with both of them, couldn't touch. Someone out of Stefan's world; someone who existed only in his, Al's, world.

Of course, Al told himself – as he always told himself when he started going out with someone new – he couldn't really imagine why Marina should want to exist only in his world. He wasn't particularly bright, he didn't have a fantastic job, and, though he guessed he was good-looking enough, he had never actually felt good-looking; or been able to believe that good looks could affect anyone's opinion of him for more than about ten seconds. Nevertheless – and there was no point in indulging in self-doubt, he knew – he did hope that Marina might want to share his world; and he did wish that she had started sharing it tonight. He didn't like stories of theft; he didn't want to feel sorry for an ageing Englishwoman, and wonder how she had come to be what she was, where she was, now. If only because it led him to wonder what and where he would be when he was her age, and if he too would feel he had wasted his life. He wanted only to be lying in bed with

Marina, making love with her, talking with her, and thinking of the children they would have together. Because they would have children togther, several of them, and, unlike with Su, the children he had with Marina he would live with and stay close to, watching them grow, watching them discover the world, watching them, maybe, go to some of the places where he, because of a lack of drive, or self-confidence, or intelligence, had never gone. Oh Marina, Marina, Marina, Al thought as he sat at that table with a man who loved him, a more than usually hysterical actress, and a sweet-souled if unstable rock singer: why aren't I with you?

He could just imagine how last weekend would have been: if, instead of ending up sharing a room with Stefan, he had been alone with Marina in that hotel in Amalfi. Coming out onto the balcony; looking down over the sea; still practically joined to one another by sleep . . .

If Al had tried to escape from talk of theft and thoughts of Nora over dinner, there was alas no escape from either over the next few days, dream of Marina and try to concentrate only on her though he might.

Not only did Judy indeed go round telling anyone who would listen that in her opinion it was Nora who had stolen Bruno's screw-driver; she seemed to have become obsessed by her British coach. It was clear to Al why she did: she knew she had to behave herself if she didn't want to risk either the sack, or the scorn and dislike of everyone on the set including her companion; at the same time, the panic, tension or 'insecurity' that the presence of Jimmy on the set induced in her had to find some outlet. She couldn't be calm and relax; she must, like a snake that would be poisoned by its own venom if it didn't strike, find a victim. Hitherto, she had lashed out and spat at anyone who came within range; in other words, above all, at Kostas. Though also at the wardrobe people, the make-up men, the camera-man, the boy responsible for loading the camera, and whoever in her opinion wasn't doing his or her job precisely as it should be done. 'Fucking incompetents', 'Fucking amateurs', 'Fucking *Italians*' were just some of the remarks that Judy had been heard to make. Now, at last, she had been presented with a perfect target. A person who was already, if for no real reason, unpopular on the set. A person whose role was not of any great importance, and therefore didn't have to be respected, and couldn't, even if she didn't do her job properly, actually ruin the film. (One could always dub in any suspect words later.) And a person, above all, who seemed to be crying out to be made a victim of, and who from the moment she had walked on the set seemed practically to be quivering in anticipation of the fangs that she knew sooner or later would sink into her.

It was, Al thought, almost terrifying, the way Judy went at it the morning after their dinner together. 'Nora!' she called across the church as she slumped into her chair, having greeted in her friendliest, most cheerful who-me-be-a-bitch-surely-not-but-if-I-was-a-little-difficult-please-forgive-me-it-won't-happen-again manner everyone she had met in her progress across the set. 'Nora!' And when the Englishwoman, walking unhurriedly down the nave to show that she was unruffled by being summoned so peremptorily, got to the bottom of the steps leading up to the high altar, by the side of which Judy was sitting, and said, very calmly and sweetly, 'Good morning Judy,' the actress, instead of replying, said, 'Would you get me a coffee please.'

There was a moment's silence then, as everyone, while not stopping work, listened and, either openly or out of the corner of an eye, watched to see what would happen. Would Nora tell Judy that fetching coffee was not her job? Would she lose her temper, and shout at the actress? Or would she show the depth of her hostility by being submissive?

The last, Al guessed, in the moment that Nora stood there, still, gazing up at the blonde American actress who this morning was looking particularly pretty.

He was right.

She held that pose at the foot of the steps for a fraction longer than she would have if fetching coffee had been part of her job. She seemed to raise herself very slightly, as if saying to everyone working round her: 'I hope you're taking note.' Then she gave Judy just the faintest suggestion of a smile, and said, clearly, 'Milk and sugar?'

'Milk but no sugar,' Judy said, not looking at Nora, but turning, as she spoke, to see where the director of photography was. 'Derek darling,' she called. 'How are you?' She bounced up out of her chair and, long-legged, frothy, light-as-air, floated over to where Derek was talking to the head electrician; no doubt to drive home the point that, while Nora had come to her, she would put herself out for Derek – or indeed, Al suspected, for just about anyone on the set – and go, if she wished to say something, to him.

And that was just the start.

Having taken the cup of coffee Nora brought her with a 'Thank you' of Marie-Antoinette-ish hauteur, Judy, once again in almost the same breath, called, 'Bruno dear, good morning,' went over to the bespectacled young stage hand, and, having kissed him on the cheek, said, loudly, 'Have you found your screw-driver yet?'

Still watched by practically everyone on the set, because it was obvious she was putting on an act, she took the young man by the arm, and led him away from the piece of wood he was nailing to one of the flaps. 'Come with me for a second,' she said, 'I think I know what happened to it.'

She led him over to the side chapel where Nora had had her nap yesterday; and there, not quite audibly – for Stefan hadn't yet set up his equipment for the morning – but not altogether inaudibly, she gave him her version of the facts.

'Nails,' Al heard. 'Unhappy,' he caught. 'A menace.'

Nora, he noticed, was sitting a good deal closer to the

chapel than he was.

Judy's denunciations of Nora weren't made so openly to the other members of the crew; during the course of the day Al heard her just happen to mention the case of the missing screw-driver, and the name of the person she had decided was responsible, whenever she found herself chatting to someone. Nevertheless, they were made openly enough; and while, maybe, he was listening out for them, and was aided by his microphone and headset, he guessed it must have been pretty hard for Nora not at some stage to have caught the gist of what Judy was saying, even if she hadn't the first time, when Judy had spoken to Bruno.

'Nora!' Judy shouted at the end of the third take of the morning, after she had fluffed her lines. 'Where's my script?'

'I've got it here, Judy. Would you like to run through the scene before you do it again?'

'Nora!' Judy snapped at the end of another take, when instead of saying to Jimmy, as she was meant to, 'I can't go to New York,' with an 'ar' sound in 'can't' and a dipthong in 'New', she came out with an unmistakably American 'a' as in 'cat', and something that was closer to 'Noo' than it should have been. 'I'm sorry, but will you *please* not look at me while the camera's rolling. You distract me, and I just can't – oh fuck it, caaaarn't – concentrate. Couldn't you – oh, I dunno – sit over there, maybe,' waving towards an altar screen, 'or – anywhere. Just – out of sight.'

'How about over there?' Nora asked sweetly; and indicated the side chapel where she had slept yesterday. 'That way I can hear you, but can't be seen.'

The trouble was, Al told himself, and what was perhaps most distasteful about Judy's now openly declared war on Nora: despite the fact that the actress, whatever Nora had done, was behaving, as she herself would have termed it, as a real bitch, there was something very slightly exciting about this campaign of public humiliation. Nor, he knew, was he alone in feeling this. With, say, ninety per cent of himself he disapproved of Judy's persecution, and wished she would stop it. As with ninety per cent of himself he disapproved of the fact that he was, however slightly, excited by it. But, with the remaining ten per cent, it did give him a real, he guessed, sexual thrill, witnessing this unsettling, perverse performance – on both women's parts – and, much as he tried to, he couldn't disapprove. He could simply watch, and as it were lick his lips, and wonder what was going to happen next.

It didn't make his voyeurism any more acceptable when he realized that Judy herself was aware that most people were watching her and, in spite of themselves, egging her on; wanting to see the outcome of this battle, and hoping in any case for a good scrap. When he realized, too, that, had not he and everyone else responded with such sadistic enthusiasm to her show of brutality, Judy would not, could not perhaps, have kept it up. She was feeding off those shamefully licked lips, charging her batteries from those furtive, hot glances.

Even the normally sweet Jimmy, who actually liked Nora and, if he did think she was a thief, felt only sorry for her, was, Al saw, against his better judgement titillated by his girlfriend's cruelty.

'Poor old Nora,' Al heard him say with a laugh. 'She'll be lucky if she gets out of 'ere alive, now that Judy's got her claws into her.'

Even – oh no, not you too, Al wanted to tell her – yes, even Marina couldn't help taking a less than entirely charitable stance.

'I know I shouldn't enjoy it,' she said over lunch, shaking her head – but laughing. 'And I really don't. Only some-how – '

'I guess what it is,' Stefan said quietly, still looking a little guilty, Al felt, for having had a hand in starting or re-starting this war, 'although Judy seems to have all the weapons on her side, you can't help feeling that if and when it comes to it Nora will be able to give just as good as

· 89 ·

she gets, and maybe better. She's just letting Judy waste her ammunition. Then when she pauses to reload – you watch out.'

'But I wish,' he added a few seconds later, 'they wouldn't fight, all the same. It's not good. And if Nora *didn't* take Bruno's screw-driver . . .'

'The only thing is,' Marina said, sounding regretful herself now, 'it's really making Judy act well now. She was terrific this morning. And she was nice to everyone else.'

'I guess she's chosen Nora as the sacrificial lamb,' Al said.

'That's what this film's all about, isn't it?' Stefan said with a smile, that still managed to seem apologetic.

Whether Kostas was aware of what was going on Al couldn't tell. He must have been fairly distracted if he wasn't, since over the course of the next few days those cries of 'Nora!' became ever more frequent, and the Englishwoman seemed to be waving her debasement and self-abnegation as visibly as a flag at a funeral. Kostas, however, unless something concerned him directly, was fairly distracted; and Al guessed that most probably he noticed but didn't care. He was just grateful that for whatever reason Judy seemed to have pulled herself together, was no longer being rude to him or generally insufferable, and was working far better than he had ever dared hope she would.

But, on the Friday of that second week at Cinecittà, the shit, as Alan would put it that evening, when discussing the scene, hit the fan; and after that not even Kostas could ignore the blood that was being shed directly under his nose.

The trouble started at lunch-time, when the prop man discovered that a small silver chalice on the high altar – that served as a dining table for Jimmy in the film – was missing. Once again the word 'thief', 'ladro', could be heard being muttered around the set; once again suspicious glances were cast. Only this time, since everyone by now knew Judy's theory as to who had taken the power-tool, these glances were cast in only one direction.

There was a problem, however. All right, Nora had, once again, remained on the set during the lunch-break, as had four or five other people. But Nora, who was always preaching the gospel of simplicity to anyone who would listen – 'Not so much less is more,' Jimmy quipped, 'as "Nothing is everything",' – had come on the set this morning wearing only her usual beige slacks, white shirt, and moccasins, and carrying only a small canvas airline bag. A bag that she always left around on the set, and was always open; and contained, as anyone who was interested could see, just a purse, a comb, a handkerchief, some tickets for the Metro, and a paperback; generally of short stories by Henry James.

'What else do I need?' she had asked Al one day last week, when she had actually fished out what was in her bag and shown it to him. 'I've got my paper money in my back pocket here; everything else – well, anyone who wants it's welcome to it.'

Today, a number of people were interested in the contents of Nora's bag; and all of them saw immediately that it did not contain a silver chalice.

That meant either that Nora had hidden the thing somewhere, and was planning to remove it at a later date, or that Nora hadn't stolen anything, and someone else – probably some outsider who had managed to sneak into the studio during the break – had.

An opinion, this latter, that soon came to be held by practically everyone; since most people on the set were on the whole decent and good-natured, and in circumstances such as these were happy to allow the ninety per cent of them that disapproved of Judy's persecution of Nora to prevail, and to repudiate that ten per cent of them that got a kick out of youth and success's torment of age and failure.

By practically everyone . . . but not, it almost went without saying, by Judy Nason. She was back on the set by two-fifteen, having had her lunch in her dressing room with Jimmy. She became, immediately, aware of the muttering and sense of disquiet.

By two-thirty she was telling Derek and Luciano, the assistant director, Stefan and Al – telling them quietly, but very firmly – that she could not go on working on a set with a thief, and that 'either that woman goes, or I do'.

'No, I'm sorry,' she muttered, when Luciano said, 'Oh Judy, come on.' 'I mean I know I asked Kostas to fire her last week – and it would have saved a lot of trouble if he had. But that was just because I didn't like her, and thought she was incompetent.' She paused, and looked around at the men, waiting for someone to challenge this patently untrue statement. When no one did, she went on. 'Now – I'm sorry. But I really cannot have someone around who – I mean, apart from anything else, where's it going to end? She's pinching things this week – next week she'll be poisoning us or something.'

'Oh come on, Judy love,' it was then Derek's turn to protest. 'You don't know that she's pinched anything. Anyway, she can't have. Where's she put it if she has?'

'Oh, up her cunt,' Judy snapped. 'I don't know. Somewhere. But I *know* it's her. I just feel it. And really – either she goes, or I go. I don't care. I will not work with a thief. And that's all there is to it.'

'Well, just do me a favour, love,' Derek said, clearly exasperated and regretting that even with one per cent of himself he had encouraged Judy in her anti-Nora campaign. 'Sit on it till this evening. Otherwise we're not going to get any work done this afternoon, Kostas will have a shit fit, and everything's going to fall to pieces. Will you do that for me, love? Just sit on it till we've finished this evening, and then, if you still want to – talk to Kostas then. And in the meantime – try to avoid Nora and, if you can help it, don't talk to her.'

Judy looked again at the men standing round her; saw that their opposition was total and united; and gave in with as bad a grace as possible. 'Oh, okay,' she pouted. 'Just because it's you.' (This to Derek; to make it plain that he was the only one present whose opinion carried any weight; or, in other words, who, for whatever reason, she feared.) She kissed him on the cheek, and prepared to sweep off. 'But this evening,' she said as she left, to prove that this was just a momentary lull in the battle, and in no way a ceasefire or a truce, 'it's bang-bang bye-bye, Nora. I mean, for Chrissake,' she shook her head. 'The woman's a *thief*.'

It probably would have been bye-bye, Nora, too; if, that evening, when Judy gave her 'either she or me' ultimatum to Kostas, Jimmy hadn't intervened on Nora's behalf. Not because Kostas necessarily thought Nora was guilty, any more than anyone else did; just because he couldn't take any more nonsense from Judy, and, unfair as it undoubtedly was, was prepared to offer her whatever she asked for so long as she kept on working as well as she had for these last few days. Particularly as Michael Toscanini was due to start working again next Monday, and Kostas couldn't be putting up with silly actress tantrums when he was having to deal with serious actor tantrums; or just with a serious actor being – 'God help us,' Kostas muttered – serious.

Jimmy however, either because he too thought it time to repudiate that part of him that applauded Judy's antics, or just because he liked to be awkward, did intervene on Nora's behalf. And that, as Jimmy himself remarked, rather put Kostas on the spot. 'I mean if you fire old Nora, I go. And if you don't, she' – jerking his head towards his companion – 'goes. 'Oo d'you want, Kostas, mi old friend? 'Er, or me. Go on, tell us.'

This scene took place in the viewing room, where Kostas, Luciano, Derek, Jim Parkinson who was going to be editing the film, Pino the new cameraman, Riccardo the focus puller, Stefan, Marina and Al had gathered to see the dailies. They were just about to start, Kostas having muttered to Luciano to call the projectionist to say they were ready, when 'Mr and Mrs X' as Kostas called them marched into the room, already, it was obvious from Judy's high colour, having had words and still more obviously about to have further words here. For a moment or two Kostas pretended not to see what was so obvious, and merely grunted, 'Hi, Jimmy, hi, Judy, I'm sorry, you can't come in here, it's not good for actors to see themselves in the dailies. It makes you self-conscious.' But, when Jimmy snapped, 'Oh fuck off, Kostas, I 'aven't come to see the dailies I've come to talk to you,' the director gave up the pretence; and sitting down with his head in his hands, as if prepared to hear that the world was coming to an end, he sighed, grunted, 'Oh Christ,' and then said, in the tone of one talking to a difficult child, 'What is it, Jimmy?'

Jimmy looked down at Kostas. He looked around at the assembled company, unsure whether he wanted to talk to Kostas alone, or whether he wanted an audience. And finally he glanced at Judy. 'It's 'er,' he said, indicating his girlfriend.

If Jimmy, however, felt some small doubt about how to go about this interview, Judy felt none. Looking suddenly so authoritative as to seem more like Jimmy's mother than his mistress – yet at the same time making it clear why Jimmy had taken up with her and stayed with her; hysterical she might be at times, but when it came to the crunch she knew how to take control – she said so firmly, 'Kostas, will you look at me when I'm speaking,' that Kostas, albeit wearily, and with another little sigh, did.

'You can sigh all you like, and I'm sorry to interrupt you. But I won't take up much of your time. It's very simple. There's a thief on our set. I think I know who it is. I'm *sure* I know who it is. And I want her sent away. If you don't send her away I'll go. I cannot work in an atmosphere of distrust. That's all.'

'That's not fucking all,' Jimmy said sullenly. 'She doesn't

know who it is. She's got no proof. And I won't 'ave it, Kostas. You understand me?' He paused, unwilling now to look at Judy. Then, undoubtedly because he was conscious of defying her, and it unnerved him, he retreated into his famous rock star personality, and did what Jimmy X, rather than Jimmy Bastow from Hackney, would have done. In a transformation so sudden it shocked his spectators, his face became red, his bright blue little eyes became tiny, and he lost his temper. 'D'you fucking understand me!' he shrieked at Kostas. 'I'm not 'aving anyone sent off this set. And if you try to I'll fucking *kill* you. You can't just be accusing people and dismissing them like they was dogs. D'you understand me? And I'll tell you one thing, Kostas. You try to send Nora away then I'm leaving. I'll be on the plane to London tomorrow. And then you'll be 'earing from my lawyers. I – I – I won't 'ave it, is that clear? I don't care 'oo asks you. Not the fucking Queen. Not the fucking Pope. No one. All right. All right?'

Kostas hadn't flinched during this outburst. When it was over he stood up, put his arm round Jimmy's shoulder, and walked down the short aisle of the viewing room with him. Down as far as the screen. Where he turned; and walked Jimmy back up. And down again. And up.

'Jimmy,' he said at last. 'I'm not your enemy.'

'I know you're not,' Jimmy said, sounding contrite now. 'And I'm not really shouting at you. I just –' he laughed, the mischievous schoolboy asserting that he wasn't really bad. Once more he looked round at the people watching, and practically winked at them. 'Poor old Kostas. I've rather put you on the spot, 'aven't I?'

When he concluded with his ' 'Er, or me? Go on, tell us', there was a moment's silence. Not because anyone really doubted what Kostas would say regarding Nora. It was just that everyone was waiting to hear how Judy would react; and to see how Kostas got out of the ultimatum he had been presented with. As he had to get out of it. He couldn't afford to lose Judy now. Any more than he could afford to lose Jimmy.

Kostas, short, dark, stocky, folded his arms over his chest, visibly suppressing his desire for a cigarette as he realized that to light one now would be a sign of weakness. He gazed up at Judy, as unflinchingly as he had gazed at Jimmy throughout the singer's tirade. And then he did perhaps the only thing he could have done. Expressing neither disapproval nor approval, neither admonishment nor forgiveness, he handed the hot potato to her. 'Well, Judy,' he said. 'It's up to you.'

Judy, when she needed to be, was strong. She was also, when she needed to be, sensible. She might walk to the edge of a cliff, and have the nerve to peer right over it. But she was not about to step off. She shrugged. She looked down at her lover, and said, 'Come on, Jimmy, they want to get on with the dailies.' Then she, as Jimmy had done, looked around at the assembled company. Instead of winking at them, however, or asking in some way for their complicity, she nodded at them as if to say, 'Mark my words.'

In a voice of a seriousness, of an authority that Al would never have believed her capable of, she murmured, 'You'll regret this.' And without any further ado she turned, and left the room.

Still, for a moment, as Jimmy followed her, closing the door behind him, no one moved. Judy's pronouncement – that had not been a threat; it was a warning she had issued, as if she really did know something about Nora – seemed to hang in the air as palpably as cigarette smoke. Then, this image having perhaps reached him, Kostas finally lit up; and he muttered, 'Okay, let's start,' as calmly – as mournfully – as he would have had there been no interruption at all.

'Oh, the wonderful world of movies,' Stefan said an hour later, as he and Al and Alan Miller got into Marina's car, and the four of them set off for a restaurant on the Appia Antica where they could eat outside and it would be marginally cooler than in the city. Yet he was unable to keep a note of genuine sadness out of his voice; thus expressing what all of them, Al guessed, felt. That matters had got a little out of hand this evening, had gone beyond the bounds of what was permissible even by the silly standards of the cinema; and that they had all witnessed what they would have preferred not to witness. He also, Al couldn't help feeling, expressed a more personal grievance: that of being unable not to wonder, when things like this happened, whether he had been right to leave Russia. At times, 'working in the movies' seemed such a flimsy pretext for abandoning one's country, one's culture; and obliging one's parents to do so, too . . .

They undoubtedly were cooler sitting outside at the restaurant on the Appia Antica. Also they ate well, the restaurant was neither crowded nor noisy, and, since it was Friday, they could drink as much as they liked without having to worry about getting up early the following morning, and possibly having to work with a hangover. Despite this, that note of sadness or regret that Stefan had sounded as they climbed into the car seemed to remain with them all evening; an exile's tune being faintly hummed beneath the chirping of the crickets, and the clink of plate and glass.

'Go back?' Stefan said, in reply to a question of Alan's, fingering his glass and gazing at the eucalyptus tree that hung over the table as if it were a silver birch, snow-covered, standing on the edge of the steppes. 'I don't know. In one way of course I'd love to. In another – ' he hesitated, and smiled wistfully at the image that rose before his eyes – 'I'd be scared to. Just in case I liked it too much. I mean, I've made my choice, haven't I? And it was one of those choices you can't go back on. I suppose I was young at the time when I made it. And I don't know, now, if I'd make the same choice. Especially with all that's happening in Russia now. I have a feeling it might be an interesting – ' he smiled again, still more wanly – 'even exciting time to be there. But that's a false premise. Because I'm sitting here, aren't I? Sitting under a tree on the Appia Antica in Rome. And tomorrow if I wanted to I could fly off to England, France, back to the States – anywhere. I mean it's a sort of luxury, isn't it, wondering whether one made the right decision, and telling oneself that if one had to take that decision now it might be different. The sort of luxury that perhaps only someone who's got a job like mine, and lives where I do, can afford. All the same – I suppose the answer must be yes. I would like to go back for a visit. And if that did make me want to stay, or make me regret my decision to leave – well, that'd be too bad, wouldn't it? I couldn't go back now. My parents couldn't take another move. So – even my regret would be futile, just – ' he stopped, and sipped his wine; and for a second all of them felt the cold wind, blowing in from Siberia.

After Stefan, it was Alan Miller's turn; to tell them of a youth spent traipsing round the world as his father, who worked for a banking corporation, was transferred from one country, from one continent to another.

'I don't think we ever spent more than three years in any one place,' he said. 'In a way I loved it. I think I'd seen more of the world by the time I was twenty than most people see in their lifetime. But in another way it was unsettling, obviously. We never had a fixed home. And though we always lived in a sort of portable American cocoon – mixing with other Americans, going to American schools, living in American-style apartments, eating American food, reading American newspapers – we were always conscious – or I was – that it was only a cocoon we were living in, and that out there, all around you, there was another world, that seemed like the real world. And my own real world, the States, I hardly knew at all, and despite living in an American cocoon I felt more like a foreigner there when we went back every summer to visit my grandmother than I did in, oh, I don't know, Paris, Kuwait, Jakarta, **Singapore, Lima. And this probably sounds very trite. It** probably *is* very trite. But I'm sure this constant hiking round from one place to the other was why I took to photography so early, so naturally. I mean I was a kind of perpetual tourist, taking snaps of other people's reality. But never really getting involved. Oh, later, when I started to get to know more about what I was doing, I could tell myself – I do still tell myself – that my skill, or talent, or art, or whatever you will as a photographer was my way of getting involved. I think that's just self-justification though. An excuse for being a perpetual observer. And making money out of it. And having fun. And really being very happy doing what I'm doing. But still, I could never make a movie myself. I mean as a director. I couldn't even act in one. That would be too much like taking part, really having to get my hands dirty. And I guess, deep down, I'm sorry. And feel envious of people who do – oh, I dunno, belong. Or feel they do. I mean they may not have seen as much as I have. But maybe they've – done more.' He smiled. 'Maybe not. Anyway, like you said, Stefan, it's no use having regrets, is it? Just play the cards you've been dealt, and make it as good a game as possible. And that's not,' he concluded, 'an original remark.'

Then, finally, it was Al's turn to listen to that exile's lament being hummed somewhere in the background; and to be inspired by it to sing a little song of his own. Though, as he said, he couldn't really join the club, since until the age of sixteen he had never left Hollidaysburg, let alone the state of Pennsylvania. Nevertheless, he murmured, he didn't reckon you had to be an exile to feel like one. 'I mean I never have, but both my parents – I think the reason they wouldn't go beyond the Hollidaysburg city limits was a bit like you, Stefan. I think they were afraid that if they did they'd start regretting whatever decision it was that brought them to where they were. And if they'd ever gone back to – well, I was going to say: where they came from. My father was born in the States, for God's sake. But I still **think he had a sort of vague idea of being from somewhere** else, somewhere better. 'Cos he was never really happy, and nothing he did ever turned out well, and I have a feeling he thought, if only he stayed where he belonged, things would have gone different. They wouldn't, of course, he did belong where he was. If anywhere. Even so . . . And my mother – she was born in Brazil. She didn't come to the States until she was sixteen. Oh and sure, the family hadn't any work in Brazil, and they were poor and all that, and they did okay in Pennsylvania. Even so, she had some kind of dream of home too, and – oh, I dunno, maybe I'm exaggerating. Being sentimental. But I always felt I was brought up in an atmosphere of regret.' He paused, to allow that sad background music really to well up, and sound now quite clearly through the night. Then he grinned, sat up, poured himself some more wine, and looked straight at Marina; as if to announce, all right, that's enough, no more dirges, let's get on with the show. 'That's why I decided to get out,' he said. 'To enjoy myself, and never regret anything if I could help it. And so far – ' he lifted his glass, first to Marina, then to Stefan and Alan, 'I've succeeded. So here's to hot summer nights, to movies – and to us.'

They drank, all four of them; and for a while Al's brave gesture did manage to banish the ghosts that had been haunting them all evening. Only for a while, even so; then, as he began to feel that his contribution to the theme of exile had been rather weaker than everyone else's, and that his final rally had had something about it of whistling in the dark, Al became aware that the frost had descended once more, and was, if anything, still sharper than before. A frost caused by the very realization, on everyone present's part, that while Marina, Stefan and Alan would probably, in one way or another, always be all right, the one person who was likely to have real cause for regret in his life was he, Al. By that; and by a return, for them all, of the memory of what had happened this evening in the viewing room.

'I wonder what Judy and Jimmy are doing tonight,'

Stefan said. 'Having a stand-up fight, or just ignoring the whole thing?'

'I wonder what poor Nora's doing tonight?' Alan said. 'Eating alone in some restaurant, or sitting alone in her hotel room, sipping wine out of a stolen chalice?'

That did it. The eucalyptus leaves stiffened; a chill passed over them so palpably that Marina shivered.

'An angel flying over your grave,' Stefan murmured; but all of them knew it was no angel. It was desolation, sadness, dishonesty; it was loneliness, desperation, death.

Naturally one had evenings like that; when nothing one did or said could clear the mists of melancholy. Al knew that, and knew that for every down evening, one tended to have ten, or twenty if one was lucky, up. Nevertheless, this return of the frost to what should have been a warm and happy table, along with the fact that Marina alone had not come up with any tale of regret, made him not just more determined than ever to ask her to go away with him next weekend, if not indeed this weekend, tomorrow, tonight, but made him sure that he was, seriously, 'in love' with her.

Al, as Stefan tended to in conversation, always put those words in quotes when he said them to himself. To protect himself, should he ever be called on to explain what he meant by the really unexplainable expression. The defence of irony, he guessed it was. But in fact, he reflected, as he caught himself looking at Marina, and smiling at her as if no one else were present, he didn't feel at all ironical about Marina, nor about his feelings for her. She was attractive – though he saw her, with her blue eyes, blonde hair, smooth skin, near plumpness, and gentle expression, as beautiful. She was, as her expression suggested, kind – with that kindness that comes from having a fellow feeling for most of the people and creatures of the world, tempered by an antipathy for the requisite few – and unpretentious, bright, and sweet. Above all, however – and it was this that made him see her as beautiful, and want to put his arms around her and kiss her even here at the table – she did have that sense of belonging that Stefan and Alan had professed not to have; and he, though he guessed it was sentimental claptrap to say this, had never had as firmly as he would have liked. Marina *couldn't* have sung a song of exile; she couldn't have told a winter's tale on this summer night. Marina was almost as firmly rooted in her country, in her culture, as – as, Al thought, looking around him, those cypress trees over by the edge of the restaurant. Not for her any fashionable sense of 'alienation'; not for her any doubt as to her own reality. Just by looking at Marina you could see she didn't have a ghost anywhere in her family; and, while he had gathered that she wasn't particularly religious, he felt that she was one of those people who had an instinctive understanding of who, or what, God was; and an instinctive relation with God. Marina might feel a wistful attraction for those who had gone adrift; which was why, possibly, he had tried to make it seem that he had, like Stefan and Alan. But she herself would never go adrift, whatever happened to her; and, however adrift one went oneself, if Marina was there on the shore, waiting, one would never, entirely, be lost. She was one's way home; she was safety, rest and peace.

All this, on a hot yet frosty summer night, Al, having drunk a fair amount, told himself. All this, having drunk still more, he tried to tell Marina – with his eyes and smile – half an hour later, after Stefan had gone to the bathroom, and Alan had gone to the car to check that it was locked and his cameras were all right. When he asked her if tomorrow they could go away somewhere, just the two of them. Please, he tried to add, once again just with his eyes. Please.

Did Marina not get this message he was wildly signalling to her? Had she drunk too much herself to see clearly? Or did she simply have something to do tomorrow, that made it impossible for her to go away for the weekend?

Al couldn't tell; Alan was already returning from the car; and, anyway, there were certain questions one couldn't ask. All he knew was that Marina looked at him with an expression that seemed to him a combination of sorrow and embarrassment; that she reached out across the table and squeezed his hand; and then, with a smile of what he could only think of as god-like sweetness, she murmured, 'No, I'm sorry, Al, I can't.'

That she just didn't want to go away with him, or that having indeed seen and understood his message she had chosen to ignore it, Al refused to consider until he was back in his hotel room, an hour and a half later, and was lying on his bed. But when the idea did come to him, and he couldn't dismiss it, he told himself that if it were true he wasn't sure if he could, or wanted to, continue working on this film. He wasn't even sure if he could or wanted to continue working with Stefan. He had had enough of outcasts, he told himself; he had had enough of hysterical actors and actresses, of stories of theft, of unhappiness. He wanted to go home, to be back on the shore. Otherwise he would end up like his parents, regretting the loss of something he had never possessed. Or worse, he would end up with ninety per cent of himself becoming excited by persecutions, humiliations, and cruelty; and only ten per cent cleaving to the good. I am not self-sufficient or brave like Stefan, he told himself; I am not cold and content to observe, like Alan. I must be able to feel the earth beneath my feet; I must have safety. And, if Marina will not help me to find it, then I shall have to look for someone else who will.

Oh Marina, Marina, Al cried silently, lying on his bed, conscious of being drunk but telling himself that that altered nothing: please, please – love me.

CHAPTER 6

ALL WEEK they had been saying, 'What are we going to do next weekend?'; unable to decide between going to Florence ('Too hot'), going to the sea somewhere ('Too crowded') or driving round the Tuscan hill towns. Yet now, on Saturday morning, it seemed they were not going anywhere.

She didn't see how they could be going anywhere, Marina told herself when she woke up at eight, got out of bed, and went to make herself some coffee. Not because it was too late; she could have been ready in an hour, and in two or three they could have been in San Gimignano, or Montepulciano – or Viareggio, had they decided on the sea after all. Nor because she didn't want to go; she did, she would have loved to; even return to Amalfi, and repeat last weekend's excursion. That had been wonderful. After all, what was the alternative? Spending today and tomorrow shut up in her small dark apartment, tending the plants on her minute balcony, reading, and trying in vain to keep cool?

No, it was just because Al had asked her that question last night; and, having refused, she had felt obliged to say, when dropping Stefan and Al off at their hotel, and Stefan had asked her what they had all decided, that she was sorry, she thought she was busy, but she would call them. She had had to say something, otherwise Al would have thought – Al would have realized – that it was him she didn't want to go away with. Which would have offended him, or hurt him, and might well have caused some sort of dissension. As it was, by saying she might be busy, it looked as if she had refused for that reason only. Obviously, if Al asked her again, as she was afraid he would, she would have to tell him no, she was sorry, but she didn't want to be alone with him. She would have preferred to be alone with Stefan; if that couldn't be managed, then it was either with both of them she went out, or neither. Maybe, however, before she was forced to say anything like that, something would crop up to resolve the situation. She didn't see what, but one never knew, did one? Perhaps Al would suddenly have to go back to America. Perhaps Judy would walk off the set, and the film would be suspended. Or perhaps – she smiled at her own foolishness – Stefan would take her aside and ask her to marry him . . .

If only they *had* arranged something earlier though, she told herself as she looked out of the window up at the bright blue sky, and pictured herself lying next to Stefan on some beach, rubbing oil into his back and legs, watching his blond hair go blonder still in the sun, and feeding him grapes. Or: just talking to him, listening to him, and slowly, under an umbrella, falling asleep by his side. Then Al couldn't have asked that question; she wouldn't now be standing in her kitchen sweating, unsure whether to take a shower or go back to bed, and at this very moment they might be on the road with music playing, Stefan sitting beside her as she drove, and Al sitting behind.

They might even, had they gone away last night, be waking up in some hotel overlooking the sea; stepping out onto their adjoining balconies and smiling at each other with the warmth and intimacy of two people who had spent the night together. Two people . . . Marina and Stefan . . .

Telling herself to stop this nonsense immediately, Marina went to the telephone, called the hotel, and asked for Stefan.

'I'm sorry to wake you at this hour,' she said. 'But I just

spoke to my mother. I'd promised to have lunch with her and my father. They've just bought a small house in Fregene – that's up the coast, thirty kilometres from Rome – and they want me to see it. But I was telling her about you and Al – I mean I'd already spoken of you – and she said why didn't I invite you out too. So – it's not quite Viareggio, or Montepulciano, or Florence. But if you'd like – I could pick you up around ten-thirty, quarter to eleven. How would that be? We can spend the night there if you like. Otherwise we can come back and – I should have arranged all this before, but my mother's so unpredictable – '

Poor mother, Marina thought, as Stefan said yes, that sounded wonderful, and he was sure Al would be happy to come. Poor mother. She would be delighted to meet Stefan and Al, of whom it was true she had heard a good deal since they had all come back from the States. But she really was the most predictable of women . . .

At least, Marina thought, she hoped she was; in that she hoped she was going to Fregene this weekend, as she had every weekend since the house had been bought.

She also hoped that neither her mother nor her father would mind having guests; and that they hadn't invited anyone themselves.

She guessed, in another half an hour or so – give them a chance to wake up, and have a coffee – she had better call them, too.

She did; she caught them just as they were setting off for Fregene. And no, of course they wouldn't mind having guests. On the contrary. With the result that by midday at least one of the fantasies that Marina had had that morning – that of lying next to Stefan, rubbing oil into his back – had become reality.

Yet though she thought she had arranged matters tact-fully, and things turned out pretty much for the best – all right Viareggio or Montepulciano might have been more fun, but there were plenty of other weekends – Marina was aware that Al wasn't completely happy. She had murmured to him, in the lobby of the hotel, as they were waiting for Stefan to come down, that she was terribly sorry about this, and she hoped he wouldn't mind having to put up with her parents. But she had had to see them – she really hadn't seen them since she had returned from New York – and when her mother had suggested that she invite 'you and Stefan' she hadn't known how to say no. The inference being that, if she hadn't had this prior engagement, she would have gone away with him. Or even that, if her mother hadn't specifically asked for both of them, she would have invited him alone out to Fregene.

Yet either he hadn't believed her – or hadn't caught what she was trying to infer – or he had sensed what he had never seemed to sense before: that, when she was with Stefan, she became fractionally more alive, more alert, more something, than she was when she wasn't with him – or than she was when she was with him, Al.

With the result that now, as he lay stretched out on her other side, lying on his back with his eyes closed, although he appeared to be sleeping, Marina could feel him radiating waves of resentment, of petulance even. It might just have been that he had drunk too much last night, and had a hangover; he had told her he had when she arrived at the hotel this morning, and kissed him, and muttered her apology. Or that he was depressed and worried for some other reason. But she suspected not. There was the unmistakable whiff of the hard-done-by in the set of his shoulders; the unmistakable shape of 'poor me' on those slightly open I'm-not-pouting lips. So much so that Marina wondered whether they were going to get through this weekend without a fight; and started to think that, after all, she might have done better to stay home by herself and tend her plants.

He had a handsome enough body, she reflected, as she

looked down at his chest and stomach and arms and legs; as he had a handsome enough face, with his long black hair and somehow antique features. And though he would soon – or had already started to – run to softness, if not fat, and his fashionable two-day growth of beard accentuated rather than hid, as it was no doubt intended to hide, this tendency, he still hadn't quite done so; and she couldn't deny that for the moment it was a pleasure to look at him.

Yet – it was nothing more than a pleasure; than the sort of pleasure looking at a splendid dog or big cat might have given one. A dog or cat that was not, moreover, one's own; and to which one felt, therefore, no particular emotional attachment. Sure, it was a beauty, and isn't nature marvellous, but – what was it you were saying, and I'm sorry, but I really must be going.

Whereas Stefan – oh, Marina told herself, that was something else altogether. It wasn't statue-like, his body, as Al's in its heavy sculpted way might have been thought to be. Nor, really, though this she knew was mere prejudice, was she very fond of fair skin, and blond hair in men. There again, though, she couldn't help telling herself: yet. Yet Stefan's body, to her, was perfect; and, while she knew she was seeing it through eyes that were idealizing what they were looking at, she could not only see no fault in it – in the long legs, in the smooth back now shining with oil – but it was all she could do not to lean over, touch it, kiss it and cling to it.

Yes, she was being ridiculous, she knew; she had no patience with women who fell in love with homosexual men and thought that maybe, somehow, something magic would happen. But what could she do? She didn't think anything magic would happen; or even, possibly, want it to. All the same, she did love Stefan, she was mad about him – literally, she told herself: mad – and calling herself ridiculous didn't alter that. She loved him for that air of otherness that he had – an otherness that she believed had little or nothing to do with his homosexuality. She loved him for what she could only call his moral grace; the grace that comes from knowing where one stands in the world, knowing what price one has paid and made other people pay to stand there, and of maintaining one's stance without bombast, without defiance, without pretension; and with as great a good humour as one can muster, and enough but not too many doubts as to whether one should be maintaining it at all. And she loved him, finally, for that very love she knew he felt for Al; a love, she told herself, though she wasn't certain what she meant by this, that would prevent him from ever being overwhelmed by his otherness, cast utterly adrift by it; and would eventually, for all his exile's soul, see him safely home. Back to Russia? Back to a belief in something other than movies? She didn't know; but home, she was sure, Stefan would sooner or later reach.

Loving him, she saw him as beautiful; seeing him as beautiful, she loved him more.

Ah Marina, she told herself, looking down over the sand, to the children playing by the water's edge, to people swimming further out to sea, to the windsurfers, the water-skiers, the sail boats and the speed boats: really, you're such a fool.

Smiling, she lay down herself at last; and, closing her eyes, felt almost entirely at peace.

'Al, what's wrong?'

It was eight o'clock that evening; and they were taking a final walk along the beach before going home to shower, change, and have dinner. The sun was setting, the crowds had gone; and the sea, so smooth it broke on the sand with a scarcely audible 'plllop', was beginning to acquire the colours of the evening sky: dusty pinks, faintest mauves, and palest, most translucent greens.

Of course, Marina told herself, as soon as her words were out, she shouldn't have asked that question. She had known all day what was wrong; and it was nothing different now from what had been wrong that morning. Suddenly, however, she had felt unable to contain her irritation any longer. There they were, on this warm lovely evening, with the only sound that hypnotic plllop, plllop of the waves; and all Al could do was walk five or six paces ahead of her and Stefan, head bent, silent, and visibly sulking. It was infuriating. It had been his sulks that had stopped her sense of peace being absolute this morning when she had laid down beside Stefan; it had been his sulks that had stopped Stefan being as content as he otherwise might have been. Well, she told herself, he could either snap out of it, or go back to Rome this evening. She wouldn't have him spoil what would otherwise have been a flawless weekend. She liked him; she liked him very much. He was generally fun, and good-natured, and kind. But if he couldn't accept gracefully the fact that she did only like him, and not love him, it would be better if they just saw each other on the set, and left it at that. That would probably mean that Stefan would stop seeing her out of work hours too, but that was just one of those things. I mean I can't put up with nonsense, can I, she asked herself. Not indefinitely. Not even for love.

Can I, she repeated to herself, as Al, in answer to her question, muttered, 'Nothing, I'm fine;' and continued on down the beach with his head bent.

Yes, of course you can, a small half-weary, half-amused voice told her. It's all very well being brave now. But you know that, if Stefan suggested you all three go out together some evening, you'd accept even if Al was in the worst of moods. I mean now – you won't send Al back to Rome. Because, if you do, Stefan will go with him. So shut up, make the best of it, and be thankful for what you've got. That is, precisely, a beautiful evening; the company of a person you love; and the not excessively irksome company of a person who loves you – and is in turn loved by the **person you love. It's just a little comedy. And, honestly,** there's no point in getting steamed up about it. Relax. Smile. And go up to Al now, and give him a kiss.

That'll make everything pass.

Marina had been having this conversation with herself. Yet either because Al – and Stefan – had guessed what she'd been saying, because both had been having similar conversations with themselves, or because the evening, that had been settling down towards perfection, suddenly, in its colours, its light, its stillness, struck perfection – and struck it so completely that no one could have failed to be moved by it – as she came to her conclusion, the two men seemed to come to conclusions of their own. Conclusions that took the form of Stefan, by her side, reaching out and taking her hand, and of Al, in front of them, now turning, looking at them – though more at her – and saying, softly, 'I'm sorry. I've been kind of – ' He shrugged, gave a smile that made him look for a second like a ten-year-old, and waited till they caught up with him. 'I'm sorry,' he repeated, only to Marina this time, and, putting his arm around her shoulder, drew her to him, and kissed her on the cheek. 'It won't happen again. I was just being stupid.' Briefly, Marina let her head rest against his warm dark chest; then she kissed him on the cheek, and held Stefan's hand more tightly as Al nodded at Stefan, grinned, and looked out over the sea to where the sun had just set.

'My God,' he said, 'isn't it beautiful?'

They stood there, all three, hardly moving lest they should disturb this moment of rapture. And now, without Marina's quite being aware of how it happened, she had her arm around Stefan's waist, Stefan had his arm around Al's shoulder, and Al was standing so close to her that her breasts were pressed into his back, and his legs seemed entwined with hers. They clung to each other, they seemed to melt into each other; until eventually, quite still, they felt as if they had become one large, many limbed creature. For ten seconds, twenty seconds, thirty seconds they held it. Then, again in a single almost instinctive movement, they

· 111 ·

separated; smiling at each other like three people who have just seen something they have never seen before, and may never see again.

They walked on for a little while, none of them for the moment willing to talk, lest they disturb that peace that lay over them as softly, as comfortingly, as the evening sky itself. Then a dog came racing along the beach, barking and splashing in the water as it chased a ball its owner had thrown; and Marina gave her head a slight shake and said, 'Come on, let's go back and eat. I'm *hungry*.'

She was still holding Stefan's hand.

Having thus in a sense glimpsed heaven, Marina hoped they would be able to hang on to at least a fragment of their vision for a while. Naturally a hundred things could cause it to evaporate as rapidly as a morning mist in summer, and all it would need to bring them down to earth would be a touch of indigestion, a bad night's sleep, a persistent mosquito, a disagreement about politics over dinner, or their having taken too much sun. Naturally, too, once they were back in town, the various problems inherent in their friendship would rise to the surface again. There was no getting away from that; nor from the fact that Al would undoubtedly have further attacks of the sulks, she would probably, despite herself, start to feel upset about Stefan's being ultimately more concerned about Al than he was about her, and Stefan, finding himself in danger of being sucked down into a swamp, would remove himself to higher ground, where he could stand alone, more isolated, more other, than ever. Nonetheless, if they were careful, there was no reason why they shouldn't make it through until the morning; and if they made an effort as well, through to their departure for the city tomorrow evening. A little bit of goodwill on all their parts, a little bit of luck – and there they were.

There was goodwill on all their parts, and they did have luck; in that they didn't fall out over politics, and weren't tormented by mosquitoes. All the same, they didn't quite make it through until the following evening. They made it through the morning; they made it through lunch. And maybe they would have made it beyond that: if Stefan hadn't come to Marina's room as she was resting after lunch, sat down on the edge of her bed, and started, in a voice quiet enough not to disturb anyone else in the house, to talk to her.

'This has been a wonderful weekend,' he said, taking her hand as he had on the beach yesterday, squeezing it, and then holding it. 'Thank you. I – ' he paused, and smiled. 'It's so difficult to say these things, isn't it? But really, I'm so happy to have met you. I mean I know it's always like this when you're making a film, but I can't help feeling this is different. I've felt it right from the start, in the States. I mean I'm not sure how, but I'm sure – we'll always be friends. Always – I don't know – together.'

Marina looked at him, gave him a squeeze of her own, and returned his smile. 'Thank you for coming here,' she said. 'You – you both – have made me very happy. And yes, I can't help thinking – '

She stopped, and for a while then the two of them stayed still. Listening to the sounds of a very hot Sunday afternoon. Looking at the shiny blue tiles on the floor, at the white walls, at the sparse beach-house furnishings, at the open windows and the closed brown shutters, through which the scents of the garden outside drifted in; the scent of thyme, and roses, and jasmine. Wondering, possibly, whether there was anything more to be said; or if they couldn't just go on like that for an hour or two; communicating despite their silence, as intimate as two people can be who are not actually in bed together.

And oh, Marina was to tell herself later, if only they had just gone on sitting there; and if there hadn't been anything more to be said. But after ten minutes or so Stefan had started speaking again; and that had ruined everything.

To begin with, she thought he just wanted to talk about Al, since he started: 'Al's happy here too. I can't remember when I've seen him so happy.'

'He wasn't so happy yesterday,' Marina smiled. 'Not till yesterday evening, anyway.'

'Al's romantic.' Stefan looked down at her, and ran a finger across her forehead. 'He likes you. I mean – well, you know.'

'Yes,' Marina sighed. 'I do. I wish he didn't. I mean I'm happy he likes me. But – '

But then, as Stefan went on, sounding awkward, and slightly off key, she began to suspect what he was getting at, or trying to get round to. 'You – ' he paused, and his mouth gave an almost imperceptible twitch, as if he too were conscious of being out of tune. 'You don't find him – attractive?'

Perhaps she was imagining things, Marina told herself, as she found herself suddenly flushing, and starting, like a dog that senses danger, to bristle. Perhaps it was her ear that was defective, and not Stefan's voice. 'Yes,' she said cautiously. 'Very. I mean – he's very good-looking. But I – '

It was Stefan's expression that told her no, she was not imagining things. The strained, uneasy way he gazed towards the window. And, as she realized it, she felt so angry, so hurt, that she wanted to hit him as he sat there on the edge of her bed. It wasn't just what he was about to suggest that made her feel so furious; it was also, or more the fact, that he – her perfect, beautiful Stefan – should be suggesting it. She didn't want to hear him sing off-key; she didn't want him to be strained and uneasy. She wanted him to be pure, above the world, above – she supposed this was what it came down to – the flesh. No, she wanted to shout at him, stop it, please, please stop it. Don't soil yourself. Don't lower yourself. Don't – just don't don't, whatever you do, say anything more.

But Stefan, at this stage, couldn't stop. He might be

ashamed of himself; he might realize he could be endangering his friendship with Marina. Having gone this far, however, he had to go all the way; and actually come out with what Marina already knew he was going to come out with.

'Marina,' he muttered, letting go of her hand now, and gazing down at his knees, 'I know I shouldn't be saying this. I mean I suppose it's sort of – I don't know. But I mean – I mean – well, what I mean is, in a way it would be a perfect solution, wouldn't it? If you did like Al. That way, we could all be together always. Couldn't we?' He gave a soft, agonized laugh, and now his lips twitched quite perceptibly. He clasped his hands together. He unclasped them. And then he bowed his head.

She tried to make a joke of it; to pretend she was as unaffected by it as she would have been by a fluff of thistledown drifting past on the wind. 'You mean you want me to make love to Al to keep him happy?' she said. And she might even have managed it, had Stefan himself not been in such agony; had the whole subject not been so conspicuously unfunny, not in the least light, to him. As it was, when he bit his lip, and gave another little laugh that sounded half-crazed now, and muttered, 'Well, as I say it would be sort of – satisfactory, wouldn't it?', she could keep up the pretence of good humour no longer.

She had to force herself not to shout something – she didn't know what; just anything – at Stefan; and she realized that, without her wanting to, she had started crying. 'Why?' she eventually said, her voice thick with her tears. 'So you can make love with him vicariously? So you don't lose him? Oh – oh fuck you,' she almost spat, sitting up in bed, grabbing his hair, and pulling it as hard as she could. '*Fuck* you. We've had such a beautiful weekend, and I've been so happy. And now – what am I? Some sort of – ?' She grabbed Stefan's hand then, and bit it as hard as she could. 'Fuck you fuck you fuck you.'

Stefan made no sound as she pulled his hair, nor as she

bit his hand. He just sweated; felt two scarlet spots appear on his cheeks beneath his already red skin; and started to cry himself.

They cried, they snivelled, they sniffed for perhaps five minutes; then Stefan got up and without a word left the room; and a couple of hours later, without having said another word to each other, they drove in silence back to Rome; the fact that they had for some reason fallen out, and fallen out badly, so obvious, that Al made no attempt to discover what had happened. He just sat in the back and hung on as Marina whipped the car, very fast, round corners; and contented himself with a muttered, 'Thank you, Marina, that was great,' as she practically pushed them out of the car in front of their hotel.

'Fuck him fuck him fuck him,' Marina told herself as she drove, faster than ever, across town back to her apartment behind the forums. And 'fuck him fuck him fuck him,' she repeated to herself as she reversed swiftly into a parking space, hitting the car behind, got out, slammed the door, and, going up to her dark little hot little rooms on the first floor, threw herself on her bed and wanted not so much to cry now as grab a knife and stick it into Stefan. He had spoiled everything; and he had not only thrown away whatever scraps of perfection that had been left over from yesterday evening; he had, with his suggestion, managed to cancel retroactively the perfection there had been. Fuck him fuck him *fuck* him. Damn him damn him damn him.

She was still lying on her bed two hours later – it was ten o'clock – when Stefan called; though she had by this stage stopped cursing him, and was asking herself, trying to be rational, exactly why she had been so hurt, angry, outraged. She guessed it was partly because she felt, as she had said, that Stefan was trying to use her as a means of keeping Al, and partly because it was Stefan himself she wanted to make love to; and was humiliated by the suggestion that she should make love with someone else. She was still hurt, angry and outraged; and still felt humiliated by what had occurred. Nevertheless, the very fact that she was trying to be rational meant that with any luck the worst was over; and was undoubtedly the reason why, instead of hanging up on Stefan as she would have done if he had called immediately she came in, she not only didn't hang up, but was, despite everything, happy to hear from him.

'Marina,' he said, as if he expected her to hang up, 'I'm sorry.'

She said nothing, not knowing what to say, and waited.

'Marina?' Stefan said.

'Yes,' she said in a voice that sounded tiny even to her ears.

'I – I truly didn't mean to hurt you. I wouldn't, for anything in the world. You know that, don't you?'

Did she? 'Yes,' she repeated, in a still tinier voice.

'I just – oh – there's no point in going into it. But – I really am sorry.'

'That's all right,' Marina said, her voice just above a whisper now. 'Perhaps I over-reacted.' She attempted a small, audible smile. 'I mean – you're right. It would be a good solution. Only – ' she stopped and, when she went on, her voice was almost at its normal level. 'Why's everything so complicated?' she said, and sighed, and smiled again. 'It would have been much easier, wouldn't it? But really,' she added, 'I had a lovely weekend, and I was very happy to be with you – both,' she slipped in, with practically a laugh now. 'And – I'll see you tomorrow.'

'Bright and early,' said Stefan.

'Oh God, don't remind me.'

'And, Marina?'

'Yes?'

'I *am* sorry. And I had a beautiful weekend too.'

'I'll see you tomorrow,' Marina said.

So, on the surface, everything had been smoothed over. It

was only on the surface, however, this return to general harmony. And by eight-thirty the following morning Marina realized she had been right to think, even before the drama in her bedroom, that the problems inherent in her relations with Stefan and Al would bob up again; like, it seemed to her now, an insufficiently weighed-down corpse.

Two things brought this home to her; the first of which started soon after she arrived on the set. When, having checked all her notes and filled in the various forms she would need during the day, she went to say good morning to Kostas, who had just come down from his room.

Even before she spoke to him she saw he was looking haggard, and had clearly had no rest. 'Christ, Marina,' he moaned, 'I had a bloody awful weekend.'

Marina put her hand on his shoulder; not wanting to be familiar, but to give him the comfort he was obviously in need of.

'What happened?'

'I had a whole weekend of actors. I can't take any more. D'you want to come to the bar and have a coffee?'

'Sure.'

'Friday night I got back to the villa at about eleven. At quarter to twelve, I had just gone to sleep – the phone rings. Judy. "I'm sorry to wake you, Kostas, but I've got to talk to you." .'

'Again?'

'That's what I said. Yes. It seems that she and Jimmy had a stand-up fight – I mean it was obvious they were going to, wasn't it? – and – she wanted to come over then. I said no, I'm sorry, you can't. "Well, I'll be out at nine o'clock tomorrow morning," she said. And she was. Wearing a track suit and glasses, like some businesswoman, and with her lawyer and agent here. God knows why. They weren't allowed to say a word. She didn't say hello or good morning or anything to Lizzie – fucking rude bitch – and just sat down and started firing away. She had been gravely insulted the night before. Not by me she hadn't, I wanted to tell her. By her bloody husband, maybe, or whatever Jimmy is, but that's not my fault. She had been put in a position where it was impossible to give of her best. She understood I couldn't fire Nora – '

'All this for *Nora*?' Marina said.

'I know, you can't believe it, can you? I mean what would these people do if anything serious ever happened? Anyway – she didn't see why she should be held up to public ridicule, or be put in a position where she couldn't give her best. So she was giving me an ultimatum. Another one. No, she wouldn't walk off the movie, she didn't see why *her* career should suffer. But she was going to insist on one thing. That from now on, and until the movie finished, she did not want to see Nora. If the woman had to be on the set – fine, it seemed there was nothing she could do about it. But she had to stay out of sight. She could listen to every word she said on a headset. She could listen to the tapes again at the end of every take. She could do what she wanted – but she had, from now on, to stay out of sight, and she must not, from now on, address a single word to her. If she had any complaints, and comments about a word, a syllable, an inflection, she was to tell Stefan, or Al. *They* were the sound department. And they could communicate the problem to her. Or to me. Was that clear? If I did not agree to her request, she had instructed Vittorio, who was acting on behalf of her attorney in Beverly Hills, to file a suit against the production, and against me personally, for professional damages. "That is all I have to say, Kostas. I would be grateful if you could give me your reply by midday. I will be waiting in the residence for your call. Goodbye."

'I tell you, Marina,' Kostas muttered, putting his arm around her now, as he guided her across the pine-shaded road that separated the sound stages from the bar, 'I would so dearly have loved to fire her, or have told her, Oh, go ahead, sue, that I couldn't even look at her as she walked back to her car. But – oh God, I've got problems enough as it is. And if I had said anything – who knows, the fucking producers might have fired me. So – I got Lizzie to phone at midday and say yes, okay. But no, Madam wanted to hear it from my own lips. And then – she was all sweetness and light like nothing had ever happened, and she was sorry not to have seen Lizzie this morning – not see her, she walked right through her! – and we must all have a drink together, and what were we doing this evening? I'm busy this evening, Judy, I told her. I'll see you Monday. Okay, Kostas darling, have a good weekend, and you'll see, everything's going to work out fine from now on. I tell you, Marina, it was exactly as if she needed a sacrifice, and – I hung up, lit a cigarette – by the way, what are you having?'

'A coffee.'

'Due caffè,' Kostas told the woman at the cash desk in the bar; then murmured, 'I haven't got any money, Marina, you'll have to pay.'

Marina smiled, and did so, and Kostas went on.

'I mean literally not more than five seconds had passed, when the phone rang again. I thought it was Madam again, and got Lizzie to answer. But no. It was Michael. He'd just arrived. The flight had been great. The residence was great. The fruit and the flowers and the wine and the books we'd sent were great – he told me in the States he liked poetry, so I got someone in production to send a whole lot of bullshit poetry books over,' Kostas interjected, 'but something was troubling him, and if I didn't mind he was going to come out right now and talk to me. He'd told the driver to wait downstairs; he'd be out in just as long as it took to get there.' Kostas sighed. 'At least he said "Hi" to Lizzie. Anyway, the problem was, he'd been thinking about the ending these last two weeks, and he'd decided it just wasn't possible for him to be killed in the end. It undermined the whole structure of the movie. It was – oh Christ, I don't know what he said. But I swear to you, Marina, he talked non-stop from quarter to one to six o'clock that evening. All through lunch. All through the afternoon. All . . . I kept on saying, Michael, we've discussed all this, we're going to shoot both endings, then we'll decide what's better. Yes, yes, he knew all that, but he couldn't work like that, he had to know what he was aiming at, what the ultimate meaning of the film was, what the sub-text was – Jesus, I thought I'd scream. I said to him, "Michael, you don't know if someone's going to smash your head in this afternoon. None of us do. But we all have to act on the assumption that no one is. So that's how you – I mean, Robert" – you can't say "you", it confuses him, for Chrissake, "has to act. As far as you're concerned, you're not going to be killed. If you are – well, that's tough shit." Yes. He knew all that. But the thing was, if Judy – I mean Elizabeth – was capable ultimately of killing him, she'd be a certain sort of person, and he'd relate to her in a different way from a person who wasn't ultimately capable of murder. And so on and so forth. Until, as I say, six o'clock. And d'you know why we stopped then? Because the telephone rang again, and guess who was on the line now? Master Jimmy, sounding very cool. " 'Allo, Kostas, Michael still there?" Yes, I said, how did you know? " 'Ee came by to say 'allo this morning when 'ee arrived. Said he was going out. Said he wanted to discuss the film with you." "Yes," I told him. "Well, Kostas, I think that's fucking insulting. There are three of us in this bloody movie. And I don't think you should discuss with one actor what may affect the others. I suppose Michael wants to change the end."

' "He doesn't want to change it," I said. "He just doesn't want the bloody one. He says it's too negative."

' "Fuck 'im. Don't you think that's something that concerns us all?"

' "Yes, Jimmy."

' "Well then, what are you going to do about it?"

' "What do you want me to do about it?"

' "You told Judy you were busy this evening. Busy with

· 121 ·

Michael, I suppose."

' "No. I just wanted to have a quiet evening alone with Lizzie."

' "Well, don't you think this movie is more important than a quiet evening alone with Lizzie?"

'I – what could I say,' Kostas moaned, drinking his coffee, lighting another cigarette, and making his way slowly out of the bar, back into the bright morning sunlight. 'Anyway, to cut a long story short, Mr and Mrs X came out together and stayed there till two in the morning, and then all three of those bastards decided that the conversation we had had had been so positive, so useful, that they wanted to continue it, finish it, tomorrow. They came back at eleven, and they were there until eleven last night. I mean I don't believe it. They didn't want to discuss the bloody film, none of them. Not really. They just wanted to be sure that the other two didn't get a bigger share of my attention, or of the film, or – God knows. Like a lot of maniacs. I mean I like Jimmy. I think he's a really nice, really sweet guy. And he only puts on all this bullshit to stop himself being crushed altogether by Judy. But even him – Jesus. And do you know what we did all end up talking about? Bloody Nora, yet again. Nora – and whether art does require blood, or sacrifice, for it to flourish. Which according to them is what the movie is all about. Only by the end I didn't know whether they were talking about the movie, or Nora, or – I mean why is it that on every film they ever work on actors end up confusing the film with real life? Or the other way round. I – oh, I don't know. Why do we do it, Marina? Why do we *do* it?'

'By the way,' he added, as they stepped into the air-conditioned cool of the set, 'can you tell Stefan and Al that they're going to have to act as go-betweens from now on. And they're going to have to provide Nora with a headset, in some place where she's invisible. I'm sorry,' he shrugged. 'But that's how it is.'

In fact, by the time Marina went over to Stefan and Al to

relay this message, they already knew, having been told by the assistant director. They had also already set up a chair for Nora in a small room off to the right of the high altar, and run wires round the studio so she could sit there and listen to what Judy said. Now, they were simply discussing with Alan, Bruno, Riccardo, and Rita how Nora would take this banishment when she arrived, as she was due to any second.

'Stoically,' Alan said; and that was the general opinion.

Yet, while most of the members of this little group were agreed that the whole business had at this point gone completely over the top – for word of Kostas's weekend had spread – and it would really be better if this nonsense stopped, one of them – Al – seemed to view it not just as professional stupidity, but as some kind of personal affront. And though when Marina had arrived that morning and kissed him he had appeared his usual cheerful if slightly reserved self, when she got back from the bar and caught the tail end of that discussion he was having with Stefan and the others, he seemed to have plunged back into the gloom that had afflicted him on Saturday.

'What's *wrong*?' she asked him again, taking him aside and speaking softly.

'Oh, I don't know,' Al said. 'It's this whole ridiculous business. It's so small, and squalid, and stupid, and – it makes me want to quit movies altogether. Or makes me wish I had one thing – I don't know – decent, beautiful, good to hang on to in my life. I mean – I've got my daughter. But I'm not allowed to see her too often. And anyway – I just want – oh, I don't know. I just want something aside from pettiness, and meanness. That's all.'

'Silliness like this isn't the whole business,' Marina said. 'It's just a small part of it. And there's silliness in every job. I'm sure you'd find just as much working in a lawyer's office, or on a building site, or on a farm.'

'Yeah, I know,' Al said. 'Only – ' Only, the look he gave Marina told her, if I can't have you, I'm determined only to see the trivia and the foolishness surrounding me, and not the good things: the skill, the dedication, the imagination. 'Oh,' he muttered, 'I'm just fed up, Marina. I'm sick of everything.'

The Nora case, and the treatment being given Nora, was the excuse then that Al used for feeling once again hard done by, and for reassuming the role of petulance. Or, to be more charitable, it was that one taste of bitterness too many, that made him determined, somewhere and somehow, to find, and attach himself in this rough sea of life to, a buoy of love.

The other thing that brought it home to Marina that her problems with Stefan and Al were unlikely to remain submerged was, however, less specific.

It was just that, after she had taken Al aside and listened to his lament, she had seen Stefan get up from his chair, cross the set, and go to break the news to Nora, who had at that moment walked in. And, as she had seen him, she had realized that whatever he had done, and whatever he did, she wouldn't for the moment be able to give him up. Nor think of him only as 'a friend'. He was, in her eyes, too beautiful; too much, pale and apart as he was, like a Russian saint; too full of the promise of being, in some fashion, 'the way'.

How gently, she could see, he was talking to Nora; even if the Englishwoman seemed unconcerned by what he was telling her. How patiently, how almost nobly, he was ignoring the fact that, though he was being kind, Nora – it was clear from the way she held herself – didn't like him.

Damn it, Marina told herself. Damn him.

Yet if, within forty-five minutes of her arrival at Cinecittà, Marina had realized that things could not again be as they were, before the morning was over she was beginning to think that, though they might be different, they might in fact be better. Sure the corpse would rise to the surface again – but mightn't that mean it could be disposed of altogether?

Perhaps it was that seeing Al looking so upset at Nora's fate – far more upset than Nora herself, who continued to take her banishment to the little back room as stoically as Alan had predicted, almost as if she welcomed punishment – she felt that there was no point in her being miserable too. Perhaps it was that she was just a naturally easy-going person, who might flare up and lose her temper, but who rarely allowed it to stay lost for long. Or perhaps it was that, like most people, she had a perverse streak in her – that streak that had responded with slightly guilty enthusiasm to Judy's initial campaign against Nora – and thought it both useless and foolish, if not ultimately dangerous, to try to deny that streak. Whatever the reason, by the time the lunch break approached, her anger of the night before had not merely disappeared, but been replaced with an also slightly guilty – though nevertheless gleeful – sense of 'Oh, what the hell, why not, it might be fun.' And she found herself not merely repeating what she had said to Stefan on the phone last night, 'It would be a good solution,' but actually thinking that it would be. Oh, of course it's wrong, she told herself, and no doubt reprehensible. But, after all, it's true that you only live once, I'm not committing myself irrevocably to anything – at worst it'll be a game that wasn't fun, a mistake I'll mildly regret – and who knows: it *might* work out.

It would be wonderful if it did . . .

Conscious that she might be substituting one set of problems for another, and conscious too that she might be fooling herself in thinking that what she was about to do was anything other than toss aside every scrap of dignity in order to hang on to Stefan, when it became clear that no more work was going to be done before lunch, and everyone was just hanging around waiting for the break to be called, Marina went into action.

First, she hurriedly finished calculating the amount of film remaining in the camera, taking precise note of every detail of the last scene they had shot, and marking those takes that Kostas wanted printed, those that were to be held in reserve, and those that were no use.

Then, keeping an eye on Kostas, in case he should need her to take part in the discussion he was having with Derek about whether Judy should have exited camera left just now, or if she shouldn't have moved camera right, she went over to Al, standing holding his microphone boom like a disconsolate knight with a lance, and, touching him on the arm, asked if they could have lunch together, just the two of them.

'Yes, sure,' Al said, looking still more disconsolate; looking positively tragic. A knight certain he was about to be dismissed from his lady's service.

And finally she went over to where Stefan was making adjustments to his equipment, glanced around the set to make sure Al was not watching – and, more to the point, had not replaced his headset – and touched him on the arm.

Stefan paused in what he was doing, looked up, and smiled; still half-nervously, half-apologetically, as if convinced that, despite his phone call last night, and the fact that they had said hello and kissed each other this morning, Marina had not yet forgiven him for what he had proposed yesterday.

'I – ' Marina said, and then stopped; uncertain what to say, or whether after all she should say anything. She looked down at Stefan, and told herself that she didn't just love him, but, now that she had cast aside her dignity, found him so physically desirable that she wanted to tear off his clothes and run her lips over his body. She gave him a smile of her own – a smile of wistfulness, a smile of complicity, a smile that implored understanding – and touched him again: on the neck. Then she came to a decision. 'I'm having lunch with Al,' she said.

Did he understand her? Oh yes, of course he did; he blushed, and lowered his eyes, and looked so confused that for a moment Marina thought he was not going to make any comment of his own. At last however he pulled himself together; and, glancing across the set to where Al was still standing, listening to the Kostas/Derek discussion, he took her hand, raised it to his lips, and said, with just the palest of smiles now, 'He must never know.'

'Well, *I'll* never tell him,' Marina practically whispered.

'You're sure you – ?'

'Yes,' Marina nodded; and smiled again. 'I mean I'm not sure. But – it can't hurt, can it?'

'I don't know about that,' Stefan said, and gave a brief laugh.

'Well, it – ' Marina hesitated; and then, suddenly, felt happy again. 'If I can't have you directly,' she said, quite cheerfully, 'I might as well have you indirectly. And, if you can't have Al directly, you might as well have him – '

'Sssh,' Stefan said with another blush, as he glanced back at Al. He returned his eyes to Marina, and murmured, shyly, 'I do love you.'

'Yes, and I love you,' Marina said. 'So there we are.'

Stefan nodded, and across the set a voice called, 'Grazie, signori, thank you everyone, lunch.'

Automatically, Stefan's hand went to turn off his machine, set out on its stand in front of him. And, as he turned it off, he didn't just blush but went literally scarlet.

'Oh, *fuck*,' he said.

'What is it?'

'Bloody Nora.'

'What about her?'

'I forgot to unplug her.'

'You mean she's been listening to us?'

'If she had her headset on, yes.'

'How hilarious,' Marina said, and couldn't resist leaning over and kissing Stefan on his forehead. 'That'll give her something to think about.'

'But if she tells Al?' Stefan said, looking not just not amused, but panic-stricken.

'Oh, of course she won't,' Marina smiled; and had to stop herself from kissing him again. 'Don't be ridiculous.' She squeezed his shoulder. 'I must go. I have a date.'

'I'll see you later,' Stefan said, still looking miserable.

'I wish you were having lunch with us.'

'I wish I was too.'

Their eyes met, as they both wondered if they wished this for the same reason. Then Marina winked at Stefan, and murmured, 'Bye.'

When she glanced back, from halfway across the studio, Stefan hadn't moved from his chair. He was looking down at his recording equipment as if it were diseased.

CHAPTER 7

'H<small>I, MARINA</small>, hi, Stefan, hi, Al. How y'all doing?'
'Hi, Alan.'
'Hi.'
'Hello.'
'What y'all talking about so secretively?'
'There's been another theft.'
'I love it! What now? The camera?'
'No. Derek's wallet. He left it in his jacket. He just hung it over the back of his chair. Next thing he knew – '
'The witch has been at it again.'
'D'you think – ?'
'Yeah, of course. Who else could it be? I mean she's classic. It's gotta be her.'
'Judy'll be delighted. She'll say I told you so.'
'Maybe Judy did it. So she could blame Nora.'
'Kostas says no one must tell Judy. Otherwise she'll go nuts again.'
'She's been fantastic all this week.'
'That's 'cos the witch is out of sight.'
'That's 'cos she's scared of Michael.'
'She'll find out anyway. Christ, it's like a village here. Gossip gossip gossip.'
'You're looking pleased with yourself, Al. What's happened?'
'No, nothing. Am I? I just – '
'Ooops, here they are.'
'Their majesties.'
'Good morning, Kostas.'

'Good morning, Derek.'

'Good morning, Judy. Hi, Michael. Hi, Jimmy.'

'Hi, darling, how are you?'

'Well.'

'Give me a kiss.'

'You're looking beautiful this morning.'

'Thank you, darling. Good sex.'

'Who with?'

'Aow fuck off, Derek. Just 'cos you'd like to bonk 'er.'

'Believe it or not I'm a faithful person.'

'Of course I believe it.'

' 'Ee doesn't, but 'ee's got to say that, 'aven't you, Derek?'

'How you doing, Jimmy?'

'All right. Fucking film. Wish it was over. I'm sick of bloody getting up at dawn. What we got this morning?'

'You come back and find Michael with Judy.'

'Oh, great. Heavy drama. To be or not to be. Now is the winter of our discontent. All that sort of thing. What you think of Laurence Olivier, Michael? Sir Larry.'

'Lord Larry.'

'Pardon me. Jude's a great one for the lords.'

'Yeah. I – '

'It's okay. You can say if you don't like 'im. We Brits won't be offended. I think 'e's fuckin' awful myself. Can't stand fuckin' ham. I'm Jewish, you know.'

'Are you?'

'No, of course he's not.'

'Excuse me, I just want to go off and – '

'Michael doesn't like all this frivolous chit-chat. 'Ee thinks we should only talk about acting, and art, and that sort of thing.'

'Jimmy, please . . .'

'Eh? What you say, Kostas? Speak up. You afraid 'ee might 'ear? Mike!'

'Yeah?'

'I was saying you care about acting and Kostas thinks

· 130 ·

you'll be offended if you hear me.'

'No, Jimmy, I'm not offended. I do care.'

'Yeah, so do I. Stupid prick.'

'Sssh.'

'Arr "sssh", yerself. Derek, mi old mate.'

'Tell me, Jimmy.'

'While I was 'aving my make-up put on a little bird told me you'd lost your wallet. Is that true?'

'I just mislaid it.'

'That's not what I 'eard.'

'Oh Christ.'

'What you say, Kostas?'

'Is that true? That you've lost your wallet?'

'Really, Judy, I just mislaid it. I think I left it in the bar when I went home last night. I'll go over and get it afterwards. There wasn't much money in it, anyway. Doesn't matter.'

'It's that *fucking* Nora again. I thought it was too good to be true. Three days of peace, and now – where is she? Skulking in her back room?'

'Sssh, love, lower your voice. She can probably hear every word you say. She sits there all day with her headset on.'

'I don't give a *shit* if she can hear. I hope she can hear. Nora, are you listening to me? Why don't you give Derek his wallet back? And replace the chalice while you're about it. And Bruno's electric drill, or whatever it was. And then why don't you just fuck off? Nobody wants you here. Nobody needs you here. Nobody *likes* you here. So why don't you fuck off back to Britain and leave us all alone. Goddam lunatic. Kleptomaniac. You should get help, you know.'

'Aow shut up, Jude.'

'No, I will not fucking shut up.'

'Derek?'

'Yes, Kostas.'

'Will you come over here for a moment?'

'Sure.'

'Now you've pissed Kostas off.'

'I don't give a shit. I will not have that woman – '

'Oh shut *up*, Jude. Just shut up, will you. Christ. I'm going to go and look at my fucking lines. Christ Almighty. Why don't you – '

'I can't take any more, Derek.'

'Don't worry. I'll tell her I found my wallet.'

'I swear I'll hit her if she starts carrying on again. And I don't know who told Jimmy about it but, whoever it was, I want 'em off the set.'

'Probably someone in make-up.'

'Well, I want them off. I told everyone – Oh, Christ. What did Jimmy have to go and say it for, anyway?'

'Just making mischief.'

'Christ, I hate actors. I *hate* them. But I'll tell you one thing. I wish I had fired that damned Nora. It would have saved a lot of trouble.'

'Caused some, too.'

'Yes, I know, but – I can't stand her myself.'

'I don't think anyone can. Still – I was going to say she means well. But I'm not sure if she does.'

'It's all your Empire bullshit. It affects some people. Not you, I mean. But – oh well, let's get on with it. But please, Derek, if you can, keep Judy away from me. I mean – tell her you found it.'

'Will do, Kostas. Don't worry.'

'Jesus.'

'Don't you love it,' Alan said. 'Don't you just love it? It's only eight-fifteen. And the shit's already splattering all around the room.'

For a while, as she sat in her cool dark room, Nora felt numb; as if someone had taken away her body, or as if someone had given her a pain-killer so strong it had deadened everything but her brain. They suspected her of having stolen Derek's wallet. They suspected her of having stolen that chalice last week. They suspected her of having stolen Bruno's power tool. And now, having sent her into this exile, yet knowing that with her headset she could hear every word spoken on the set, they were quite openly accusing her of it. What had that Alan called her? The witch? What had Judy said? What had Kostas said? 'I can't stand her.' No one could stand her. Everyone hated her and thought she was a thief. And now, instead of sitting at home in her quiet safe flat, going shopping in Kensington High Street, walking across the park and looking at the tourists, and the children flying their kites, and the people sailing their toy boats on the Round Pond – instead of giving her lessons, and watching the six o'clock news, and seeing the sky change from blue to grey from black to white all within the space of a few hours – instead of looking at the trees and the flowers and the squirrels – instead of being enveloped in that great soft blanket that was London – she was stuck in air-conditioned darkness at the back of a film set in the suburbs of Rome, being tormented, being almost physically spat at, being humiliated, insulted and despised.

Get up, she told herself, as she started to become conscious again of her body. Take off your headset, march out of here, and demand an apology. Or simply – march out of here, go back to the hotel, pack your bags, go to the airport, take the first flight back to London, and let them realize, when the next thing goes missing – as it undoubtedly will if there is a thief on the set – that that thief was not you, and you have been misjudged, ill-used, and unfairly condemned. Go on, she told herself, you must do something; even if it is just scream, and cry, and demand, probably in vain, that Judy retract her accusations.

Stand! Nora commanded herself. Move!

Yet, though she gave herself these orders, and though feeling had now returned to her body, Nora did not move.

What is more, she knew she wouldn't have moved if she had heard herself accused of murder.

And why?

That too she knew. Though this was harder to admit, and a minute or two passed before she could bring herself to form the words in her head. Then she told herself: why not? That is what you are thinking, so there's no point in being shy, or denying it.

She continued to sit there because it satisfied her to hear herself reviled. It almost excited her, in some dark unsettling way – or perhaps even that was a subterfuge: it did actually excite her. And most troubling, most inexplicable of all, although she had not stolen either Derek's wallet, or the chalice, or Bruno's screw-driver, she felt she deserved those insults that were being whispered all over the set, and, had she been hauled before some sort of kangaroo court, she might well have pleaded guilty.

No, not because she felt guilty of the crimes of which she was accused; but because she felt guilty of others. She felt guilty of having turned her back on her talent. She felt guilty of a lack of courage, of strength, of honesty. Above all, though this was really just a summation of all those other crimes, she felt guilty for having turned her back on God. Yes, this was what it meant, to reject the gifts one had been handed at birth; those unique gifts that had been given to you, and could never, in that form, be given to anyone else. That was what it meant to say no, I'm sorry, I'm afraid, I'm weak – and, besides, I really wasn't given any gifts. To turn one's back on God. Of course God was forgiving, and perhaps most people, in the end, gave in, pleaded exhaustion or excessive fear, and turned their backs on Him. Most people, however, didn't turn their back on Him completely, she suspected; didn't reject all their gifts. All right, they might reject some; they might reject most. But one or two, always, they kept. The gift of loving, perhaps; perhaps the gift of having children. The gift of merely being kind, and decent, and, in whatever way one chose, good. And keeping them, and making use of them – obviously it disposed God to feel charitably towards them: to think, well yes, all right, despite everything, you'll do.

She though – oh, she had tossed all those other gifts out years ago, the better to concentrate on developing, exploiting that one great gift she did have. She had stripped herself of everything, the better to wear the simple white dress of her talent; to improve its cut, make it even simpler, even whiter, even more striking.

And then one day, just like that – she had taken it off. Certainly she had been discouraged; by the constant stains, by the lack of appreciation, by the *cold* that wearing only that simplest of shifts had caused her. But other people were discouraged, and they didn't give up. They struggled on, shivering and in rags. And, if eventually they did collapse by the wayside, die there in the gutter, they died with their eyes fixed on heaven; confident that they had been true to it; that they would be received in it; that they had lived.

She, Nora Mellon, had not lived. She had turned her eyes from heaven, and been false to it. And now, quite rightly, she had been cast into hell, and would have to stay there until she had atoned for her sins.

Nora the thief. Nora the witch. Oh yes, Nora told herself, sitting in her cold back room. Yes. Condemn her. Brand her. Burn her.

Naturally, after a few more minutes, she tried to rid her head of this lunacy. You're in a state of shock, she told herself. You're quite justifiably upset. God indeed! Heaven and hell! You haven't believed in anything like that since you were sixteen years old. Nor did you turn your back on your talent. You simply found yourself unable any longer to earn a living with your acting. So rather than performing a whole song and dance, and being a burden on your friends, or the state, you did what you had to do to keep yourself alive. It's all very well carrying on about genius and talent when you've got enough to eat, but the instinct to survive is the strongest of all; and the gift of life is that which must be preserved first.

Furthermore, she just about succeeded in ridding her head of most of it; if not all. What she did not succeed in doing was getting to her feet, taking off her headset, and walking out of her 'hell'; nor in stopping herself from feeling gratified and yes, dammit, excited by the insults she had heard, and the prospect of hearing others. She sat there, the image of probity, of purity, of simplicity; and she wanted to be covered in slime.

CHAPTER 8

WHEN Marina had asked Al to have lunch with her on Monday, she saw that he expected to be given the gentle brush-off; to be told that, while she hoped they could go on being friends, he really mustn't expect anything more from her. She had had one marriage, that hadn't worked, and for the moment she was fine as she was, thank you very much. She didn't want to make any further emotional investments at present, her capital still being depleted after her previous attempt at playing the market; and if she did manage to scratch together a few more pennies she was going to put them in some safe, solid place, and start saving for the day when she did once again feel like taking a gamble.

This being so, she had her work cut out, in the intimacy of the crowded, chair-scraping, plate-clattering canteen, convincing Al that that wasn't why she wanted to eat alone with him. They sat at a table at the far end of the long, brightly lit room, and, trying to speak softly despite the din, she started:

'I'm sorry if you didn't really have a good time this weekend.'

'I did,' Al said, not sounding as if he meant it. 'It's just that – ' he shrugged. 'Oh, you know.'

Marina nodded. 'Yes. But – ' she lowered her eyes to her plate, then raised them again. 'I'm very fond of Stefan,' she said.

'Yeah, so am I,' Al said. 'Obviously.'

'And it's just that – ' she paused again – 'I don't want to

hurt him.'

'There's no reason why you – we – should.'

'Oh, Al, come on. There is.'

Now it was Al's turn to lower his eyes to his plate, and as he did it occurred to Marina that, though physically different, he wasn't unlike her first husband. He too had seemed more often than not perplexed by the difficulties and subtleties of life, rather than intrigued by them; and he too when faced with any sort of firework display had tended to turn away, and prefer the darkness to the risk of being dazzled. Did Al, like Patrick, also wish that he did like the lights, and pretend to like them, and anyway find people who stood in the middle of them attractive? She suspected so. Hence, at least in part, his affection for Stefan; whose background, whose departure from Russia, whose quiet constant love of him must have seemed tinged with a sort of dim brilliance. And hence, too, his affection for her?

Not really, Marina suspected. Rather, she had the feeling that she represented the darkness for Al – as she had for Patrick – and the warmth and safety of the darkness. Which was unfortunate. Because not only did she herself like the firework-handlers, and indeed the fireworks themselves; she had the feeling that ultimately, though she might have seemed as placid as the night, she was on their side, or was even a firework-handler herself.

Ah well, she told herself, it's probably poor Al's fate to be dazzled; though, God knows, I've never till this moment thought of myself as dazzling.

The idea was so incongruous that she couldn't help a tiny smile coming to her lips, as Al raised his eyes from his plate and gazed at her.

'But we – I – can't spend my whole life not doing anything so as not to hurt Stefan.'

'I'm not saying you shouldn't do anything,' Marina said, the smile still on her lips. 'Just that you should – we should – go slowly.'

'Oh, go where?' Al said wretchedly, still under the impression he was being let down.

'Wherever you like,' Marina murmured, suppressing her smile in case Al should take it to be a smile of compassion, or of gentle mockery. 'I mean,' she went on, conscious that, if this would reassure Al, she was burning her own boats, 'just because I like Stefan doesn't mean I don't like you. Just – as I say – that we've got to go gently.'

Did it reassure him? For a second Marina thought that he wanted still more; that she was going to have to practically proposition him. Then that wounded hurt little-boy look there had been in his eyes seemed to take a step back, and Al allowed himself a tiny albeit doubtful smile of his own.

'So you will some weekend – or some evening – come out with me? I mean – just the two of us?'

'Yes, Al,' Marina told him.

'It doesn't have to be this weekend, or even the one after. Just as long as – '

'Whenever you like,' Marina almost mouthed. 'Just as long as – '

'No,' Al couldn't stop himself from grinning now. 'Of course we won't hurt Stefan. I would never hurt Stefan,' he said, suddenly serious. 'Just – ' he grinned again, and swept his hair back with his hand, 'I was thinking that you sort of – you know – wanted Stefan. That maybe you didn't realize that – ' he stopped. 'Christ, I've been – '

'I'm not a fool,' Marina murmured.

'I know you're not. Only – ' he stretched out across the table, and took her hand. 'You'll probably think this is stupid. But I sort of – fell in love with you the day we met.'

'Did you?' Marina smiled, not prepared to tell a lie, and say that she had fallen in love with him; nor able to help feeling slightly embarrassed by the idea that she had, however, almost from the moment she met him, fallen in love with Stefan. 'I don't think that's stupid at all,' she said. 'Why should it be?'

'Oh,' Al said, starting to eat rapidly, and looking all at

once radiant. 'Love at first sight, and all that sort of crap.'

'First, second – what does it matter?' Marina shrugged. 'I suppose all it means is, anyway, that you find you like someone as a person whom you're sexually attracted to. Generally they happen at different times, if at all. But, if they do happen together, why not immediately?'

'Why not?' Al grinned, practically licking his lips. 'Why *not*?'

That evening the three of them had eaten together, as normal; on Tuesday, not wanting to be too obvious, Marina said she had to have dinner with an aunt. But on Wednesday, as they were all having lunch, and she was trying to think of some natural way of saying to Al, 'All right, tonight if you like,' Stefan said that he had a date that evening and, if the two of them didn't mind, he wouldn't join them.

He did it so smoothly that for a moment Marina thought he really might have a date, and was tempted to catch his eye and ask, 'Really?' Then, though, she thought that under the circumstances it should be Al's eye she caught; and, doing so, gave him just the quickest of winks.

'Oh, Al,' she wanted to tell him, 'I hope you never find out. You are, after all, so nice; and I do like you, so much.'

They ate at home that evening; Al standing behind her in her tiny kitchen as she prepared dinner, occasionally just touching her shoulder or her hair, as if he couldn't believe his luck, and were afraid that if he made too abrupt a move she might still change her mind and throw him out. And after dinner they went out to have a coffee, and take a walk by the forums. But after they had had their walk they came home again; and five minutes after that they were in bed together.

As a lover, too, Al resembled her former husband in some respects; in that he was thoughtful, gentle, and seemed more intent on giving pleasure than on taking it himself. Unlike Patrick, Al was indefatigable, and unlike him too, as Marina lay in bed with him, she was conscious of the presence of a third person; a tall pale blond person with a faint Russian accent. Both of which details caused her not only to enjoy Al's lovemaking more than she ever had Patrick's, but to think that perhaps her initial outrage at Stefan's suggestion was due to her suspicion even then that she would enjoy it. Could it be right to feel such pleasure when one was in a way betraying the person who was giving one that pleasure? Could it be right to be feeling such pleasure in part just because one was betraying the person who was giving it one? No, she told herself, as she tried to do something other than smile at the memory of her anger. Of course it couldn't be right. And she truly was perverse. But oh, how wonderful it was, and oh, if they could go on like this, the three of them, how happy, how happy she would be.

'Oh, Al,' Marina murmured, as around four o'clock in the morning they whispered to each other that they guessed they had better get an hour or two of sleep. 'Oh, Al.'

She should have realized by now that Al found it difficult to conceal his feelings. All the same, when they arrived at work the following morning, she was almost embarrassed by how very much Al resembled a cat who has just discovered a bowl of cream. She, after what had turned out to be slightly less than two hours' sleep, felt terrible. Her eyes burned, her skin was tight, and her hair, though she had washed and dried it before she left home, already felt grubby again and was wet with sweat by the time she got to the studio, with hardly the energy to wave to the guard who lifted the barrier for her. Al, on the other hand, looked fresh and young and rested; and far from being upset by the fuss about Derek's missing wallet, that broke like a storm soon after Judy and Jimmy arrived, and rumbled around all morning until Derek announced he had found the wallet, he hardly seemed to notice it. He certainly didn't appear to view it as evidence of man's unkindness to man, or proof of the existence of original sin; nor did it make him gaze at Marina as if she were his only shelter in this vale of tears, deceit and cruelty. Instead, when Marina did catch him looking at her – which she did whenever she looked at him – he merely raised his eyebrows, or grinned, or briefly rolled his eyes; which messages clearly meant, I love you, and as long as you're with me I'm going to love the whole world too, and everyone in it.

Even Judy? Even Nora? Yes, even them today. For, while most people on set seemed to side with Kostas that morning, and fairly radiated hostility towards the leading actors and the invisible Englishwoman, Al spent his time radiating only good-will. Michael, whose reaction to Jimmy's earlier frivolity and Judy's complaints about Nora had been to become more trying yet, was insisting on ten, twelve, in one case fifteen takes. Well, why not, Al's stance proclaimed as he held his microphone above his head as if it were a victory banner; it's worth it to get things right. Judy, who seemed determined to make up for having been pleasant for the first three days of this week, was being so disagreeable as to make one feel at times that she was unbalanced? Well, poor thing, Al's smile proclaimed, as he took the actress aside, when no one else would talk to her, and told her a joke; you've got to understand that she's been put in a difficult position, thrust into this part just because of who she's living with. And Nora, whom no one actually saw all morning, was up to her tricks again, pinching things? Well, she's lonely and unhappy, Al's tone of sympathy proclaimed, as he whispered, into his microphone, 'Nora, can you hear me? Kostas said if Judy's "No" wasn't right, will you yell, or beat on the wall, or let him know.' And anyway, what is all this nonsense about her having pinched Derek's wallet? I thought he said he'd found it again.

Indeed at times that morning Al was giving off such immense waves of charity that Marina had the feeling he had taken it upon himself to stop the whole set disintegrating into acrimony; as it might well have done had someone not managed to release the prevailing tension. It was Al who went up to Michael, after Kostas had said five times he couldn't hear him, to ask if they could maybe have just a little more volume on that line about 'You've got to live in the world or die'. 'I'm sorry,' he said, earnestly, 'but these mikes just aren't sensitive enough.'

'I'll try, Al, I'll try,' Michael sighed; and on the next take he succeeded.

It was Al who went up to Judy when she burst into tears after Jimmy had said something to her, and everyone was standing around watching her with a combination of exasperation and satisfaction as she cried in a corner.

'Come on, baby,' Marina heard him murmur to the actress. 'It's all right. You're doin' a great job. Don't let 'em get to you.'

And it was Al who went into Nora's little back room to ask if she was okay when repeated calls from Kostas as to whether such and such a word had been pronounced right – it was the director's way of getting his own back on Judy – had failed to elicit a response.

'Yes, thank you, Al, fine,' Nora had replied, Al told Marina and Stefan over lunch. 'It's just that it's so obvious Kostas is only asking me to annoy Judy, and I know if I actually appear it'll only make things worse, that I thought the best thing to do was pretend I hadn't heard. Anyway, there wasn't anything wrong with her accent,' she said, slipping back into her professional role. 'If there had been I would have said something, whether Kostas asked me or not.'

Yet this cheer that Al exuded, this single-handed holding everyone up, while it amused Marina, and heartened her, and touched her, also, when she stopped to think about it, alarmed her a little. He was so very much the guiding light of the set that the other members of the crew were beginning to comment on it, pull his leg about it; and she was afraid that before the day was out someone would either guess the reason why, or Al would actually tell someone; if not straight out, then dissembling so little that even the dumbest of them would be able to work out who or what he was talking about. And she didn't want, for the moment at least, to be exposed in her hypocrisy. She had the sensation that the mask she had put on, as Al's girlfriend, lover, mistress, was attached too flimsily, and that anyone who wasn't blind would be able to see that it was only a mask. Later perhaps, if there was a later, it would fit better. It might even, with time, hide her real face so well as to become, to all intents and purposes, her real face. For the moment though – no, surely, it was obvious it was a mask; and through it her blushes, her shame, could be seen.

Besides, she told herself as she stood by Kostas and tried to concentrate on her work, she didn't want people to think of her as Al's 'girl'. Or for people to think of Al as 'her man'. She wasn't Al's girl, he wasn't her man; and it was humiliating for anyone to believe otherwise. If word did get out, it would be as if a banner had been raised proclaiming her falsity to the whole world.

She felt her cheeks reddening at the idea.

Marina wished Al would learn to conceal his feelings better. Around five o'clock, however, when she was beginning to feel so tired she was afraid that if she sat down for a moment she would fall asleep, Al said something to her that gave her genuine cause for alarm. All right, to be thought of as false, perverse, or simply as Al's girl, was bad enough. But she would have been able to laugh it off, or deny it, if someone had actually accused her of being one or the other. Besides, she was on good if not excellent terms with practically everyone on the set, and she couldn't really imagine anyone going around making trouble, or even trying to, just because she had spent the night with the boom man. What Al told her, on the other hand, largely because it concerned one of the few people on the set with whom she was not on excellent terms, caused her not to blush now, but to shiver; and to think that, if what she feared was going to happen did happen, she would never be able to laugh it off.

Since she had had her brief conversation with Stefan on Monday morning, when she had let him know that she was going to take him up on his idea regarding Al, she had forgotten his panic at the possibility of Nora's having overheard their conversation. And, not only had it never occurred to her to worry that the Englishwoman had been listening to them, she would have continued to think 'how hilarious' if it had. Until, that is, today, when their fantasy had become reality; until, that is, now, when Al, still apparently not feeling the slightest effect from his lack of sleep last night, said, 'Hey, guess what, Nora's invited me to have dinner with her next Monday.'

'Just you?' Marina said, forcing herself to smile as that chill came over her. 'Just the two of you.'

'Yes,' Al grinned. 'I guess. You jealous?'

'No, of course not,' Marina said. 'Just that – it's a bit odd, isn't it?'

'Is it?' Al shrugged, the grin remaining on his face. 'I don't see why. I'm just about the only person on the set who talks to the poor woman.'

'I thought you didn't like her,' Marina said – sharply, she heard.

'I didn't. I don't. But – oh, poor thing. She's not so bad really. I mean you can't help the way you're made, can you? And at least she's got some sort of dignity. She doesn't go round moaning at the way she's being treated, does she? Besides, I was talking to her just now, and she sounds as if she's had quite an interesting life. You know she worked with Hitchcock, and Preminger, and Wilder. She made some good movies.'

'You mean you've accepted?' Marina said, still forcing herself to smile, but her voice sounding even sharper to her.

Al too must have caught it, because he stopped grinning

all of a sudden, and said, 'I won't go if you don't want me to.'

'Oh no, don't be ridiculous. I just – '

'Or we could both go.'

'She didn't invite me.'

'I know, but – '

'No, you go. I – I'm tired,' she said, summoning up her last reserves of energy to make it sound as if this were the only problem. 'Of course you must go. I was just a little surprised, that's all.'

But that wasn't all, Marina told herself as Kostas cried, 'Marina, where are you?', and she called back, 'Coming!' That wasn't all at all. It was true that she was tired, and that she might therefore be feeling particularly nervous or on edge. Even so, had she slept twelve hours the night before, and taken a siesta this afternoon, she was sure she would still have found reason to feel troubled about this invitation from Nora.

What had she said to Stefan on Monday morning? She couldn't really remember. But enough, surely, for anyone with half a brain who had heard them to understand what they were talking about. And Nora had more than half a brain; she was an intelligent, alert woman who never, Marina was positive, missed a trick. Of course it was true that Al was one of the handful of people who spoke to her. And today, when he was so very cheerful, and Nora had, at least this morning, been exposed to such a barrage of abuse, his friendliness must have been particularly welcome. Even so, she was sure that didn't explain the invitation. No: she was convinced of it. Nora had indeed had her headset on the other day, when she had been talking to Stefan. And next Monday, over dinner, she would find some nice, simple, undramatic way of letting Al know that he was being made a fool of, that he was being used, that – she didn't know what Nora would tell Al. She didn't know what she and Stefan were doing to Al. Perhaps they weren't making a fool of him; perhaps they weren't using him, and he would have been happy to go along with their game, had he realized they were playing one. What she did know was that she didn't want Al to realize this, that she was determined he shouldn't, and that if he did it would make the continuation of their game impossible. How could she lie in bed with him and murmur, 'Al, Al,' when he was thinking, rightly or wrongly, that she meant, 'Stefan, Stefan'? How could she pretend to be clinging to him, when he knew that she was doing it only to hang on to the person who was in truth clinging to him? She couldn't; not for more than a week or two at the outside, anyway, whatever Al's own attitude; and she couldn't, probably, even for an hour or two. Only, if she didn't, she would lose Stefan, and if she lost Stefan – oh sure, her life would continue. She wasn't the type to die of love. Or even to suffer unduly for it for more than a couple of months. Nevertheless, she didn't want to lose Stefan, and, if she could help it, she wasn't going to. All right, maybe even if nothing awful happened this odd triangle they had formed would disintegrate after a little while. But maybe it wouldn't, maybe it would never disintegrate; and, until it did, she was going to do her utmost to ensure it remained intact. It might be somewhat, or more than somewhat, unorthodox; but it wasn't bad. On the contrary, it was good. And what was good was worth holding on to, even fighting for. If one didn't – what was there left in life? One's job. One's friends. A husband and children, possibly. Underneath, however, the desert would be growing, day by day; until finally the sand enveloped everything: job, husband, children, life itself. Nora, it suddenly occurred to Marina, hadn't fought for what was good. And look what had happened to Nora. Condemned to a cold back room in life, listening to other people's stories. Well, she wasn't going to end up in any cold back room; nor, if she could help it, was she going to let Nora drag her so much as a centimetre in that direction. No, goddammit, she would fight; and no, goddammit, she would not allow that woman to tell Al what she had heard. Or, if she couldn't prevent it, she would keep on at him, and do everything she had to do – even marry him – until he believed her, or said he did. She had to, Marina told herself; she saw no other alternative.

Such bravery! Such resolve! Such – she confessed it – hysteria! Yet though, over the next three days, Marina calmed down, and the thought of Al's having dinner with Nora stopped making her shiver, her determination not to allow Nora to interfere with her life remained as firm as ever; if anything it became, just because she had calmed down, firmer yet.

This was to some extent because she remained convinced that what she had told herself on Thursday afternoon, however wildly expressed, was essentially correct. It was also to some extent because when she told Stefan about Nora's invitation he too, without any prompting from her, immediately came to the same conclusion she had; that Nora had invited Al with the sole purpose of making mischief. But it was principally due to the fact that having, on Thursday evening, had a quick dinner with 'the boys', and then allowed Al to drive her home, come upstairs with her, and more rapidly than the night before but no less satisfactorily make love with her, she had had a good night's sleep. After which, and after a relatively uneventful Friday at the studio, she had had another wonderful weekend. Or rather, considering the ups and downs of the previous weekend, a far better weekend than the one before, and one that equalled her weekend up in New England.

They had done, the three of them, what they had talked of doing seven days before: driving round the hill towns of Tuscany. Only, if last weekend, had they taken it, their trip would have been disturbed by unresolved tensions, and tantrums, and sulks, this weekend everything went so smoothly, and they all got on so well together, that more than ever Marina had the impression of their being a single animal with six arms, six legs, and three heads. A graceful, well-coordinated animal, what was more; whose limbs all moved in harmony, and who didn't, even for a moment, feel itself wanting to move in two or three different directions at the same time. Along winding mountain roads they drove, Al at the wheel, Marina beside him, Stefan sitting in the back seat. Through rocky sun-scorched landscapes they drove; their arms out of windows, the hot air blowing back their hair and drying the sweat on them even as it formed. And into grey, and ochre, and burnt-red villages they drove; where they parked the car if possible in the shadow of a tree, and walked around the apparently heat-stunned streets, looking up at towers and façades, and going, when they could, into the cool of churches and small museums.

They spent Friday night, having left directly from Cinecittà, in San Gimignano; and Saturday, as planned, in Montepulciano. There was no question now of who slept where; Al and Marina as if by instinct went into one room; Stefan, as if by choice, went into another.

They went to a concert on that Saturday night in Montepulciano; sitting in the main square in the warm night, with stars above them, food and wine in their stomachs, and Mozart, Marina felt, being trailed coolly, elegantly and sometimes sadly over them.

And on Sunday they watched a regatta on Lake Trasimene; scores of boats cutting across the silver still surface of the water, weaving patterns and forming shapes that made the trio, up on the hillside where they were standing, feel they had been hypnotized, placed under a spell. The different coloured sails looked like butterflies, skimming through a haze . . .

Yet it was neither the concert in Montepulciano, nor the regatta on Lake Trasimene – nor simply sitting in a restaurant eating sweet hard pears and a sharp local cheese, nor lying wet and slippery and entirely happy in bed with Al – that really constituted the high point of the weekend for Marina, and really finally convinced her that what she had was worth fighting for. Rather, this peak of her contentment, this moment when everything seemed to come together and strike a note of such purity, such beauty, that she felt both totally made one with the world by it, and paradoxically made nothing of by it, came in the chapel of a tiny cemetery in the middle of some cabbage fields. A chapel she had insisted they visit, despite its involving a long detour, since it contained what was for her the most beautiful painting in the world.

She was prepared for her final ascent by the fact that, having driven up to the cemetery, they had found the door to the chapel locked, and were standing there, wondering how to get in, when from down below in the fields a woman wearing a straw hat and a large flowered apron called 'Siete venuti a vedere la Madonna?' – Have you come to see the Madonna?

'Si,' Marina called back, as all three of them smiled at the question; and the woman left her work in the scorching field and, taking a large rusty key out of her apron, came up towards them.

But what actually hauled her those last few metres to the summit was this. They had gone inside, and gazed at the painting for some thirty seconds, maybe. Then Stefan had turned to her; and, in a voice that seemed to her as rapt, as luminous, as serene as the picture itself, he said: 'It's wonderful, isn't it? It really is as if one had seen the Madonna.'

Of course, Marina told herself, it was only because she loved Stefan that his words had the effect on her they had; made her feel, dizzyingly, that she had been afforded a view of the entire earth. Normally the comments people made as they stood in front of paintings irritated her, struck her as being fatuous, at best. Also they were limiting, since they never expressed what she was feeling. In this instance though – oh yes, Marina wanted to shout, as Stefan's words seemed to echo inside her head. Yes. That was exactly what she'd been feeling. And, hearing her thoughts expressed so exactly, it was as if the last barrier between herself and Stefan had fallen away, and they had literally become one. She scarcely dared breathe for a few seconds, in case that view she had been granted should be taken from her. She felt, absurdly, that she had been married to Stefan in that moment; married with the blessing of, married in the presence of, the Madonna. Then – then she took Al's hand, held it, and said, 'It's amazing no one's ever stolen it, isn't it? There's no security here at all.'

Wasn't such a view worth doing almost anything for, Marina asked herself again and again as, around nine o'clock that evening, they approached Rome – and, as they did, the shadow of Nora seemed to loom larger and larger over her?

Of course it was, she told herself. Almost anything.

Naturally, she admitted afterwards, had Nora been determined to tell Al what she had overheard, there wasn't a thing that either she, Stefan, or anyone else could have done about it – except deny it, and claim that Nora was mad. Fine words were all very well; but how did one fight someone who only intended to have dinner with one's lover – as she supposed she must think of Al now. Punch her on the nose? Threaten her? Shoot her? No. The only weapon she could have used was that of the lie; of indignation, protestations, scorn. And if that hadn't worked – well, she guessed she'd either have had to come to some compromise with Al, or say goodbye to him and conclude that subconsciously Stefan must have realized that Nora was still plugged in and probably listening to their conversation last Monday; and that, therefore, for all his subsequent panic and distress, subconsciously he had wanted Nora – and thus Al? – to know what he and Marina were up to.

Exactly a week after her conversation with Stefan,

however, on the day after they returned from Tuscany, there was an accident on the set; and after that not only did any idea of Al's having dinner with Nora get put aside, but the whole matter of what Nora might or might not have heard seemed suddenly very unimportant.

CHAPTER 9

Al, BASKING in the sun of happiness, had become friendly with Nora; apparently seeing her as some sort of symbol of his good fortune. Just as, before he had been blessed, he had seen the general opprobrium in which the woman was held as a symptom of his ill fortune. Jimmy too, though he now professed to detest Nora, whether to irritate Judy or out of a desire to be different, occasionally talked to her. Other than Al and Jimmy however – and the make-up man and the wardrobe supervisor, who had decided that it was politic not to speak to her, though they seemed to like her – Nora had just two friends on the set. One was Renato, the gaffer – the chief electrician – a great bear of a man in his late fifties, who smoked continually, had a deep gruff voice, and took it upon himself to stand by, to stand up for, anyone who found themselves in the position of the outcast. There was no proof that Nora had stolen anything? Good, then Nora was not guilty, and it was his duty – it was every man's duty, Renato's massive serious presence seemed to suggest, though that was up to every man to decide for himself – to act towards Nora with the courtesy due from one worker to another.

'I have been a member of the communist party all my life,' he had informed Stefan the other morning, when the two of them were watching Judy tell Derek she didn't believe he had found his wallet, he was just saying that to keep her quiet and didn't he realize it was to everyone's benefit that that woman be gotten off the set as fast as possible? 'And I have always believed in what I thought the

· 153 ·

party stood for. You cannot allow personal feelings to blind you. Not in a negative way. I don't really know Nora. But she always says good morning to me; she is always polite and good-mannered to me; and she does her job without any fuss. That one,' jerking an immense thumb in Judy's direction, 'only says good morning when she feels like it; is almost never good-mannered or polite to anyone; and does not do her job without any fuss. Despite the fact that she is being paid probably fifty times what Nora is getting. Why shouldn't I be friendly with Nora? I think it's a scandal what is going on on this set, and I won't put up with it. Until anyone can show me different I will continue to believe that she is a good honest woman; and I will not listen to anyone who tells me otherwise. I have always considered lies and gossip dishonourable; and people who don't I have always classified as right wing, whatever they say their politics are.'

A speech that in its earnestness, yet evident sincerity, had made Stefan slightly ashamed of his feelings for Nora; and more than slightly ashamed of his treatment of her over the past few days.

Ever since Nora had, or might have, listened to his conversation with Marina, in a combination of deliberate cruelty, Stefan was afraid, and a desire to make Nora stand up and walk off the set, he had left her headset plugged in, and turned on, the whole time; so that she might hear every word that was said practically anywhere on the set. And, when he had become aware that someone – generally Judy – was speaking ill of her, he had even increased the volume.

But if the burly, bespectacled, tobacco-reeking Renato liked Nora, at least in part, for ideological reasons, her other friend on the set allowed no such considerations to sway his feelings. Dark, Zapata-moustached Sergio, who had a grandson in the business, but who had maintained the somewhat stocky figure of the stuntman he had once been by working as a scene-shifter and carpenter these past thirty years, was simply, incurably good-natured. Perhaps he, like Al, had felt the sun of love rise on him when he was young; and that sun had never set. Perhaps he had had a particularly happy – a uniquely happy, it occurred to Stefan – childhood. Or perhaps, as it might once have been put, all the planets had been in conjunction on the day he was born. However you explained it, good-natured, apparently inexhaustibly good-natured Sergio was; and not only would he not accept that anyone was guilty until proved so, but he seemed incapable of conceiving the idea that anyone, anyone on *this* set, anyone he *knew*, should so much as take a pin that didn't belong to him, let alone be evil. Judy? Well, she was nervous, *poverina*; she was under a lot of stress; you could see that she wasn't really difficult; she was just trying, perhaps trying too hard (the nearest Sergio ever came to a criticism) to be good. Michael? A real gentleman; a quiet, intelligent, *serious* person, who lived for his work, was a perfectionist, and expected – quite rightly, too! – everyone else to be a perfectionist. Jimmy? Oh, a sweet boy, you could see that just by looking at him. And as for Nora – she, in Sergio's opinion (expressed always and only in Italian; he spoke not a word of English), was a real lady. In the sense that she had just as much respect for him as he had for her; and as a *person*, not just a fellow worker. 'Una signora, signor Stefano,' Sergio told Stefan, grasping him by the shoulder, wagging his finger at him, and beaming, 'Una vera signora.'

Of course Stefan could, and did, tell himself that Sergio was a little simple; and that, pleasant as it must be to live in such a rose-tinted universe, life just wasn't like that, and one had to be pretty near-sighted to believe it was. All the same, he found it impossible not to like Sergio – he guessed everyone found it impossible; he guessed it was impossible – and if Renato's strictures and fraternal solidarity with Nora made him feel guilty, Sergio's warm-heartedness, his very simplicity, made him feel only glad that there were such people around; to counterbalance those who had been born when the times were out of joint. He also hoped that, near-sighted though Sergio might be, his eyesight never improved. It made him happy to see Sergio, the most gallant of cavaliers, escorting Nora to lunch in the canteen; utterly unaware that the other members of the crew made jokes about the attendance he danced upon the English-woman – when they didn't actively disapprove. (Though, while people made their jokes to Sergio's face, they never expressed their disapproval openly.) Sergio was equally unaware of the fact that Nora herself, while clearly grateful for his company, yet couldn't help treating him with the faintest air of condescension. That I should be reduced to this, Nora's stiff back, fixed smile and up-turned chin expressed; having to feel grateful to a simpleton for escort-ing me to lunch. Of course I like Sergio, and of course I prefer to eat with him than eat alone, or not eat at all. But really, we have nothing in common; it is, ultimately, pity that prompts him to ask me if I will have lunch with him; and I am, let's not forget it, a distinguished actress. Whereas he . . .

Not only did it make Stefan happy to see this; it made him feel that, if anyone could disarm Nora, draw her poison, render her – as far as he Marina and Al were concerned – harmless, then Sergio would be the man. For his own part, he couldn't resist keeping Nora plugged in to the things that were being said about her on the set, and he did do it in the hope that the humiliation would drive her away before she could do any harm. Even if, from the way Nora smiled at him, and said good morning to him, and came to tell him that Judy had pronounced some word wrongly, he had the feeling that she thrived on the diet he was feeding her, and that, far from driving her away, he was only likely to make her stay longer, and become more dangerous yet. Never-theless, seeing Sergio taking her on a tour of some of the other sets, showing her the fantastic creatures that were being made for some children's film, and introducing her to his friends in the special effects department, Stefan wished he could be a little more like him.

'Stop it,' he told himself when, after he had seen Nora amidst that crowd of goblins and winged horses and unicorns, he once again automatically flicked the switch that would allow her to hear all that was going on.

'Stop it,' he told himself on another occasion, after he had seen Sergio present Nora with a tiny bunch of rather wilted wild flowers that he had picked on some back lot; and he found himself preparing to transmit Judy's comments on this gift.

And 'Stop it,' he told himself when, on that Monday after his weekend in Tuscany with Marina and Al, he saw Sergio, during the lunch break, clambering way up in the rafters of the studio, showing Nora the lights, showing her how they shifted sections of the 'roof' of the 'church', showing her what the set looked like from up there, sixty or so feet above the floor. 'Just stop it. If you're worried about what Nora's going to tell Al at dinner tonight, cut off her drip of hatred and contempt. Only let her listen to Judy when Judy is actually working, actually saying her lines. Allow Sergio, and Sergio's charity, to take the knife from her hand; so to wrap her around in kindness that even should she want to strike she would be unable to. And then just sit back, and relax. That'll do the trick; that'll save you. Love, not hatred; kindness, not cruelty . . .'

Stefan was still sitting making adjustments to his recording equipment, talking to himself and almost smiling at his own foolishness, when Sergio fell. He knew what had happened the second he heard the man's cry; followed immediately by a strange, somehow awkward thud, and yells from those few people who had either stayed on the set during the break, or like him had returned before the hour was up. And for a fraction of a second he was paralyzed with shock. Then, stunned, with the rest of the world having slipped away to leave only that one fact – Sergio has fallen – he got to his feet and, having glanced up and noted a rope dangling from the hole in the roof the man must have slipped through, he rushed across the set to see if there was anything he could do.

For the next hour or so there wasn't so much chaos on the set as a feeling of everyone being in a state of collective trance. Bruno called the emergency services; an ambulance seemed to arrive in no time at all; and before some people had even returned from their break, or learned what had happened, Sergio had been taken off to hospital. The only sign of the accident was a small bloodstain on the cushioned pew onto which Sergio had fallen before bouncing to the floor; and that Mario, the prop man, was considering clearing up.

'You better not,' Stefan heard someone mutter. 'Not for the moment. Just in case – '

Just in case what? No one seemed to know what to do. Everyone just stood around; except Kostas, who sat on a pew with his head bent, smoking and muttering, apparently in Greek, to himself. The accident was discussed, re-discussed and the spot Sergio had fallen from was pointed to again and again, as if it, or the rope hanging from it, might provide some clue as to how or why he had slipped. And time after time the same question was asked; though no one, so far, could give an answer to it.

'Is he alive?' people whispered to one another. 'Is he all right?' 'Is he dead?'

Then the police came, and everyone who was on the set at one fifty-four was asked where exactly they had been, and what they had seen. To which everyone, except one person, replied, 'Over there,' or, 'Over there,' and in any case, 'Nothing.' Not till Sergio fell. Not till he hit the ground.

The one exception? Nora, naturally; and she went off into her little back room, that had become by now her private domain, and told the police everything she had seen.

Afterwards, very pale, very still, very straight, and telling Renato, yes, please, she would like a brandy – which Renato sent someone to the bar to fetch – Nora gave the electrician, her bearlike protector and friend, the details of what had happened.

She gave them sitting on a delicate gold-backed chair by the side of the high altar; Renato sat next to her on a similar chair, that looked as if at any moment it would crumple beneath him; and everyone else stood in a circle round them.

Nora spoke in English; translations were muttered by those of her onlookers who understood the language.

'He was showing me how things worked. I just told him I wanted to go up there and see the set from above. He took me all around. We were on the catwalk – ' she paused, as she saw Renato's puzzled expression. 'You know, the balcony – no, those things up there,' she said, pointing to the walkways high above them, that ran around the edge of the studio, and criss-crossed the roof. 'And – nothing. I was just looking. Then Sergio told me – I mean I think he did – you know we really just communicate in sign language and – but we *understand* each other. We really do.' She paused again, to sip her brandy now. 'He said he had to shift a bit of that roofing material there, because the ceiling was going to be visible in the next shot. He edged out along that beam there – and he had that rope – ' she turned, and pointed at the hanging rope, that reached to within twenty feet of the ground. 'He signed to me that he wanted to throw it over that beam there – ' again she turned and pointed; again perhaps forty heads turned with her, to follow the direction of her finger. 'I think he wanted to – I don't know. Anyway, he tried once, and he didn't get it over. He just grinned at me. He tried again, and got it a quarter over. But it didn't fall down completely the other side, so he could get a hold on it, and attach it to – so he pulled it back and threw a third time. But – he seemed to take a step back as he threw it, to give himself some extra leverage or something. Only of course there was nothing to step back onto. He was holding the rope – but of course the weight of his own body – and suddenly falling like that – he couldn't keep hold of it. I mean I don't know how long he held it for, and whether it was enough to break his fall at all. But – it just happened so quickly, from one moment to the next. If only I'd been closer. I suppose even if I had been I couldn't have done anything. We would both have fallen perhaps. But – '

Then Nora stopped; and no one knew what to say. Once again people just stood around, aimlessly waiting for some word as to what they should do, for some sort of direction. But the director continued to sit off in a corner, smoking and with his eyes now closed; and his assistant director seemed as perplexed and at a loss as everyone else. To return to work was unthinkable; to go home until some news came from the hospital was out of the question. And so – some people sat. Some people stood. And, apart from the occasional offer of a cigarette, hardly a word was spoken. Stefan sat at his table with his headset on, listening to the silence; Marina sat on the floor by his side, her arms around her legs, her chin resting on her knees. And Al sat beside her, at times with his arm around her shoulder, at times binding and unbinding a piece of tape at one end of his mike.

Somewhere, off in a side chapel, someone coughed. Somewhere else, a man's voice could be heard mumbling something indistinguishable. Every now and then the noise of the air conditioning unit could be heard, though in fact it was on the whole time, and it simply broke into one's consciousness before, as thoughts took its place, fading again. Footsteps walked down the supposedly stone-flagged nave; the studio doors could be heard opening and closing.

Finally, however, at a quarter to four, word arrived. A grave-faced messenger came into the studio and muttered something to Kostas. Kostas listened, nodded, and called Luciano, his assistant. Luciano too listened and nodded. Then he turned to the waiting, watching crowd, and announced: 'He's all right.'

A collective sigh went up. One or two people applauded. Then Luciano went on. Sergio had broken both his legs and one arm. He had a fractured pelvis and a suspected fracture of the skull. It seemed likely that he had chipped one of his vertebrae. And he had severe burns on his hands. But – he was going to be all right. He was alive. He wasn't paralyzed. And with any luck – the messenger murmured something else to Luciano now, who instantly relayed the information to his listeners. He must have managed to hold onto the rope for a while. Hence the burns on his hands. But it must have saved his life. In effect he had fallen from twenty feet, not sixty feet. If he had fallen from sixty feet . . . Luciano stopped; and once again there was silence on the set.

Luciano turned to Kostas and asked him something; Kostas shrugged fatalistically, and Luciano gazed down on him for a second before taking matters into his own hands and turning back to the crowd. 'Ladies and gentlemen,' he said, first in Italian, then in English. 'I don't know whether we want to go back to work, or – Renato? Pino?' he asked, addressing the key grip. 'Judy, Jimmy?' There followed a further minute or two of muttered discussions; though these now entirely on the part of the crew, the actors simply waiting, in silence, for whatever decision was reached.

A report was made to Luciano; who referred it to Kostas. Kostas again nodded, and lit another cigarette.

And then: 'Okay, everyone,' Luciano said. 'Back to work. Thank you.' He added, somewhat sanctimoniously: 'I think Sergio would approve.'

The crew ignored this; everyone returned to his or her task, the key grip himself going up into the rafters to throw the life-saving rope over the beam; and forty-five minutes later Kostas could be heard grunting, as if it were the last thing on earth he wanted to say, 'Okay, sound,' – Stefan pressed the buzzer for silence, and turned off the air conditioning – 'Camera' – 'Camera rolling,' the cameraman murmured – 'Action.'

'You can't kill people,' Elizabeth/Judy whispered.

'I didn't try to kill him,' Jimmy/Jimmy told her.

· 161 ·

Was it these lines that planted a seed in Stefan's – and not only in Stefan's – mind? Or had it been there all along, and it was the return to work, the getting back of everything to normal after those stunned couple of hours, that made him aware of it? He had no idea; though he did know that it wasn't until after he had heard Kostas grunt, 'Action,' that he felt that a short terrible parenthesis had been closed, and he was able to recall what he had done at the instant of that parenthesis being opened: look up at the spot where Sergio had fallen from, and see that dangling, still-swaying rope. The dangling rope – and above it, gazing down through the gap in the roof that had almost proved fatal to Sergio, Nora's white, staring face.

In any case, whether planted by those opening lines of the afternoon's first take, or whether it was just the resumption of ordinary life that made him conscious of something that was already there, by the time Kostas said, 'Cut,' not only had that seed made its existence known, but, encouraged perhaps by the memory of Nora's white face staring down, it had started to put out shoots.

Stefan tried to uproot it, telling himself: No, this is grotesque, just a result of the shock, and of course I saw Nora staring down: what was she meant to do, *not* stare down? And there's nothing sinister in my having seen her; from where I'm sitting now I can not only see the beam Sergio must have been standing on, but the catwalk behind him on which Nora must have been standing. It's not more than a yard or two back; and in fact I suspect that Sergio was just putting on a show for Nora, by standing on that beam: he could very well have tossed the rope over the rafter from the catwalk itself.

He also told himself that he was simply feeling vindictive; afraid of what Nora might know, and be planning to tell Al.

But whatever he did, and whatever he told himself, that seed would not be uprooted. And when, after four good takes of the scene between Jimmy and Judy, Judy was told there'd be at least half an hour before the lights were ready for the next set-up, and she came over and said, without any preamble, 'She pushed him, didn't she?' Stefan couldn't help admitting, to himself and Judy, that he had something similar growing in his brain.

'No, Judy, of course she didn't,' he said; his eyes and his frown giving the lie to his words. 'He slipped.'

'Did you see him?'

'No, but – '

'Oh don't give me that shit, Stefan. I can see what you're thinking. Yeah, sure, you've got to be noble, you've got to be fair, you don't like gossip. Well I do, and I don't have to be either.'

Stefan hesitated before replying, and gave a quick uncomfortable shrug of the shoulders. 'I don't know, Judy. I mean – it's ridiculous. She can't have. People don't. We're all just shocked, and – you know how movies get. We're all tired, and – '

'Oh tired, *balls*,' Judy snapped. 'For Chrissake, Stefan. Okay, you've made your protest. I take the point. You're a nice guy. You're a gentleman. Now forget it. You goddam well *know* that that bitch pushed him. I mean – okay, I feel sorry for her. She's getting old, and her career's gone down the spout, and it must be difficult for her, the great Shakespearean actress or whatever she was, having to play nursemaid to someone like me. I even understand her, the anger and the humiliation and all the rest. But feeling sorry for her, understanding her, isn't enough, is it? I mean – it's an absolute miracle Sergio wasn't killed.'

'I guess he'll be able to say whether he was pushed or not,' Stefan murmured; though the suggestion sounded weak even to him.

'Of course he won't,' Judy spat. 'Apart from the fact that I don't suppose he'll be able to remember exactly what happened, even if he was pushed he'd never admit it. You know what he's like. He's very sweet and all that. But – if he were a Jew, he'd be insisting Hitler was a nice guy even as they shoved him into the gas oven. He *couldn't* admit that Nora had pushed him. It'd be stronger than him. Anyway, you can be sure she did it on the sly. Just gave him a little tap, or even – I dunno, tripped him or something.'

'What are you going to do?' Stefan asked; sounding, he heard, miserable now.

'I don't know,' Judy said, sitting down on the floor beside him.

'You want a seat?' Stefan murmured.

'No, darling, thanks. I'm fine here. I really don't know. I mean it was all very well when it was just a power drill, or a chalice, or even Derek's wallet. I could go sounding my mouth off about them, and I didn't care what the witch thought. I hope she heard me. And all that business about me walking off – I was sort of serious, I guess, and God knows it would have been better if I had, or if I'd insisted on Nora being fired. But now – I don't know. I have the feeling if I accuse her of trying to murder Sergio – I bet ninety per cent of the people here would believe me. But just because it's – well, ridiculous, like you say, because it's sort of *too* serious – they wouldn't allow themselves to. I have a feeling there'd be a walk-out. And then the film would be suspended, and I'd be fired, and Nora would bring an action against me, and everything would be a mess. On the other hand, if I don't make a fuss, no one else is going to, are they? I mean *you're* not, are you?'

'No,' Stefan admitted. 'I don't see – '

'Yeah, whatever. But there you are.' Judy frowned. 'Only if no one says anything – what's she going to do next? She won't stop here. She's sick. Obviously. I've said it before and I'll say it again. She needs help. Urgently. I was just hoping that you'd seen something, since you were here when it happened.'

'I just saw her looking down.'

'You *sure*?'

'Yes, of course.'

'Oh fuck. Fuck fuck fuck. This movie's turning into a

nightmare.' She gave a faint, grim smile. 'Every movie I work on turns into a nightmare. *I'm* a nightmare, I know. Christ, I call Nora a bitch. She's a fucking saint compared to me. Only – I don't go round stealing things. And I don't go round pushing people off beams.' Judy stood up. 'Where is she now?'

'Back in her hole, I guess.'

'She hasn't been listening to all this, has she?'

'No,' Stefan said, with a faint grim smile of his own. He tapped his machine. 'I made sure. I unplugged her.'

'That's another thing.' Judy frowned again. 'Before, I got a kick out of saying evil things about her, knowing she was listening. But after this – Christ, I'm scared. I mean who knows what she might do.'

'Oh I think you'll be all right,' Stefan ventured, with an apologetic smile now. 'I don't think she's interested in fellow bitches, if you'll excuse me. I think she's the type – I mean, if she did push Sergio, it was just because he's the one absolutely nice guy on the set. I think people like us – people who don't like her – I have a feeling she approves of us in a way. I – I suspect she might actually like to hear herself accused of attempted murder. I think she might like to hear herself accused of murder.'

Judy sighed. 'Shit,' she murmured. 'I'm sorry to have bothered you, Stefan. I better go and talk to Jimmy. See what he says.' She looked sad all at once, and wistful. 'He'll probably say I'm the one who needs help. He's probably right. Though he thinks Nora pushed Sergio, too. Only – oh, what the hell. I'm going up to my dressing room for ten minutes. I'll see you later, baby. And whatever you do – don't go climbing anywhere near Nora.'

'I won't,' Stefan promised. 'Nor you.'

'Oh *I* won't,' Judy laughed, without humour, as she walked away. 'Don't worry about that.'

Judy was right; Jimmy did believe that Nora had 'given poor old Sergio the shove'. So, Stefan gathered before filming finished that day, did Al, Marina, Alan, Riccardo,

Bruno, and – according to them – just about everyone else on the set. Judy was also right, however, in thinking that, although ninety per cent of the crew did believe they had a seriously disturbed and dangerous woman in their midst, practically every one of them was as determined to uproot that idea they had discovered inside themselves as he had been – and as he remained, even after he had realized it was not a rare plant that had seeded itself.

He remained determined just because it was such a poisonous plant; just because not to try to uproot it did somehow expose one to a danger still greater than that which Nora herself posed. After all, Stefan argued with himself: it was as he had said. As long as one didn't like Nora, one was probably safe. It was only by loving her, or pitying her, that one put oneself at risk.

'Yeah, sure she pushed him,' Bruno said to the three-some as they stood by Marina's car, the long eventful day finally over. 'But there's nothing we can do about it. I mean you can't just go round accusing people of murder, can you? Otherwise – I don't know. You sort of make it possible, don't you?' He suddenly gave an exaggerated glance over his shoulder. 'My God, she's not listening to me, is she?'

'No, don't worry,' Al said. 'She went home early.'

'The shock?'

'No. I heard her asking Kostas if she could go. She didn't mention the accident. She just said that, as Judy didn't have any more lines this afternoon, would it be all right if she left.'

'Good old Nora,' Stefan murmured. 'Professional to the last.'

'Actually, I was kinda miffed,' Al smiled. 'She'd invited me to have dinner with her tonight. And it's not like a lady, is it, to forget her invitations?'

·   ·   ·

Cruelty, and the hope of getting her to quit, had made Stefan keep Nora plugged in before the accident. A still tiny hope of getting her to quit, and that vague if irrational belief that by showing himself antagonistic to her he would be protecting himself from her, contributed to his decision, the day after Sergio's fall, to keep Nora plugged in. They contributed only to a minor degree however; and the principal reason why he continued to let Nora listen to everything that was said on the set was because at eleven o'clock on Tuesday morning, in a break between takes, Nora came round to where he was sitting and asked him to.

Had she not asked him, neither his hope nor his belief would have allowed him to go on with this game that he considered not merely cruel now, but as adding to the danger that Nora posed. In fact it was because he had decided to cut the Englishwoman off, that she was obliged to ask him to reconnect her.

There was nothing shame-faced or underhand about the way she did it. As calm, as matter-of-fact, as normal, one would have said, as ever, she tapped him on the shoulder and said, 'Hello, Stefan.'

Removing his headset, Stefan smiled, noted the unruffled appearance, and said, 'How are you feeling this morning?'

'Oh, much better, thank you. It was such a shock yesterday. I just went back to the hotel, got into bed, and went out like a light.'

'It must have been.'

'Poor Sergio,' Nora said. 'I went to the hospital this morning to see him.'

'You did?' Stefan said, unable to disguise his surprise. 'And you did?'

'Yes. Just for a moment. They didn't want to let me in, but I pretended not to understand. And then, well, you know, a smile works wonders.'

'Was he conscious?'

'Oh, yes. I mean terribly groggy, obviously. All bound

up from head to foot. But he managed to smile, and gave me a sort of wink. He's *such* a nice man. I took him some flowers.'

'Whatever time did you go?'

'Oh, I must have got to the hospital at about a quarter to seven. As I say, I only stayed a second. His wife was there, and son and daughter and daughter-in-law and grandson. Then I just got the Metro and came on out here.'

'How did you know what hospital he was in?' Stefan asked, still so surprised by Nora's visit that the questions seemed to fall out of him, without his forming them in his head.

'The police told me yesterday when they came.'

'Well, I'm – ' amazed, he guessed, would be a rude, or anyway the wrong, word – 'sure he was very happy to see you. Maybe in a day or two – ' he didn't finish, but allowed Nora to think he had been going to say, 'I'll go to see him, too.'

Then, changing the subject, he murmured: 'It's all going very smoothly this morning, isn't it?'

'Yes,' Nora smiled. 'The accident seems to have taken all the tension out of the air for the moment. I don't expect it'll last, but – I never have understood why some actors find it necessary to work from tension. I always used to seek absolute calm. Just a difference in temperament, I suppose. But in fact that's what I wanted to ask you, Stefan. I get so bored back there in my little cell, I was wondering if you could keep me switched on the whole time, if you see what I mean.'

Stefan saw exactly; and blushed.

'You haven't changed equipment or anything, have you? I mean last week I could follow everything that went on. Then this morning – silence.'

'No,' Stefan muttered, his confusion growing. 'I just – '

'Aside from stopping me getting bored,' Nora went on, not only showing no confusion of her own but seemingly unaware of Stefan's, 'it helps me to follow discussions. So when we actually come to the takes I know what inflection Kostas wants. Film acting is such a matter of inflection. I mean it's *so* subtle, the camera picks up the faintest – internal hesitation, if you follow me. You can do with a thought in the cinema what you have to wave your hands around to do in the theatre. But if Judy – oh, I don't know. Like that scene yesterday afternoon. When she says, "You can't kill people." There are a thousand different ways of saying it. You can boom it out, like some eternal truth. You can be disapproving. You can be frightened. You can be saying the very opposite of what you seem to be saying. You can be pitying. You can be – well, as I say, whatever you like. But, if I don't hear what Kostas says to Judy beforehand, I can't tell if she's given the right reading. Or has put in all the various meanings Kostas wants. And poor Kostas can't hear himself. I think he knows what he wants; he just doesn't know when he's getting it, or always how to get it. That's actually one of the disadvantages of not having any theatrical background. Also, if you don't have absolute mastery of a language – or a terrific intelligence, or I suppose *sensibility* – which I'm afraid poor Kostas hasn't – I mean he's awfully nice, and great fun, but he's not really a true director – he doesn't have any overall vision that he makes every little detail fit in with, does he? – and – and, if you don't have that, you're fighting against almost insurmountable odds. It's rather like a painter, isn't it?' Nora rattled on, 'who has a great technique, but who doesn't really have any idea of the finished painting.'

For another ten minutes she kept it up; managing, in that time, to cut down to size – to whittle down to practically nothing – not only Kostas, but Jimmy, Michael, the actor who was playing Jimmy's sinister secretary, the actor who was playing Jimmy's bodyguard, Derek, the cameraman, and, for good measure, the man who designed the set: 'who clearly has never been in an English church of this sort. There again, the details are all right, but the overall effect, the *feel*, is somehow wrong.' Then, with a renewed and breezy-as-can-be plea for Stefan not to 'turn me off', Nora sailed away, her eyes as bright and blue and clear as the sky on a sunny spring day in England.

It was only as he watched her white-shirted, beige-trousered figure disappearing round the back of the set, and his hand went to his machine to do Nora's bidding, that Stefan realized that the one person Nora hadn't thought it necessary to put the boot into had been the one person who might have been held to deserve a good kick: Nora's arch-persecutor, and charge, Judy Nason.

Stefan was so upset, disturbed, perplexed – he wasn't sure what – by Nora's visit and request, that it wasn't till lunch time that he told Al and Marina about it.

'I couldn't tell you before,' he said over the blue plastic table in the canteen, as he pushed a dark thin slice of overcooked beef around his plate; feeling more unhappy now than anything else. 'She might have been listening to *that*.' He looked across at Al and Marina, and felt himself giving a troubled frown. 'It's her transparency that gets me. Her simplicity. When you look at her – it's like looking into a pool of absolutely clear water. You can see everything. Every pebble on the bottom. Every grain of sand. Only you realize – ' he shrugged his shoulders, practically twisting around in his sense of discomfort, 'you haven't actually seen anything. Or it's all a blind. Or that – oh, I don't know,' he repeated. 'Everything's going on *under* that bottom you can see. And if you dig down – ' he gestured with his hands. 'God knows what you might find. Also – ' he pushed his plate away from him, 'you get the impression that *she* thinks she's just a clear simple pond. That she doesn't know what's churning away under-ground. She must do – I mean I suppose she must do. But – ' he breathed out, heavily. 'She makes me feel unclean. I don't want her to listen to everything that's being said any more. I don't want her to – she makes me feel I'm involved with her, that we're sort of plotting together. And – I don't want to.'

'Just unplug her again,' Al said. 'Say Kostas told you – '

'She'd go straight to Kostas, you know that. Anyway, she might – oh, who knows. It's sick. I'm sorry. But that's the only word for it. And it gives me the shivers.'

As it seemed to give everyone, when Nora's request became generally known. Even Judy, whom Al muttered the news to when she returned to the set after the break, found this latest development a little too disturbing; and, instead of taking the opportunity of doing what Nora presumably wanted her to do, mentioned neither her name, nor Sergio's fall, all afternoon.

'It's not *really* because I'm frightened of her,' she whispered, eyeing Stefan's recorder apprehensively, when she came to get a first-hand report of the conversation Stefan had had with Nora. 'But – yuk. It's just too weird, isn't it? What are we meant to do? Go round chanting – ' she raised her voice very slightly – ' "Okay, Nora, the game's up, we all know what you did"?' She grimaced. 'God, I hate feeling sorry for people. But really I do for her, and – she really might go completely off her head and do something, mightn't she?'

Stefan nodded.

Judy glanced at the machine again, waved an admonishing finger at it, and squeezed Stefan's shoulder.

'Sssh,' she whispered; kissed him on the cheek; and tiptoed away – looking over her shoulder as she went, smiling, and raising now a finger to her lips.

Nora's longing for humiliation gave everyone the shivers. It also, as it had with Judy, achieved the very opposite effect from that which Nora presumably had intended it to achieve. For Judy was not alone in finding her coach's desire to be publicly condemned too perverse to be indulged; and in finding her now an object only of pity. Even the faithful Renato, who still refused to listen to any gossip concerning his English co-worker, professed himself sorry for Nora, Al reported over lunch the following day.

' "Not because she did anything," he told me. "Just because she wants to hear people say she did." I think Renato thinks she's some sort of casualty of the class war,' Al said. 'Who misjudged the tide and got stranded on the beach and now doesn't know how to get back to the water.'

'Poor Nora,' Marina smiled. 'Just when she thinks she's got it made, everything goes wrong.'

Stefan looked across the heads of the men and women eating in the canteen, and saw Nora, sitting alone, surrounded by extras for what appeared to be a Latin American adventure movie, since most of them wore peacock feathers in their hair, and were dressed in costumes of vaguely Inca – or Aztec, or Maya – inspiration.

'She looks happy enough,' he said, still feeling fretful about what had happened.

'Ol' sparkle eyes,' Al said, turning to look himself, and shaking his head.

'I just wish to God she'd go away though. Because I can't help feeling if she doesn't get what she wants – ' Stefan smiled, as unhappily as he had the day before. 'Oh, I'm probably just being Russian now. But you know, if everyone goes on feeling sorry for her, I have a feeling everything could end in some real tragedy.'

'Sergio falling off the roof wasn't a real tragedy?' Marina asked.

'Yes, of course it was. Only it didn't have a tragic ending. I mean it was bad enough. But maybe next time – oh, I'm probably just getting carried away. Being overdramatic. Probably Sergio did just slip, Nora is just as transparent as she seems, and I'm hysterical.' He paused. 'We're all hysterical. But I do wish this film were over. Do you realize we've got another month to go? I wish the film were over, we could all go to the sea for a week, and then – home.'

'And me?' Marina said, with a smile.

'Oh, you come with us,' Stefan said, smiling back at her, then looking at Al. 'Doesn't she, Al?'

'Yes, of course,' Al said, very seriously. 'If she wants to.'

'*Do* you want to?' Stefan asked.

Marina herself was serious now. 'I don't know,' she said. 'I mean – ' she lowered her eyes. 'Yes. Obviously. In a way. Only – ' she looked at Al, though her question, Stefan felt, was really aimed at him. 'Do you mean it?'

'Yes,' Al murmured.

'I don't know,' Marina said, lowering her eyes again. 'I'll have to think about it. As I say, in one way yes, obviously.' She returned her gaze to Al and, resting a hand on his forearm, stroked it. 'But it'd be a big step, wouldn't it? Leaving home. Leaving Italy. Leaving my family. Leaving all this.' She glanced about her. 'I know people here.' A brief smile. 'I know practically everyone here. Cinecittà has been my life for the last ten years. I've got another job to go to as soon as this film's finished, and I'm sure I'll have another one after that. In the States I'd be a foreigner, the work would be different – '

'The work's the same,' Al put in. 'You've worked there.'

'Yes, I know. But I'd still be a foreigner. And – I'm not sure if I'd like that. I mean I suppose Italy's no better or no worse than any other country.' She smiled. 'That's not true. I think it's better than some countries. But – a country's like your own body, isn't it? You might not really like the shape of your nose, the colour of your eyes, the length of your legs. But there's not really much you can do about them, is there? Oh, you can tinker with them, but, in the long run – they're still yours, aren't they, and you have to get on with it. There's no *point* in always wanting to be someone – somewhere – else.'

Stefan said nothing.

'That's what I feel, anyway. I mean I can understand you – ' this she did address to Stefan – 'wanting to leave Russia. But I can't help thinking that, if I'd been born there, I wouldn't have left. It's a stupid thing to say, I know, because if I'd been born there I wouldn't be who I am now, and so my decision wouldn't be mine. If you follow me. All the same – '

'I'd live in Italy,' Al said quietly.

'Well, for a while you would. But it'd be the same story for you, wouldn't it.' She took her hand from his forearm, and rested it on his knee. 'We're alike. We're both essentially stay-at-home types. It's just Stefan who's the wanderer. That's why – ' she stopped; in case, Stefan felt, she should betray herself.

'Anyway,' he said quickly, to cover any confusion there might have been, 'we don't have to decide right now, do we? I mean you don't have to decide right now. By the time another month's up – '

'Nora,' Marina interrupted, 'may have pushed us all off the roof.'

'Oh, stop it,' Stefan said. 'I don't want even to think of her for the next – ' he glanced at his watch – 'twenty-five minutes. Let's go for a walk, shall we. Or have a coffee. Or we could even have an ice cream.'

'Oh yes,' Marina said. 'That sounds like a good idea to me. Let's go get an ice cream.'

Thus, by getting round to the subject of themselves, and what they were all going to do, they got off the subject of pity, and humiliation, and possible tragedies.

And more and more, over the next two days, they not only managed to stay off the subject of pity and humiliation, but succeeded in doing what they and everyone else had been trying to do since Monday afternoon; burying deeper, since they couldn't uproot it, the seed of suspicion. A process that was helped rather than hindered by Nora's own desire to see that seed grow; and by Friday afternoon had gone so far that not only did no one mention Nora or the accident – except to ask how Sergio was, and pass the word that he was likely to be in hospital at least a month – but it was almost as if Nora had been cancelled from the collective consciousness. People said good morning to her

· 174 ·

when she came in; they said goodbye to her, see you tomorrow, when she left in the evening; a lone figure walking out under the umbrella pines towards the Metro. And perhaps twice a day she would come round to Stefan and ask what he had thought of Judy's a or o or u in the last take. Apart from that, though, Nora didn't exist; even for Stefan and Marina, over whom she still had, theoretically, some sort of hold. And now, if there was any one predominant topic of conversation amongst the crew, it was that of whether, perhaps, this film might turn out to be not too bad. Or even: whether it might turn out to be quite good. For a vague, pleasant feeling of excitement had been seeping onto the set; as people began to think that, despite what Nora called Kostas's lack of vision, the final result of their efforts might be a complete picture. It was an excitement that affected everyone, from Kostas, to the fourth assistant grip, to Judy; and it was an excitement that not only suddenly made everyone feel good when they started work in the morning, and look forward to the day ahead, but made the whole unit tighter, more cohesive, so that at last everyone felt he or she was working together on something, rather than just doing a job that would be finished in x number of weeks.

One could always tell if a film was going well around this point in the schedule, Stefan reflected. If it wasn't, this was when people started falling out; when people started leaving, to go on to another film; when people began to show their contempt for the director more or less openly. If it was, however, the opposite happened. People started getting on with colleagues they didn't really like and hadn't got on with for years; timetables were juggled, plans made so one could finish this job before going on to something else; and all at once a respect was given to the director that, even if he didn't deserve it, made him a figure whom cast and crew felt they would, if necessary, have followed into battle.

The effect of this coming together was not only to make

people feel happy with their work, but to make that work go more smoothly; so that now, if there had to be five or six takes of a particular scene, there would be a general unconscious egging-on of the actors to give an ever better performance – rather than a general and very conscious desire for them to say their lines at least correctly, so one could move on to the next set-up. It also made everyone more involved in the story, as if what was happening were in some way real; so that even people who had been working in movies for years, and would have sworn that they looked on what they were doing simply as a job, could be heard discussing whether Judy/Elizabeth should kill Michael/Robert at the end, whether they should go off together into the sunset, or whether there should be a different ending, that no one had come up with yet. Most of these discussions tended to be light-hearted, the favoured solution depending on the degree of sympathy – or more often antipathy – that the participants felt for Judy or Michael. Yet underneath the light-heartedness, the quips that 'I think that Jimmy should kill both of them', 'I think they should all go off to the madhouse with Jimmy's brother', Stefan, as he listened to them and tried to make out what was being said in Italian, felt there was a genuine concern, and that in fact everyone cared quite strongly about how *The Storyteller* would end. An end that anyway was going to have to be shot in both its versions next week; as the church set was going to be dismantled, and the last three weeks were going to be taken up with shooting in Jimmy's New York apartment, Robert/Michael's New York apartment, the coffee shop where Elizabeth and Robert meet, and the hospital in which Jimmy's brother Billy is a patient, and where too Elizabeth is treated at the beginning, and reads Billy her stories.

Kostas still favoured the bloody ending; as did the writer, who arrived from England on that Friday, and could be seen hovering around the set, a bespectacled nervous slightly overweight man in his forties, explaining to whoever would listen his theories about art and life and how it was essential on a symbolic level for Robert to be killed. Michael, though, more than ever was insisting on what he called the 'positive' ending, and was still more assiduous than the writer in trying to win converts to his cause. Stefan, Marina, Al, Derek, Alan, Riccardo, Bruno, Renato – anyone who could speak or understand English, whatever his job, was subjected to a tirade on 'how we're not dealing with symbols here we're dealing with real life and in real life people don't go round killing each other, that is they do but not often enough for it to be well, realistic' – and on how even tragedy had to be 'cathartic, if you know what I mean', and that 'if Elizabeth kills me that won't be cathartic it won't be tragic it'll just be – it'll act against the spirit of the film, it'll make the audience feel that Elizabeth's just a nut, and that'll undermine everything that's gone before. It'll make people leave the theatre thinking they've seen an art movie, a Euromovie. Instead of just a – well, a movie-movie, a pure *story*, a *true* story. And if you do that – you're lost. 'Cos if people start thinking that, take my word on it, there won't be that many people *coming* to see the movie, let alone leaving it. I mean the stories that Elizabeth reads to Billy in the home – they're not trying to prove a point, they're not *about* truth. They're just stories. That seem true, because they're good. Or even become true because they're good. Which is why I want to publish them. So, if she can do it, why can't we? You try to tell a story about the truth, you end up becoming unbelievable. You try to tell a good story – if you tell it well enough, it ends up becoming true.'

'I mean it's all bullshit,' Alan Miller said, after Michael had just released him after one of these tirades. 'But, if everyone is getting this passionate, Kostas is doing something right. Christ, that'd be something, wouldn't it? If Kostas Evangalides made a good movie. They'd declare a national holiday in Greece, or something. Or say that someone had made a miracle happen, and let's find out who it is and canonize 'em.'

And yet, and yet – despite this general awakening to the fact that against all the odds a decent film, even a good film, might be in the offing, and despite Nora's apparent non-existence, the Englishwoman had not altogether vanished from people's minds, any more than she had vanished altogether from the set. To the extent that as Stefan sat in the back of Marina's car, as they drove back into the city at the end of their week's work, the idea came to him that Nora's disappearance, and the feeling of being involved in a worthwhile project, were somehow linked, and that everyone had come together, and was working now as one enthusiastic team, just because 'the witch', 'Ol' sparkle eyes', as Al had called her, was sitting back there – back there in the recesses of their minds – controlling them, driving them on, threatening them with who knows what fate if they didn't 'get their act together'. She was like a giant spider, squatting over them, weaving her web about them; and causing them to work well because they felt that only by so working could they save themselves from the evil that she represented. Or perhaps, he thought, it was simply that the suppression of everyone's doubts about Nora had caused that seed they were trying to keep buried to sprout in an unexpected direction; and that what might have been poisonous, had it grown straight upwards, was turning out to be fruitful now that it had found a less direct access to the light.

Either way he supposed it might be a wrong-headed idea, and once more it might have come to him on account of the hold that he felt Nora had over him. But he didn't think it was, and when, somewhat hesitantly, somewhat apologetically – just because he was mentioning the unmentionable? – he told Marina and Al what he'd been imagining, they didn't think so either.

'Yeah,' Al said. 'That occurred to me this afternoon. It's as if everyone's scared of what might happen if they don't behave well. I mean just knowing old Nora's sitting back there sort of keeps you on your toes, doesn't it?'

'I can't help thinking of her more as a queen bee than a spider,' was Marina's comment. 'And we're all her workers, producing honey.'

'And hoping she doesn't sting us to death.'

'We're probably wrong,' Stefan said. 'And we'll find next week that everything's back to normal. But it is a nice idea, isn't it? Even if it isn't true.' He paused. 'Anyway, that's enough of that now, and I propose we don't say one more word about you-know-who until – eight o'clock on Monday morning.'

That, however, was too much for Marina. And, as they drove on, past the shabby modern blocks of flats on either side of the via Tuscolana, she couldn't resist murmuring, wistfully: 'Poor Nora. I wonder what she'll be doing this weekend?'

CHAPTER 10

'I AM spending today and tomorrow in Rome,' Nora wrote to her brother James in Canada. 'I was up at Franca Cavallone's place last weekend, and I shall probably go again next weekend, though Franca herself is away now. But this last week has been such a strain that I just want some peace and quiet. I shall stay in bed, eat and read, and if I'm feeling really energetic I shall walk around the block. Though this last is not very likely as the temperature still seems to be rising by the minute. Yesterday was overcast, but it was way over 100 degrees, and there was a strong wind blowing. Most unpleasant.

'The film is going quite well, but a most terrible thing happened on Monday afternoon. There is a dear man on the set who works as a scene shifter and carpenter, and in the lunch break he took me up to the walkways at the top of the sound stage so I could look down and get a bird's-eye view of what was going on. He had to shift a section of roofing while he was up there, and wanted to attach a piece of rope to it. Anyway, he edged out along one of the cross-beams to throw the rope over a rafter, and on the third try he slipped, and fell.

'Miraculously, he wasn't killed, as he managed to hang onto the rope until he was halfway down. But he was very badly injured, and his accident has cast a cloud over the proceedings. In a way it is a beneficial cloud, since everybody seems to be working harder and concentrating more than they did before. Either to avoid any more accidents, or out of respect for Sergio. Even Judy, my

· 180 ·

charge, has calmed down, and has been behaving quite well. In another way, alas, it has not been a beneficial cloud, since it has replaced the tension that prevailed before – the normal film set tension, the result of a lot of people, many of them highly strung and not too bright, working together at close quarters – with a different sort of tension. There again it's as if everyone feels they have to give of their best. But not now out of respect for Sergio, rather as if that is the only way of avoiding the evil eye. Of warding off some similar curse falling on them. All very Italian, of course. Nevertheless, it's a potent feeling, and has touched everyone on the set, Italians and foreigners alike. It's almost as if everyone is asking themselves: who's going to be next? And, despite the results it's achieving, over the long run that isn't a good feeling. It creates a strain, the strain means everyone becomes more tense, and the more the tension builds up, the more it becomes likely that someone will be careless and another accident *will* happen. Perhaps I'm being silly and superstitious, and it's just the shock of seeing Sergio fall that makes me think all this. Perhaps after the weekend everything will be all right, and as it was before. I don't think so, however, and that's why I feel I must keep myself severely to myself for the next forty-eight hours. To prepare myself for what might lie ahead. If it's nothing, all well and good. If it's something, I shall be a little more able to cope with it if I'm rested, than I would be if I went gallivanting around town, or started doing the rounds of the local restaurants up in Sinalunga with Franca's friends.

'I suppose I'm getting old. But what can you do? I shall be so glad when this film is over though, I must say, and I don't think I've ever appreciated or missed London so much as I have in these last few weeks. Everything is so sane, so safe in London. Even if one gets robbed or mugged, it somehow comes under the heading of normal life. Here everything is – oh, I don't know. Does it sound patronizing, or insulting, to say everything here seems so *silly*? Silly, yet at the same time (or precisely because silly: lacking in essential seriousness) *un*safe, if not positively dangerous. In future, even if they offer me ten times what they're paying me now, even if they actually offer me a starring part, I shall say no, I'm sorry. I prefer giving my lessons, walking in Kensington Gardens, shopping in Marks and Spencer's, and then coming home and watching the television, to all the money, all the excitement on earth. And to tell the truth, after this experience, if I never see abroad again in my life, I shan't just not be sorry, but will be actually glad. I know I shouldn't be writing this to you – although I suppose Canada no longer seems like abroad to you, but has become home – but what can I do? I'm not only getting old, I'm getting crotchety, too, and set in my ways, and with every day that passes I can less and less bear wasting my time in foolishness. So – just four more weeks, and then back to my nest forever.

'I hope you are well, and had a good time in Victoria. Do drop me a line in London when you have time.

'With much love, Nora.'

And now, Nora asked herself, the second she had signed her name. And now? All right, put the letter in an envelope, seal it, walk down to the tobacconist's, buy a stamp, and post it. But after that? It was all very well telling James that she was going to stay in her hotel room, rest, and read. But she was afraid that if she did within half an hour the whale of depression would have swum up to the surface, swallowed her, and hauled her back down to the depths with it. Or, as she pictured it at times, the iceberg of depression would have ripped her keel out, and she would find herself floundering in black, freezing water.

For the last few days her whale had been swallowing her, on average, twice every twenty-four hours; around four o'clock in the morning, and around five o'clock in the afternoon. At four o'clock, soon after she had woken feeling calm and peaceful, and hoping to get back to sleep immediately, it loomed up out of the dark and took her off to the seabed until a quarter to seven, when she forced herself to get up, have a shower, call room service for breakfast, and set off for the studio. And at five o'clock in the afternoon, sitting in her little backroom, with her headset covering her ears, it did its dirty work until it was time to go home; its work being so dirty that once or twice this last week she had felt that unless she really concentrated she was going to pass out, literally be consigned to the depths, sliding down into unconsciousness as the only way of avoiding thoughts so awful they might have damaged her permanently if she hadn't taken some evasive action. Now, though, with no work to go to, and with no prospect of Luciano or anyone else calling, 'Grazie, signore e signori,' and sending her off to the Metro, she was afraid that the beast might not only hit her outside the timetable it seemed to have established for itself, but, having hit her, keep her under the water indefinitely. Moreover, she suspected that however hard she reasoned, however severely she lectured herself and told herself not to be stupid, if she did dip beneath the surface, there would be no way for her to get back up again of her own volition. She had to be called back, by the necessity of getting up, by Luciano's voice; and if she wasn't – as she saw no reason why today she should be – she might very well be trapped there for good.

All her life Nora had been subject to the occasional period of depression; as, she liked to say, anyone with half an ounce of intelligence in this world must be. She had borne these periods as things that had to be borne, had allowed them as little room, as little time, as she possibly could, and had sent them packing at the first opportunity. She had certainly never indulged them, or encouraged them to stay for a minute longer than strictly necessary; nor had it ever occurred to her that they might move in and refuse to be evicted. But the depressions of the last few days had been of an order she had never dreamed existed before, let alone had to play host to; and once or twice she hadn't been sure how she would get through till a quarter to seven, when her alarm clock sounded, or how, in the studio in the afternoon, if she had to get up and tell Stefan that Judy's accent wasn't quite right, she would be able to put one foot in front of another, form words with her lips, or give Stefan, and anyone else who might be watching, the impression that she was the firm upstanding Nora of old; the Nora he thought she was. She had been afraid that the darkness around her would become so intense that, if she wasn't indeed swallowed up permanently, she would panic, cry out, 'Help me!', or just burst, uncontrollably, into tears.

She knew why she was being so assailed, naturally; it was this punishment course she was making herself endure. A punishment course that if, before Sergio's fall, had seemed to her justified, and had even satisfied her, now, though it still seemed justified – though it more than ever seemed justified – no longer satisfied her at all. It had gone totally, horribly out of control, and all the more so because those accusations of attempted murder that she knew people had on the tips of their tongues remained on the tips of their tongues; or at any rate remained unheard by her if they were expressed. She was being deprived of the drug to which she had become addicted – a drug she shouldn't be taking, that she should have had the strength to reject, yet to which she enjoyed being a slave just because she felt she deserved it – and the deprivation only made her craving, and her feeling that her addiction was a just sentence, stronger and more terrible yet.

Still more than before she could tell herself, This is folly, I must stop this, and penitence, self-flagellation, or willing submission to punishment, if pushed beyond a certain point, becomes perversion, sickness, behaviour worthy of punishment itself. Still more than before she was unable to stop it; and, being unable, was being visited not only by the punishment itself, but by these depressions that were threatening to unhinge her.

Tell everyone – tell *someone* – you didn't push Sergio, she cried to herself as she went to work, as she sat in her back room, as she ate and went to bed, as she felt the approach of the whale or the iceberg. Or if you can't tell anyone here, go to the phone and speak to someone in England. Say you're afraid you're having a nervous breakdown, and will they please, please do something, send someone – oh, just please, please *help*. Or, if you can't bring yourself to do that, tell yourself that you do not deserve any punishment whatsoever, that you have done your best in life, and if your best wasn't good enough that's by the way. Also: women in their late middle age do not welcome accusations of things they haven't done. It is, as you would put it, *silly*. And one cannot, at sixty – or indeed at any other time in one's life – be, knowingly, silly. Yet – she was abroad; she was cut off from the safety of London; and, anyway, she didn't feel nearly so certain of the safety of her home as she liked to make out she did. Simple, sensible Nora, the Nora whom people saw, was certain of things like that. Other-Nora, the Nora who was standing right behind that seems-to-be Nora, had her doubts, and suspected that, had she got on a plane and gone home, even there she might have found herself being swallowed up, or shipwrecked. And so, tell herself what she might, she did nothing. With the result that here she was, on Saturday morning, about to go out and post a letter to her brother, not only knowing that at any moment she might feel a whale's breath on her, but knowing that somewhere in the back of her mind this thought was lurking: it is a shame Sergio wasn't killed, so I could really have been condemned.

I must *do* something, she told herself, as she proceeded to write her brother's address on the envelope. I must *do* something.

Something other, that is, than reflect on this bizarre fact: that all week, when she hadn't been down in the depths, she had spent much of her time in the opposite place: up on the heights. And that, while the rational part of her was never satisfied by those unspoken accusations of attempted murder, another part of her felt not just the faint excitement the accusations of theft had inspired, but a more than faint sense of glee. So much so that at times she had had the sensation of flying; while at other times it was as if she were standing on a mountain top; way, way above the clouds . . .

Of course she had fought against these contradictory and more perverse than ever feelings, and had insisted to herself with even greater vehemence that she should either walk off the set and go straight back to England, or face the suspicions she knew everyone was harbouring and say, 'I did not push Sergio any more than I ever stole anything.' But, as before, she might have been talking to herself in a foreign language; and not only had she not moved, but slowly, over the course of the week, she had become aware that a new dimension had been added to her glee, that had nothing to do with any thrill she might get at being insulted and despised.

As she had said to her brother, since Sergio's accident everything had been going well; as if the fall had drained the unnecessary tension from the set, and concentrated everyone's mind. What she had not said to her brother, what she scarcely dared say to herself, was that she felt that this sudden raising of the tone on the set, this sudden pulling together of all the separate strands of the film, was due to her. People were afraid of her, people thought she was a witch; and, for fear of what she might do if they did not behave well, they were now behaving better than she had ever seen anyone behave on a film set. They had banished her from their presence; they could not banish her from their minds. There she sat, looming in the back of their consciousness; a white-haired blue-eyed avenging angel, with a thunderbolt in her hand. A witch, who had cast a spell on them, and from whose domination they could only escape if they bore themselves impeccably.

The trouble with this fantasy – other than that it was irresistible, and amused her, and delighted her – was that she couldn't rid herself of the idea that, foolish though it was, it contained a nugget of truth. She was a good, possibly a very good, actress, whose talents had never been fully used or appreciated. Now, almost totally cut off from her colleagues, and therefore with her talent almost totally suppressed, that talent had concentrated itself into something tight and hard; and finding a channel by which it could communicate itself with those colleagues – their fear of her – it was now flowing down into them, as oil might down a pipeline that fuelled a power station. It was her talent they were acting with, Judy, Michael, Jimmy and the others; it was she who was raising them to levels they had never touched hitherto. And raising them up to such heights – oh, how could she not be high herself? She was at last doing it; what she had been born for. She had at last been granted the opportunity of expressing herself, and been given not just a starring part but, in a sense, the only part. It wasn't at all the starring part she had once hoped to be given, and it was not the means of expressing herself it had ever occurred she might be granted. One had to seize one's chance where one found it, however; and from one point of view this was the greatest chance of all. For it removed the 'I' from the role; it removed that awful, flesh-eating creature called vanity. The complete actress, the consummate star, she had been utterly transmogrified: into a blonde Californian girl – or a chronically shy English girl; into a foul-mouthed good-hearted rock singer; into a handsome, earnest young New Yorker.

There *was* truth in this, Nora told herself; they *were* using her. And that being so – oh, how could she not feel that this was her film, that she, not Kostas, was the true director, and that, as long as she stayed there in the back of people's minds, everything would not only continue to go well but, provided she kept the heat up so to speak, would go better and better? This is my triumph, she told herself: this is my apotheosis. And, now that my hour has come, nothing on earth – neither depression, nor fear of madness, is going to take it from me. On, on, she exhorted herself: higher, higher.

What really scared her about these flights was that every now and then, as she sat there dwelling on her triumph, she once again found herself wishing, or at any rate thinking, that it might have been better if poor Sergio had died. And this for a reason other than that it would have brought further condemnation on her head. It wasn't that she had anything against the dear man; far from it, he was one of the few true gentlemen on the set: one of nature's gentlemen, as she liked to think. It was just that, had Sergio died, her isolation from the others would have been still more complete; the fear which they felt for her still more absolute. And that would have concentrated their minds to a still greater extent; and possibly produced not just a fine film, as this was now promising to be, but a truly excellent film.

Be gone, she ordered these thoughts when they came to her; get back! That is wickedness.

But, just as she could not be evicted from the minds of the cast and crew of *The Storyteller*, so the devil would not be evicted from her mind. He lurked there in the shadows, waiting; smiling . . .

In fact, when Nora went out to buy a stamp and post her letter, she found that, while it was as hot as ever today, it was no longer overcast or humid. Instead, the sky was a clear blue, and the air had a tingle of something exhilarating in it. Which made her think she might as well risk a walk; which in turn had the effect of banishing unhealthy ideas from her mind, and making her think that as long as she was careful, and the weather stayed like this, she might get through the whole weekend without either sinking or soaring. If I can just keep calm, she told herself; if I can just keep steady.

She walked down the Spanish Steps, past the guitar players and the vendors of bracelets and belts; she walked across piazza di Spagna: where she not only bought her stamp and mailed her letter, but bought a copy of the *Herald Tribune*. Then she made her way slowly down via del Babuino, pausing to look in the antique shops, and to go into the English bookshop; she even contemplated for a moment whether to go into one of the fancy clothes shops – Armani, or Missoni – to buy herself something. All right, she wasn't the type, but she had hardly spent a penny of the money she had been earning here; and just to buy something, anything, might help to keep her mind off other matters. Added to which, a bit of frivolity every now and then did one good. In the event she didn't buy anything; but just the serious consideration of whether she might cheered her up, and made her feel confident of remaining for the next forty-eight hours what she knew she must appear to be: an eminently sane Englishwoman of a certain age, in Rome partly for work, partly for pleasure, who would soon be returning to her modest but comfortable flat in London to continue her quiet, uneventful but on the whole satisfying life.

Instead of a blouse or a scarf, she told herself, I will treat myself to something to drink at Rosati's, in piazza del Popolo. I will sit at a table, read the paper, and then – the Etruscan Museum in Villa Giulia, perhaps. I have heard that that is nice. Or maybe just the Caravaggios in Santa Maria del Popolo, on the other side of the square. After which I will stroll over to piazza Navona, take a look at the Caravaggios in S. Luigi dei Francesi, possibly have a bite to eat, because it will be lunchtime by then, and after that – a nap and, before my depression has a chance to gobble me up, out to the cinema, to see whatever's on in English. Then another drink, in another café, another light meal, a stroll home, and – that's the weekend half over. Tomorrow I'll write some more letters, go up to the Pincio to read, and – I'm going to make it, Nora told herself. I'm going to make it. Just keep your eyes on the horizon, and first stop – Rosati's.

That, alas, was her undoing. Had she bought herself a blouse or a scarf at Armani's, and skipped the drink, she might well have got through the weekend without a hitch. But piazza del Popolo was near where Michael Toscanini – and Jimmy and Judy – were staying; and, while it was doubtful if the rock singer and his companion would ever have sat out in a café, Rosati's was Michael's favourite bar. Or so he told Nora when she saw him sitting at a table, was about to nod a smile and a greeting and pass on by, and instead found herself being waved over and invited to sit down.

Michael, in the fantasy that Nora had been indulging in over the last few days, was the weakest point. Both because he was undoubtedly the most talented of the three principal actors, and because she wasn't certain if he was frightened of her; if she squatted anywhere in or even near his consciousness. At times she suspected he was hardly aware she existed – nothing to do with her banishment; she had the impression very few people existed for Michael – and that far from being attached to her by any pipeline, through which her talent was flowing into him, if she had dropped dead or been the world's worst actress it wouldn't have made one scrap of difference either to him or to his performance. Other times she told herself no, of course he is aware, of me and of my witch's spell; he just doesn't like to admit it. But that might have been wishful thinking.

If, however, Michael was frightened of her, and did suspect her of being a thief and a potential murderess, he gave no sign of it this morning. Nor did his unexpected invitation to sit down, and his muttered, fretful 'What are you drinking?' indicate a sudden decision to take her under his wing, to delve into any possible mysteries of her character, or even to be, suddenly, friendly. Nora was English-speaking; Nora was working on his film; that was the only thing that interested him. For as he said, after he had muttered, in reply to an enquiry if he came here often, that phrase about Rosati's being his favourite bar, he needed allies; and clearly, to his way of thinking, non-English-speaking allies were no allies at all.

'I've got to make Kostas *see*,' he moaned to Nora; though he didn't look at her but out, through his dark glasses, across the wide piazza. 'I had dinner with him and that Englishman who wrote the screenplay last night, and – '

There was silence now, for more than a minute; as Michael continued to gaze into the distance, and Nora began to suspect that he wasn't going to say anything more, and that at any moment she would be dismissed from his presence as abruptly as she had been summoned into it. If she hadn't been forgotten so totally that Michael wasn't even aware of her sitting there.

Then he went on.

'We've got to shoot it this week. I mean the ending Kostas wants. But I can't. I'm not ready. I don't – ' he sighed, took off his dark glasses, and still didn't look at Nora. 'If only there was some way I could get through to him. To make him understand. I *cannot* be killed. I – you don't have any influence with him, do you?'

The green Toscanini eyes did at last focus on the woman, whoever she was, sitting across the table.

'Me? Oh, good heavens no.' Nora smiled at the very idea.

Eyes away. 'You could say something, couldn't you? I mean – '

Nora knew what he meant; she had heard him voice his objections at least twenty times to different people over the last few days. Nevertheless, she managed to listen reason- ably sympathetically, and nod understandingly every now and then, and smile at what she thought was the right moment, as Michael voiced them yet again to her here. She even managed to say, so quietly as not to interrupt the flow, 'Yes, I think you're quite right there,' or, 'Yes, but you must realize Kostas isn't an intellectual,' or, 'I think Americans understand the cinema instinctively, whereas we English are essentially theatre people.' What is more, she might have ended up feeling quite flattered by this attempt of Michael's to drag her into an alliance, or have come up with some convincing argument herself as to why 'You' should not be killed, but should be given the chance of living happily ever after with Elizabeth/Judy. Had it not been for the fact that, as she sat listening to the handsome green-eyed black-haired actor whose virtually total self-regard made him to her eyes hideous, certain phrases that he kept on using – and had been using all week – continued to echo in her mind, and call up images she had hoped would stay away.

'The sacrifice necessary for art.' 'The blood that civilization feeds on.' 'The sacrificial lamb.' 'The guilt of civilized societies.' 'The violence that springs from the suppression of our animal natures.' 'The blood.' 'The blood.' 'The blood.' On and on he went, rejecting the horror that Kostas and Jimmy and the scriptwriter wanted; yet affirming in Nora's mind the idea that it was Sergio's near-death that had pulled the film and its actors together, and that, since she was held responsible for Sergio's near-death, she it was who manoeuvred the strings that kept all these puppets working so skilfully. No no no, she told herself, as Michael declaimed to the people sitting round him; and 'no no no' she almost screamed at herself, when she became conscious of her devil repeating that most dreadful of suggestions to her: that it might have been better if Sergio had died. Or if not Sergio, it whispered, someone else. After all, that's what this story is about, isn't it? Whether art, whether civilization, feeds on death. If you say no, as Michael does (the hypocrite! the liar!), then you are effectively turning your back on civilization; saying manners, decency, generosity, unselfishness – social services, laws, Mozart, Shakespeare – are, ultimately, not worth the blood that has been shed over the ages – and is still being shed now – in order to create and maintain them. If on the other hand you say yes – then why do you turn me out? Why be bashful? Of course I'm not proposing that *you* kill someone – that would be madness. Individuals who kill are unwell; as unwell as someone suffering from a terminal disease. *Societies* that kill, however, or societies that require individuals to kill: that is just nature at work. The survival of the fittest; the weeding out of the weak; call it what you will. Really, Nora, that's all I'm saying to you. That had Sergio died – or were someone else to die – out of his blood flowers might spring. (Only might; it isn't a sure-fire thing.) And were you held to be responsible for that death – or did you accept responsibility – then it would be you who could claim the merit if those flowers came up, and you who chose, so to speak, their form, their colour, their scent. That's all. Truly. And that's not so terrible, is it?

'I don't know,' Nora said to Michael. 'I'm not a philosopher. And I do think there's the risk here of theory getting mixed up with fact, if you see what I mean. In *theory* it might be true that our civilization – that every civilization – is nourished by blood. And I suppose,' she added, somewhat contradictorily, 'in *fact* it may be true, too. But what I mean is – that's one thing. The other is – does the theory, or the fact, have anything to do with our story? Aren't we in danger of dragging in arguments that are quite irrelevant to what we are doing? What we must think about is what is best for the *story*; not what is true in real life. What is the most convincing ending. What makes the story seem truest – gives the most convincing illusion of reality. Because that's what film is, isn't it? Our century's way of creating the illusion of reality. In the past we created it in the theatre, or in opera, or in books. But nowadays . . . That's all we must think about. What makes the story seem most *real*? If Elizabeth kills Robert; or if Elizabeth walks out of Jimmy's church, to go and face whatever the future might hold, with Robert, without Robert. What would Elizabeth *do*? What would *Elizabeth* do? Nothing else matters. Neither the truth about the world, nor any theory or fact about death. The *film* is the fact; everything else for the moment is irrelevant.'

Nora came to a halt; neither surprised nor embarrassed by her speech. She had said what had to be said; she had stated the rational case. And not only was there no point in being coy about it; one had to be prepared to repeat oneself if one's message hadn't got across.

There was no danger of that now, it appeared: not only had the devil within her been silenced; Michael himself seemed at a loss for words for a moment, hearing his case stated so eloquently. Perhaps a little too eloquently indeed; he even seemed slightly resentful of this Englishwoman's outburst, as if he had invited her over not to talk, but to listen. I mean, who *is* she? It should be enough for her just to be sitting, and be seen to be sitting, with Michael Toscanini. She wants to step into the limelight too? Well, I'm sorry, and of course everyone's entitled to his – oh yeah, and her – opinion. But just at the moment it's my opinion that counts. I want allies, sure; but I'm the commander, don't forget, it's on my behalf the war is being waged. And if you think that gives you the right to claim some share of the booty – forget it. You'll get just what I give you – which in this case is a cappuccino – and be thankful for that. I mean for Chrissake – you're just some actress who never made it. Whereas I – I'm the star. And it's my survival we're talking about here. So back off, lady, and don't you ever try and pull a number like that on me again. Jesus. I mean – Jesus.

All this, possibly quite without justification, Nora read on Michael's face, as he removed his sunglasses again and gave the piazza the benefit of his unshielded gaze. And all that, too – with possibly more justification – she heard in Michael's voice when he did finally go on. For he sounded not merely resentful, but actually irritated when he said, 'Yeah,' frowned, and muttered, 'That's what I've been saying all week to Kostas. It's just not *true* if Elizabeth kills me. It's not real. And shit – we're so near to having a really good picture. In spite of Kostas. Only, with this one scene, he could ruin the whole thing.' And from the way he then looked at his watch, said, 'I think I'm going to call him, and go out to his place. I mean it's just too important at this stage,' and raised his hand for the waiter, Nora realized that the audience was at an end.

'Thank you for the coffee, Michael,' she said, standing up. 'I'll see you Monday.'

He might have been irritated with her; she might have been sent on her way. Even so, Michael hadn't quite finished with her. And either to punish her for having presumed to share the stage with him, or because despite his self-absorption there were certain things in this world that couldn't help but get through to him, as she turned he stopped her with this question:

'Is it true what they say about you, Nora? That you pushed that guy off the roof?'

He asked it quite seriously; without any coyness or embarrassment on his part now. And for once his eyes did not wander as he spoke, but stayed, firmly, on hers.

'Of course I didn't,' Nora told him, the anger in her voice as much directed at her for-the-moment-silent devil as at this arrogant young man in his tee-shirt and chinos, whose manner didn't quite disguise the fact that, talented though he was, he wasn't very intelligent. 'You know that perfectly well. Do you think you'd invite me to have a coffee with you if you thought I had?'

Michael however was not in the business of answering questions; only asking them. He shrugged his shoulders as he let his eyes drift off again; once more he replaced his dark glasses; and having stared at him for a second or two, tempted to repeat her question, Nora walked away, muttering to herself, 'For God's sake.'

It was only after she had gone a few yards that she realized she was trembling; and not until she had gone some distance that she realized why. Someone had had the gall, or the courage, to ask that question to her face; and, though she had denied it so indignantly, she had been neither surprised, nor outraged, by the question itself. It was the coming out into the open that upset her; the dragging out into the light of a foolishness, a perverseness, that had hitherto been contained within her own head, and within the confines of a film set. To hear words like that spoken on a sunny Saturday morning at the beginning of August in a public place, and not really to lose her temper, nor explode – oh, she told herself, that was terrible, and was a measure of just how far she had gone. I should have hit him, she told herself. I should have threatened him with a law suit. Instead – I just did my contemptuous head-mistress act, and stalked off. And now – he'll probably go on thinking I did push Sergio, I'll be pleased in my heart of hearts to know that even the great Michael Toscanini, in *his* heart of hearts, is in awe of me and therefore in my power, and off we'll go again.

Oh God, Nora told herself, stop it; as somewhere inside her she heard her devil giving a little chuckle at this revelation that the American actor too was receiving energy, inspiration from her. And oh no, go away, please, she almost said out loud as, proceeding down via Ripetta, she became aware that, though her devil was in residence, the whale of depression was swimming up towards her, and was going to gulp her down.

After that, try though she might, she wasn't able to regain her balance; neither for the rest of that Saturday, or that night – during which she slept for no more than a couple of hours – nor the whole of the following Sunday. Down, down she went, until all was darkness, and every-thing she had ever done in her life seemed nothing but dust, and emptiness, and squalor. And then, when she was down, into the gloom popped her devil, telling her yes, all right, but now is your moment of triumph, and now at last, in this film, you are going to vindicate everything that has gone before. You are going to make sense of your life. You are going, at last, to give full expression to your genius.

Go back to England, she told herself.

Stay, and see this out, she told herself.

You must leave, she told herself.

You must win, she told herself.

Oh stop it stop it stop it, she told herself and all those

voices within her, and please, let me just sleep.

Dazed with tiredness, yet still, she saw in the mirror, outwardly unchanged, Nora went into work on Monday morning, and sat in the darkness listening to Michael/ Robert making love to – practically raping – Judy/Elizabeth. They were both of them extraordinary, managing to suggest all sorts of ambiguities with their every word, their every breath; and Nora didn't have to correct or make a comment on a single syllable of Judy's. The actress had, to all intents and purposes, become Elizabeth; the shy English girl having the world forced upon her; a world she is terrified of, and a world that may destroy what is, paradoxically, her one link with the world: her stories. Oh you're wonderful, wonderful, Nora wanted to cry to the young woman, every trace of the rancour she had felt for her eliminated by the performance she was now giving. And if you can just hold it, keep it – you're going to be better yet. Hang on to me, Nora wanted to tell Judy, keep me there in your mind; and I'll raise you higher, and higher, and higher. Oh, Judy, you can do it, Nora exhorted her. Come on, come on – do it!

Michael too she whispered to, urging him on to the summit. But Michael was already nearer, and didn't need so much encouragement.

'Good night, Nora, see you tomorrow.'

'Goodbye, Nora, have a good evening.'

These, apart from a couple of good mornings, were the only words that were spoken to Nora all day. She didn't care though; she could scarcely think, so exhausted was she for lack of sleep, and for having spent the day fighting off devils, and whales. All she wanted to do was go back into town, have something to eat – she hadn't eaten at lunch, she hadn't moved out of her little back room – and then go to bed. To try to rest; and to prepare herself for the following day's shooting. For, once again, her battle against evil and depression; for, once again, her task as priestess, inspirer, divinity.

On that Tuesday – and on the Wednesday – Kostas shot the violent ending to the film, despite Michael's objections. Objections that were, when it came to it, strangely muted. In part because Kostas, with great self-assurance, told Michael that, if he didn't want to do it, they would use a stand-in, and get round the problem by shooting him always from behind. 'Actually it would be very effective,' Kostas muttered, no doubt knowing the effect his words would have. 'I've got it all story-boarded. You want to see, Mike? We shoot everything from Elizabeth's point of view, and she can't bring herself to look at your face, just in case that weakens her.'

The other reason for Michael's anticlimactic acceptance of something he had been fighting against for so long was – according to him – that he didn't want to waste everyone's time now, and it was much better to shoot the scene, and get it over, and then convince Kostas and the producers and the editor that the positive ending was better.

'Though that probably won't be necessary,' Nora heard him mutter to Jimmy. 'They'll see it for themselves.'

Once again all the actors involved gave superb performances; once again at the end of the day Nora went home with her eyes burning, mouth dry, and sweating with exhaustion; fairly sure now that however tired she was she wouldn't get more than an hour or two's sleep, and even beginning, now, not to care. She was afraid that if she did sleep she might lose her concentration. And if she lost her concentration, if she allowed her puppets at this stage to slip out of her grasp, everything might be lost. Sleep doesn't matter, she told herself as she rode home on the Metro – as she had been telling herself all day, willing her creatures on. Nothing matters. Except to get this made, except to keep everything going. Then, once it is all done – then you can rest. But for now – you cannot, must not relax, not even for a second. Keep going, she ordered herself, keep going. Just for another few days. Just until all the big scenes, the decisive scenes, are done. Because, if they go well, everything else – the scenes in the hospital, the scenes in the New York apartment – will undoubtedly take care of themselves. The picture by then will be complete, those will just be details to be filled in, that it will hardly be possible at that stage to get wrong.

On both these days Nora's isolation remained virtually complete; although not quite as complete as on the Monday, since a couple of times Marina came by to say hello, how are you, Nora. But grateful as she was for the young woman's attention Nora wouldn't really have minded if she hadn't had it, and with part of herself actually resented it. She felt it was compassion that was making the script girl be friendly; and, besides, she didn't want anyone disturbing her in what she was starting, despite herself, to think of as her holy task. She was a goddess, to whom a sacrifice had been made; now it was her duty to watch over the mortals who had made that sacrifice. She couldn't allow her attention to be taken from those mortals; and she had no need of pity. I have come this far, she wanted to tell Marina; do you think I can't go that much further? That I can't go all the way?

On Thursday however, and then on Friday, goddess or no, Nora found herself obliged to rest; at least when she was on the set. For though she would have liked to go on and shoot the other ending – Michael's ending – and thus wrap everything up, Kostas wanted to do a number of small scenes, and some retakes of shots he wasn't happy with; and thus the happy end was put off until the beginning of next week. A scene that promised to be the most complex of all, since when filming the violent end Kostas had only shot Elizabeth's actual killing of Robert, while in the alternative version he was going to have to shoot the dialogue preceding it. Dialogue that would of course remain the same whether Elizabeth walked out with Robert, or beat Robert's head in with the baseball bat – to avenge her rape, to save herself from having to go out into the world, and, most essentially from her point of view, to ensure that she would be able to keep her grasp on the world, on sanity, on life, by continuing to write her stories.

In fact, as Nora was told, she need not have come in while Kostas was doing those small scenes and retakes, since Judy had no lines in them. But by then she had come to feel that not only Judy was her child, the whole film was her child, and she didn't want to miss a moment of it if she could help it. Jimmy needed her quite as much as Judy – maybe more – and Kostas himself, she was afraid, could no longer have worked without her.

Nora, Nora told herself, you've gone completely crazy. But she didn't care; and she sat in the darkness with a small smile on her face, and her bright eyes gazing up as if at a mountain top that was now within reach. Who gives a damn if you're crazy, she told herself. Who gives a damn about anything? So long as you're enjoying yourself. So long as you're happy.

As she realized by now she was, most of the time. Just very occasionally she found herself being taken off under the waves; just very occasionally she heard her devil whispering to her of death. For the most part she thought of nothing but her film; and of how she was determined to make it great.

She didn't want to stay home. All the same, having less to do on those last two days of what was by now the fifth week of filming, Nora was still more grateful than before for the visits Marina again paid her – and less resentful. Possibly it was compassion that prompted the young woman to come by and say, 'Hello, Nora, how are you?' But so what? At least it provided her with some human contact, made her feel that, even if she was a goddess, she didn't have to be entirely isolated in her heaven. Her heaven that had so recently been her hell . . . Good, honest Renato had abandoned her; if no doubt, had it come to it, he would still have been prepared to be her champion. Handsome, soft-eyed Al had abandoned her; after that brief flush of friendship prompted by his conquest of Marina. A flush of friendship that had been abruptly halted by Sergio's fall. And all those other people on the set who had formerly stopped by to say hello, and have a chat – all those people who had thought they were doing her a favour by stopping by – they had not so much abandoned her as started pretending they had never seen her before in their lives. Toadies, lackeys, worms . . . She was supposed to be sorry to be cut by them? They must be mad! Marina though, whatever her motives for being friendly now, was a different matter. Physically pleasant to look at in her blonde, comforting way, she was, there was no getting round it, good. She was, she made one feel, of the earth, as trees are of the earth, as rivers are of the earth, as hills are of the earth. And, being of the earth, she also made one feel good oneself.

She didn't stay very long when she came by; she couldn't, she worked harder than anyone else on the set, keeping tabs on everything that went on. But she stayed long enough to touch Nora with her sweetness, to ask Nora whether she was going away this weekend – 'Yes, I'm going up to near Siena, a friend of mine has a house there she's lending me' – and, on Friday morning, to make Nora ask her, very cautiously, and without much hope of hearing her say yes, if she would like to come up to the country for the weekend with her.

'Franca, my friend, won't be there,' Nora said. 'But she told me if I'd like to invite anyone – ' She stopped, not wishing to embarrass Marina by pressing the invitation.

And embarrassed Marina looked. She blushed slightly. She smiled. She lowered her eyes to the ground. Nevertheless, she did not refuse, but simply said, 'Can I let you know in an hour or two?' Then she murmured, 'I must get back to Kostas,' pointed over her shoulder, and turned away.

How very, very nice she was, Nora thought; by far the nicest person on the set. And how she hoped this peculiar relationship she had entered into with Al and Stefan wouldn't cause her any grief. Of course it was nothing to do with her, and she wouldn't dream of mentioning it to Marina, or anyone. That, however, someone who was so very rooted to the earth should be so attracted to someone who was so very unrooted as that Stefan seemed to her a recipe for disaster; especially when she was using a third person, the amiable Al, as a cord to tie them. Maybe not; maybe everything would work out for the best. Stranger things had happened, and she was hardly in a position to lecture anyone about disastrous choices. Even so, she couldn't help but be afraid for Marina; and couldn't help wishing she did know her well enough at least to warn her: tell her what she undoubtedly already knew, but might not want to admit to herself. That she was, to put it mildly, playing with fire, and that, while she and Stefan might be aware of what they were doing, poor Al would probably be greatly hurt if he ever found out the truth.

On the other hand, Nora told herself half an hour later when Marina had not come back to say either yes or no, maybe Al wouldn't be hurt. Maybe the arrangement would suit him, too.

An hour and a half later Nora wondered: was it possible that Marina had prevaricated, hadn't come out with a straight 'No, I'm sorry, I'm spending the weekend with Stefan and Al' because she was afraid that if she did she, Nora, might say something to Al? She knew that Stefan had been afraid when she had invited Al to dinner. She had seen it on his face. He had been as afraid of her as everyone was afraid of her. There again, of course she wouldn't have said anything to Al, had Sergio's accident not intervened and made her forget that she had issued that invitation. But that was neither here nor there; neither more here, nor more there, than the fact that she had never stolen anything, and hadn't pushed Sergio.

God, Nora couldn't prevent herself thinking as the time passed, and Marina still didn't return; if Sergio's fall had had the effect on people it did, what would have happened if Marina had had an accident, or even if Marina had been killed? Marina, who was the most popular person on the set. Marina, who was the nicest person on the set. If she'd been held responsible for her death, they might have made – *she* might have made – one of the greatest films of all time.

At the end of the lunch break Marina sweetly, shame-facedly stuck her head round the edge of Nora's door and said if the offer was still open yes, she'd like to come to the country. Could they leave tomorrow morning? If Nora liked, she'd come by and pick her up at her hotel.

Oh yes, Nora practically boomed. That'd be fine. That'd be wonderful. She was so glad.

Was Marina afraid of her, she wondered again as, some forty-five minutes later, she listened to Robert/Michael telling a mute Elizabeth/Judy: 'You've got to live, there's nothing else to do.'

Or did Marina simply feel sorry for her?

Nice Marina. Good Marina. Marina whose death –

Stop it, Nora told her devil.

Get thee hence.

CHAPTER 11

'W HERE?'
         'What do you mean, going away?'
'You can't.'
'It isn't allowed.'
'We're getting married.'
'Who *with*? By yourself?'
'Marina, please.'
'What are *we* going to do?'
'We can't spend the weekend together, just the two of us.'
'Why are you being so mysterious?'
'Marina, *please* . . .'
'Just tell us.'
Marina looked back and forth between her two lovers, as she had come to think of them, and smiled. 'I just need to go away and think,' she said. 'I have to make a decision. And I can't think during the week, and I can't think at the weekend if you two are around.'
'We won't talk to you. We'll just – '
'No,' Marina said. 'I'm sorry. I'm serious.'
'Okay,' Al said, and raised his hands in surrender. 'You win.'
Stefan, across the table, nodded with a quiet, private smile, as if he knew where she was going; or approved of her going, if he didn't know where.
'But,' Al went on, 'I won't take no for an answer, whatever you decide.'
'It's everyone's weekend for choosing the ending,'

Stefan murmured. 'Happy or unhappy. Confetti or baseball bat.'

'Oh, stop it,' Marina smiled. 'I can't bear it. If Michael says one more word – '

'Michael will say one more word, and you know it.'

'You know what I heard him telling Kostas this afternoon? "Errr – Mmmm – listen, Kostas, all that stuff about death – that's bullshit – civilization, art – it's about the rejection of death, it's about the refusal to be frightened in the face of mortality. Art doesn't feed on death. It spits death out. It says no to death. And, unless we do the same, we're going to end up just making a cheap horror flick. We're going to be turning our back on our own film." Kostas just stared at him, patted him on the shoulder, and walked away.'

'Poor Kostas.'

'Poor all of us.'

'Poor Michael.'

'You know he's invited everyone out to dinner next Wednesday.'

'Everyone who?' Al said. 'He hasn't asked me.'

'He will. Everyone who speaks English. Everyone whom he can possibly win over to his side, and who could conceivably have some influence on Kostas.'

'He won't ask me,' Al said.

'You think he'll invite Nora?'

'I'm sure he'll invite Nora. Nora first of all.'

'Why Nora first of all?'

' 'Cos if people don't do what Nora wants, you know what's liable to happen to them.'

'In other words, everything's up to Nora.'

'Yes, I suppose so. It's Nora who gets to decide. Does Michael live, or does Michael die?'

'Do we *all* live or die.'

'Oh, stop,' Marina said again, unable to keep her anger out of her voice. 'Stop it! That's ridiculous. I feel sorry for Nora. I'm sure she didn't do anything. I – I like Nora.'

'You do?' said Al. 'Since when?'

'I don't know. Just these last few days. I suddenly felt – '

'You'll be telling us you're going away with Nora for the weekend next.'

'Oh, don't be *ridiculous*. I told you. I just feel sorry for her. And – it's true. I like her.'

'Oh, well,' Al smiled. 'Each to his – her own. But be careful of her, anyway.'

'Oh, I will,' Marina said. 'Don't worry.'

She wasn't certain why she hadn't told the boys where she was going, Marina reflected the following morning, as she drove north along the autostrada with Nora sitting stiff and sparkling beside her, chattering on about her family and their stately home in Cumberland and the estate she had lived on as a girl before she had decided she must do something with her life. It was largely, she supposed, because she was ashamed of what she was doing; her acceptance of Nora's offer being a sentimental gesture, prompted by pity. A gesture she was already starting to regret. Though it might also have been because she was afraid that, if she did tell them, one or both would have forbidden her to go, or followed her, or prevented her physically from going. And, aside from the fact that she did – or had – felt sorry for Nora, it was also true that she wanted a little time to herself, to try to come to some decision about the future. Whether she would get any time to herself remained to be seen, but in a way even if Nora didn't shut up all weekend what she said hardly impinged on her consciousness, so she was for all practical purposes alone, and could spend her time thinking.

If, by this evening, she was too bored, she might telephone one or other of the boys, and suggest they come up and as it were rescue her.

Which thought brought her to another reason why she

had accepted Nora's invitation. Yes, she had felt sorry for her, and she wanted to be alone. Yet also, by going away with Nora, and no one knowing where, she was demonstrating to herself – and to the world, when she went back to work on Monday morning, and told everyone where she had been – that not only was she not afraid of Nora, but there was no reason to be afraid. Nora *hadn't* pushed Sergio, she told herself – even if maybe she was responsible for the thefts. She couldn't have pushed Sergio. If she had done, it somehow undermined everything that she believed in, everything she cared for in the world, or thought was worth hanging on to, fighting for. Her family, her friends, her work, decency, kindness, and – above all, at the moment – love: in the shape of Stefan Bischov, and his boom man, Al. One had to have faith, one could not be afraid; otherwise one didn't even have a hope of happiness. There was no guarantee one would find it, anyway; but at least this way there was a chance. Indeed, Marina told herself as she told Nora yes, she also had a younger brother, who was studying to be a doctor, this might have been the only real reason why she had accepted Nora's offer, and why she hadn't told the boys. She couldn't really follow all that talk about which was the better ending for the film; or rather, she didn't want to follow it. She knew that for herself she had to attempt what Michael called the positive ending; she had to step out into the world. And stepping out into the world meant for her now refusing to believe that Nora had pushed anyone, that one should be scared of Nora, and that, therefore, Nora had any control whatsoever over the quality or the outcome of the film. Nora was a sixty-year-old Englishwoman, and that was all, that had to be all, there was to it.

Even so, Marina repeated to herself, barely able to suppress a smile, as Nora kept up her chat, telling her about the horses she had had when young, the nannies, the parties, she did wish there had been some easier way of affirming her faith in the world. And she had to admit that in one respect at least she had lied to Stefan and Al. It wasn't true that she liked Nora. She tried to; but there was something about the woman that made it impossible. Maybe it was that for all Nora's transparency, for all that it could have been true, she didn't believe her gush about country estates and being presented at court and disapproving parents trying to stop their daughter going on the stage. Maybe it was that, for all Nora was constantly implying that she was a great actress, she couldn't help feeling that she wasn't and never could have been. Either because that stiffness of hers went all the way to the bone, or, if it wasn't the same thing, because she lacked the one attribute which in Marina's experience all actors possessed, whether they admitted it or not: the desire to be loved. But what, she suspected, made it most impossible for her to like Nora was a certain almost physical feeling she had that Nora, who was as limpid as a mountain stream, had, beneath that clear surface of hers, a bed of hostility and hatred deeper than any she had ever encountered. It was hatred that made Nora's water so transparent; it was hatred that filtered all the impurities from her spring. Hatred of the world in general; and hatred, at this particular moment, of Marina Schiavon. Marina didn't believe she was vain – certainly not unduly so – and she would never have claimed she was a great beauty. Yet Nora, sitting beside her, had the effect of making her feel she was as lovely, as warm, as full of promise as any woman who had ever lived. She made her conscious of her sun-gold arms, stretched out towards the steering wheel. She made her conscious of her longish blonde hair that everyone thought was dyed but was, instead, corn-coloured, summer-ripe, natural. She made her conscious of her breasts beneath her white tee-shirt; breasts that suddenly seemed to her, though she had never before felt this way, founts of life, of nourishment. And she made her conscious of her stomach, her thighs, her legs, so firm, so tanned, so *human*, and made her wonder if, already, she were pregnant with Al's – that was also

Stefan's – baby. Yet – and this was the thing that worried her, and made her wish all at once not only that she hadn't come, but that having come she had told the boys where she was going – at the same time Nora's hatred made her feel like a shrivelled pod on an otherwise leafless, fruitless tree; a pod that a bitter wind was tugging at, and doing its damnedest to tear from the branch. Despite the heat, despite that sense of her own warmth and ripeness, Marina felt like putting on a sweater, and wondered if she shouldn't clasp a hand to her head, say, 'Oh my God, Nora, I've just remembered something,' and as soon as she could turn the car round and head back to Rome. She knew she'd never have the nerve to; nor would her sense of the ridiculous have permitted it. And already she could hear herself muttering, 'Oh for God's sake, Marina, don't be so melodramatic. Hatred, hostility, withered pods – really, what are you talking about? Those are just excuses you are making, because you want to get out of spending what will undoubtedly be a boring weekend with a person you have little or nothing in common with.' All the same, she told herself after another five minutes had passed, and Nora was still chattering on, she would have done better to turn round; and while she might be being melodramatic, thinking in terms of winter winds and leafless trees – or in terms of her own ripeness and gorgeousness – she was, ultimately, justified in doing so. There was something bitter, bleak about Nora, and there was something that made her feel that, if she was by any chance pregnant, she must do everything she could to prevent the life that was growing inside her from being in any way touched or having a shadow cast over it by this white-haired blue-eyed wicked witch. Nora, smiling, spotless Nora, was a character from a fairy tale – from *The Sleeping Beauty* perhaps – and everyone knew that one should never invite or permit the presence of a witch at a baby's – well, in this case practically conception. At any rate the very first days of what was, or would be, its life. That sort of thing put a curse on a child, that could only be lifted by love. And if for any reason love should not come –

'That's enough, Marina!,' Marina told herself. 'Just pull yourself together!'

And pull herself together, as she turned briefly to Nora, and smiled, and said, 'You must have been very brave,' she did.

Nevertheless, she still wished she hadn't come; and she still felt that Nora hated her. Hated her because she was warm and golden and gorgeous. Hated her because she pitied her. And hated her because she alone of all the people on the set had, or ever would have, agreed to come away with her.

Only those who despised Nora were not in Nora's book hateful.

The villa that Nora had said was so beautiful was built on the wrong side of the hill; Marina saw that almost as soon as they arrived. Surrounded by steeply-terraced vineyards, and a garden that looked as if it had been designed by a landscape architect but was almost sinisterly bereft of flowers, fruit trees, or indeed anything very much that actually grew, it got the morning sun. But by one o'clock, just when one was beginning to look forward to an after-noon spent swimming in the obviously new but already cracked and anyway uninviting pool, it was in the shade; a shade all the more noticeable for being the only shade around. The neighbouring hills, the valley below, they all glowed and basked in the sun. It was just here, chez Nora, from which brightness was banished. Then, possibly because of this lack of sun – or because it was hardly used – the house itself was dark and damp; a great barn of a place that at a distance looked like a typical Tuscan farmhouse, but from closer to, one saw, was nine-tenths modern, and badly built modern at that. The outside walls were thin;

inside great expanses of cheap white tiles and spindly-legged furniture accentuated the impression that, instead of being 'open-plan', as had no doubt been intended, the building hadn't actually been finished – and was already starting to disintegrate. Flimsy shutters swung back on rusty hinges. Windows with warped frames didn't close properly, and chipped away the plaster from the white-stained walls if one left them open and allowed them to bang to and fro, as they did even on this windless August day. And all the scarcely furnished bedrooms smelled of mildew, and had ants and other insects scurrying about the floors.

'What I suggest,' Nora had said when they arrived, Marina's heart sinking even as they drove up the long track to this ersatz farmhouse, 'is we have some lunch, have a nap, and then swim a bit.' To which proposal Marina had nodded as enthusiastically as she could, and gone along with initially as if she could imagine nothing nicer than sitting out on a flowerless patio eating tomatoes and mozzarella and basil that, though she had brought them herself, seemed to have lost their flavour on the journey, drinking a white wine that wasn't quite cold enough (there was no ice in the fridge), and then retiring to one of those chilly bedrooms to lie on a bed whose sheets were damp and whose windows, when she opened them, admitted only flies. But when it had come to swimming she had put her foot down.

'I'm not really one for swimming,' she told Nora, as around four o'clock she emerged from her bedroom, trying to look more rested than she felt. 'I think I'll just sit by the pool, and read.'

The truth was, she didn't want to get into that cheerless, faintly squalid pool. It was too uninviting, and even on the hottest of days she didn't like to get wet unless she could afterwards dry herself in the sun. Also, while she had told herself to stop being ridiculous in the car, she couldn't help feeling slightly frightened of sharing a pool with Nora. It was bad enough having to put on her bathing things, and wear them in front of the woman; so bad that far from going topless, as she would normally have done, she had slipped on her tee-shirt over her bikini, so as not to incur further Nora's hatred by exposing more of her body than was necessary. But actually to get into the water with her – no, she told herself, she couldn't do it. She had a vision of herself swimming along, and of Nora saying, 'Marina, you really should keep your head down a little more.' Of Nora coming over to her and saying, 'Here, let me show you.' Of Nora's large sensible hands grasping her neck. And then of Nora, strong, inflexible Nora, suddenly thrusting her below the surface of the evil dark pool, and holding her there until she drowned.

Once again she tried to evict this nonsense from her mind. Now though, as she lay on a white slatted cushion-less pool bed, face down and reading a limp-paged woman's magazine that she had found in the house, she wasn't so successful as before. Even lying here she expec-ted Nora, who herself had no qualms about swimming, suddenly to leap out of the pool, say, 'Oh, come on Marina,' and push her in. And this, she told herself, was only Saturday afternoon. They had the evening to get through, and the night, before the morning and the sun, a light lunch and the drive back to Rome. What had she *done*, accepting this invitation? And oh God, she told herself, this is my punishment for being sentimental.

'Some people don't like it here because there's no after-noon sun,' Nora said, beaming from the middle of the pool and looking, with her white hair slicked down, and wear-ing a simple black costume, suddenly much younger, and very handsome, if not beautiful. 'I can't take the sun myself. My skin's too fair. So this is ideal for me. Besides, I find the shade more restful. It's as if the sun attracts clamour. Here we're on the peaceful side of the hill.'

Marina turned on her side and smiled at her hostess; in a fashion, she hoped, that would add to Nora's store of restfulness.

'I suppose you prefer the sun,' Nora went on. 'You're so lovely and brown. But in the morning there's sun enough here. Franca only bought the place a little while ago, and there's still lots to be done here. But once she's done it up a bit, and planted some flowers, it'll be beautiful. The city seems so far away here, doesn't it? Just us, and the birds, and nothing else. I'm so glad you came, Marina. I mean apart from the fact I would have been fiddling around with trains and buses and taxis if you hadn't – well, it's nice to have you here. It's nice to be able to share all this with someone.'

Marina nodded gently, and smiled again, and said, 'I'm glad I came, too.'

Nora plunged back under the water; and Marina told herself, If only we can keep it at this level everything will be all right. Friendly, and polite; and entirely forgetful of the fact that back there in the city Nora is suspected of theft and attempted murder, and is happy to be so suspected. That's all a long way away, as she herself said. Here, as she also said, it's just us, and the birds. There's not another soul for miles. Just rest, and silence, and us.

Poor Nora, Marina told herself. I wish there were some sun . . .

It wasn't cold, naturally; it couldn't have been. Sun or shade, the temperature was up in the 90s; and was likely to remain so all night. Nevertheless, by eight o'clock that evening Marina was once again wishing she had brought a sweater with her. Standing in her bedroom, preparing to go out to the restaurant Nora had recommended, some fifteen kilometres away, she even had goose-flesh on her arms. And now, when she reminded herself that she had come here principally as a demonstration of faith, she could hardly think what she was or had been talking about. Faith in what? she kept asking herself as she debated whether to wear any make-up and then thought hell, yes, while I'm at it – while I'm safe in the presence of other people – I might as well make myself as beautiful as I can. Faith in human goodness, in sanity, in happy endings? For heaven's sake, I must have been out of my mind. And perhaps the best thing to do when I get to the restaurant is call the boys and have them come up – somehow – tonight. I mean better to appear foolish than to risk – oh, I don't know what happening. Besides, I want to see them. I don't want to sleep alone in this house. I don't want to sleep alone in any house with Nora. I'm freezing, and I'm depressed, and I'm – yes, all right, frightened. In half an hour or so it's going to be dark. And then – oh, God, Marina nearly said out loud, please let there be a telephone in the restaurant. Please.

And let the boys be in.

There was a telephone in the restaurant; and Nora did nothing to prevent her using it. (How could she have? Marina asked herself.) But the boys weren't in; and having, by then, had a couple of glasses of wine, and feeling at last warm, Marina felt too embarrassed to leave a message for them at the desk, telling them where she was and that they should come and fetch her immediately. What she did do, having been about to hang up, was ask the receptionist at the hotel if Alan Miller was in, and, when told he was, ask to be put through to him.

She was too embarrassed to leave a message with Alan, either. But she could at least say something.

'Hello,' she told him with an involuntary smile of relief when he said, 'Hi, Marina darlin', how're you doin', where are you?'

'I'm in the country. I'm sorry to disturb you.'

'Don't be silly. I'm just sitting here watching T.V., trying to get the energy to go out. It's so fucking *hot* here tonight.'

'Yes, it is here,' Marina said, not certain if she were lying or not at this point. 'I – it's just that I went off without telling Stefan and Al where I was going, and I thought – I mean they're not in – '

'They've gone to a movie. They stopped by fifteen minutes ago to ask if I wanted to come.'

'Well, would you just tell them I called,' Marina said, hearing her voice sounded very small, and wispy. 'And tell them I'm having a good time, and – '

'Where are you?'

Marina hesitated. 'Well, at the moment I'm in a restaurant. You probably won't believe this, but I'm spending the weekend with Nora.'

'*Nora*?'

'I said you wouldn't.'

'Have you gone mad or something?'

'No. I just suddenly felt sorry for her. And she asked me to come. And – '

'You all right? She hasn't pushed you off the roof?'

'No, of course I'm all right. She's being very nice. And I'll be back tomorrow afternoon. But if you'd just tell Stefan and Al if you see them – I mean it doesn't matter – I just – when they said at the desk they weren't in I wondered if you were, and – '

'Yeah, sure I'll tell them. But you sure you're okay?'

'Yes, of *course* I am.'

'You know best, darlin'. Anyway, *lots* of love to Nora, and I'll see you Monday.'

'Yes,' Marina whispered, unable not to put some sort of pathos, some appeal for help in her voice. 'Bye, Alan.'

'Bye-ee.'

Did Nora know what she had been intending to do? Marina wasn't sure, but she suspected she did.

'Were they in?' she asked when Marina got back to the table.

'No.' Shame made her lower her eyes. 'Alan – you know, the photographer – was. So I just had a chat with him.'

Nora didn't ask why.

'I forgot to tell Stefan and Al that I was going away. And I thought they might be worried if I just disappeared.'

You don't have to explain to me, Nora's expression said. What she came out with was, 'They're so nice, aren't they, those two?'

'Yes,' Marina said, forcing herself to look up from her plate.

There followed then a silence. That seemed to be shared suddenly by all the other diners in the old, vaulted restaurant. Marina was very conscious of her jaws chomping, and the scrape of metal against china.

She was conscious, too, though this she knew might just have been her imagination, of Nora's starting to assume the role that she played at Cinecittà; the role of queen bee; or, still more, of a large malevolent spider, squatting over her web, waiting to see who flew into it, and watching the struggles, the beating wings, the flailing legs of those who tried, in vain, to escape. She felt that the woman was sitting high above her, looking down on her; and she had never had such a sense of her own frailness, helplessness, and vulnerability.

A vulnerability she knew she would have betrayed in her voice had she produced the 'Are you looking forward to going back to England?' she was about to produce.

Before she could, however, Nora herself had broken the restaurant-wide silence; that had also been a product of her imagination, Marina realized. Of course everyone else had been speaking. It was just that, in her nervousness, she had blocked out all sound.

'Well, what do you think of the great debate?' was Nora's question; that so startled Marina she blushed. Did the woman really want to know whether she believed her guilty of attempted murder?

In her tiniest, wispiest voice, glancing at Nora, she said 'Which great debate?'

'The happy end or the sad end,' Nora smiled; surely knowing what her companion had been thinking.

'Oh,' Marina said, so relieved for a moment as to be unable to think what either ending was. 'I – ' And then, as she looked at Nora, she not only told herself she had been wrong to feel relieved, but that the ground had been whisked away from under her chair. So that instead of sitting in some softly lit converted monastery, with metre-thick walls and candles in wrought-iron holders, surrounded by friendly waiters and on the whole smartly dressed people having a good meal out on a Saturday night, she was in some vast space, some kind of immense, empty court, preparing to plead for her life. Once again she told herself she was being silly, she was overwrought, she really must be pregnant and some great change was coming over her whole body and mind; once again – more than ever – she was unable to pull herself together, and saw Nora now soaring over her, bat as well as spider, a great terrible winged creature borne aloft by winds that howled out of the dark places of the earth.

'I think,' she said, despising herself for her softness of voice, for the lack of conviction with which she said it, 'I prefer the happy end.'

'Yes, so do I,' Nora agreed. 'I think it's better. More logical. I thought before she should kill him, but – ' she shrugged, and sipped her wine; as Marina practically blurted out, as if it really were her own fate that were being discussed, 'No.'

'It's more realistic this way, isn't it?' Nora went on, apparently unaware of the interruption. 'I mean, however frightened she was of the world, she'd still prefer going off with a handsome American to staying locked up for the rest of her life, wouldn't she?'

Would she?

'Yes,' Marina murmured. 'Unless of course she loved Jimmy, and knew that he loved her.'

'But they don't do anything about it, do they?'

'No, but that doesn't necessarily – I mean maybe – she doesn't have to – '

'Oh, I know, but even so. What would you do?'

'I don't know. I – I think I wouldn't stay with either. Or I'd stay with Jimmy but wouldn't kill Michael. Just send him away.'

'But he won't go away. He'll always stay and haunt you.'

'I know – '

'Besides, he's raped you.'

'Yes, but – ' Marina paused, not certain now which ending either of them were in favour of.

'And if you don't kill him Jimmy or his secretary will. Jimmy because Michael's everything he's not – of course he's got fame and money, but he can't live in the real world like Michael does – '

'You mean he can't have sex like Michael does?'

'Also. And the secretary because he's a horrible fawning toady who lives through Jimmy and is jealous of his wealth and fame yet despises him at the same time for being less well educated, lower class, and wants to get a hold over him. Which he undoubtedly will do if he does kill Michael and gets rid of the body. And you can't tell me that in the world that Jimmy and Judy live in people *don't* get killed and they don't manage to hush it up and say it was an accident, or an overdose of drugs or something. There was the famous case of that director who killed someone at his villa in the South of France. *That* never got out. Oh, I mean it did, but there again it was all hushed up, and made to look like an accident. No,' Nora said, appearing now to remember that she had opted for the happy end: 'I don't think you can send him away. Either you go with him, or you kill him.'

'Then I'll go with him,' Marina whispered.

'Even though you know that means exposing yourself to further rape – both physical and mental?'

'Yes,' Marina whispered, her voice still weaker. 'I suppose – '

'Even though you know you'll probably never write any more of your fairy stories, and it's only your fairy stories that keep you sane, that make the world at all bearable?'

'Yes,' Marina whispered.

'Even though you know that essentially Michael is just a vulgar publicist who is only interested in you because he sees you as a rare butterfly whom he can show profitably to the world, impaled on – well, excuse me, I was going to say a pin, but I suppose it would be more accurate to say his prick.'

'What do you want me to say?' Marina almost cried.

'No, you're right, of course,' Nora said, her face as unclouded as ever. 'I'm just playing the devil's advocate. But you have got to think of all the arguments, haven't you, before deciding one way or the other.'

What were they talking about? 'I don't know,' Marina mumbled, pouring both of them more wine. 'I mean no, not really. The point is – it's wrong to kill people, isn't it? That's the only real argument.'

'Oh wrong, wrong. What does wrong mean? I don't know if you're religious, Marina – '

'No, I'm not.'

'Well then, if there's no religion there's no absolute right or wrong, is there? And even if there is religion right and wrong are very subjective notions. That tend to be decided by the government of the day. After all, even as we're sitting here eating there are undoubtedly people dying in different parts of the world. And I don't think you have to be a radical or a crackpot to claim that ultimately they are dying – well, not so we *can* sit here eating in this restaurant, but because we *are* sitting here eating in this restaurant. Is that right? Is that wrong?'

'Oh, I don't know,' Marina said. 'I just think – well, I suppose, for me – it's what's against life. That's wrong. And if something's for life – it's right.'

'All life? Or just human life? Is it right to kill these lambs we're eating just so we can go on living? And if you fight a war – do you think the First World War was for or against life? The Vietnam War? The Falklands War?'

'Well then – for – freedom.'

'Whose freedom?'

'Oh – '

'I mean freedom's a still vaguer concept than right or wrong. And anyway, what are you saying? That it's right to kill for freedom, but wrong to kill if you want to enslave someone? In that case, to get back to our own case, Judy's right to kill Michael, surely? He's not going to give her freedom. It could be argued she'd be freer staying with Jimmy.'

'That's why I said she should reject both.'

'But she's too weak to!'

'She'll find the strength.'

'Oh, in a novel she will. In a film she might. But in real life – you think someone like that – ?'

'Well, she could.'

'Yes, she could. But she won't. You know that.'

'All the same –'

'I'll tell you one thing that's occurred to me,' Nora said, in a tone that announced that the subject was for the moment closed, 'it would have been very ironic – I mean tragically ironic – if poor Sergio had been killed. If Sergio had died, and they'd then gone on to choose the happy end. As I'm sure they would have out of respect for Sergio, in a sense. Because while they were asserting, "No, art can never or must never grow out of blood," the very existence of the film would have been stating the opposite.'

'It wouldn't,' Marina said; feeling no longer wispy, but passionate. 'Because Sergio's death would have been an accident. I mean Sergio's fall was an accident.'

'It would still have been a sacrifice for the film. And a sacrifice that determined the shape of the film, the quality of the film. After all, you must admit everyone's been working much better since the accident, haven't they? And that can't help but affect the final outcome.'

'But –' Marina shrugged. 'No. I mean – I'm not sure what we're talking about any longer, but it does all boil down to what Michael's been saying these last few days. Is civilization the rejection of death, or is it the acceptance of death?'

'Oh,' Nora smiled, as if this were a question to which she *knew* the answer. 'It seems to me that it's a rejection of death on the part of the strong, that is paid for – somewhere out of sight preferably – by an imposition of death upon the weak. And the strong know that and yes, accept it. Only, accepting it, they eventually develop a bad conscience. Which weakens them. And thus lines them up for roles as potential victims. You see,' Nora said, her eyes clearer, bluer, than Marina had ever seen them, 'there'll come a time on earth when no human beings are killed anywhere, other than by disease, accident or old age. And even disease and old age will be beaten back until they're almost invisible. But when that time comes everything else on earth will have been destroyed, sacrificed if you like, to make the triumph of humanity possible. And so, at the precise moment that humanity scores its final victory over the world, and rejects death totally – at that precise moment, the world will come to an end. For the ultimate rejection of death – the ultimate sacrifice will have been made. Gone. In a puff of smoke.' Nora made a gesture with her hand. 'Oh yes, Marina, of course civilization rejects death. That's why the film should have a happy end. But as with us, in this restaurant – to enable that film to have a happy ending, someone, somewhere, is going to die. And it's our refusal to acknowledge this – when in our hearts we know it – that clouds our vision, that makes us, how can I say? – false. And that makes our art less – less good, and less terrible than it would be if we did acknowledge it. If Sergio had died, and we had admitted he died for us – oh, Marina we really might have made a great film.'

'When I acted,' Nora added as a postscript to this speech, after Marina, unable to feel in the least guilty, had finished the lamb on her plate, 'I tried to work from this knowledge. From that absolute contradiction, that paradox if you like at the heart of our culture. But somehow – ' she stopped, looked at Marina, and shook her head slightly. 'Marina' she said, 'this is absolutely none of my business, I'm only saying it because I've drunk too much, and you'll undoubtedly tell me to keep my nose out of matters that don't concern me. Or something worse. And you'll be quite right. All the same, having gone this far – ' she paused. 'Don't marry Al. Don't. It's wrong what you're thinking of doing.' She smiled. 'There's me using the word "wrong". But let's say – it's false. It won't work. And – you're a lovely girl. You're a nice girl. You'll find someone else. You know that, don't you? On the next film, probably. And on the one after that. *Or* on the one after that. But – ' she stared at Marina now, until Marina herself felt like a butterfly, impaled on Nora's gaze. 'This way you'll never be happy. And if you're not happy – or don't at least try to be – you'll end up being a sacrifice. You'll end up – oh, I don't know – *dead*.' She leaned across the table and grasped Marina's hand. 'Work from the centre, Marina. Work from the very heart of the contradiction. At least that way you'll see the whole of life. All of it. Both the acceptance and the rejection.'

And I will end up, Marina wanted to tell her, like you. I will lose whatever ripeness I have in me, I will lose – I will make myself lose – my baby. And all I'll be able to do is, as you say, see life, with eyes as clear as yours. But I don't want to see life. I don't want simply to look. Sure, I may end up unhappy. I may end up a sacrifice. But, if I do, maybe something will grow from my sacrifice. And, if I don't, at least I will have come down on the side of acceptance. All right, maybe I am fooling myself. Maybe someone somewhere in the world is paying so I can love Stefan and have Al's child – as I probably will do sooner or later even if I am not now pregnant. But I cannot and will not reject that love, however off-centre, off-balance, it may be. And I cannot and will not reject my baby. I may be wrong, I may be false – but anything, anything seems to me better than ending up sitting clear-eyed in a restaurant at the age of sixty, seeing everything and yet still having hatred in my heart. Or seeing everything except that what perhaps is making me clear-eyed is the fact that I do have hatred in my heart. Of course I am taking a terrible risk in doing what I am doing; but better take that risk, and fail, than not take it and wish for the death of those who do.

For that, finally, is what you are doing, isn't it, Nora? In the name of rightness, in the name of sanity, in the name of truth – you are wishing for my death. For the death – of life.

She told Nora none of this, naturally. She simply held the woman's gaze for a moment, smiled, and said, as gently as she could: 'I'm sorry, Nora, but you're right. It really is none of your business.'

An hour later, after the meal had ended quite amicably with the two women splitting the bill and Nora offering to drive if Marina felt too tired – 'Oh no, really, I'm fine' – Marina reflected that her unspoken reply to Nora had probably been unfair. At least a little facile, and rhetorical. A result of her having drunk too much too, and of her being embarrassed by Nora's advice. Nevertheless, as they made their way through the dark countryside, towards that damp, no doubt by now mosquito-ridden house – and she tried to force herself to concentrate on the road ahead, aware that, if she had drunk too much an hour ago, she had drunk still more since – she couldn't help thinking that there had been an element of truth in it. An element of truth regarding her own desire 'to live', whatever that vague word meant; and an element of truth regarding Nora's desire not to see her live. That is: Nora's desire to see her die.

There *was* hatred in the woman, she told herself as it struck her how easy it would be for Nora to give a quick jerk to the wheel, and send them spinning off the road. 'Killed herself while driving when drunk.' There was a desire to tear her from the branch.

But you shan't succeed, she wanted to cry out to her now. You shan't.

I don't care if the film turns out to be a disaster.

I shall lock my door tonight.

CHAPTER 12

T HEY got back from the cinema around eleven-thirty, having spent an awkward evening together.

'It's not the same without Marina, is it?' Stefan said; and Al, though he merely nodded and smiled, agreed.

There had been a distance between them, a lack of ease; as if both, for the first time, were embarrassed by Stefan's attachment to Al, and felt it was something that separated them rather than drew them closer. 'I feel,' Stefan nearly added, 'like an old queen going out with some youth who doesn't give a damn about him.' He didn't, because Al didn't like that sort of talk. He didn't like it himself. All the same, that was how he felt, and he suspected that Al felt the same way too.

'She's *got* to decide she'll come – or I can stay,' Al frowned as they walked through the door of their hotel. 'I mean – ' he didn't finish, but it was Stefan's turn now to know what he wanted to say.

'There is a message for you, Mr. Bischov,' the desk clerk told Stefan, as he handed him his key. 'Good night.'

'Maybe it's from – ' Al once again didn't finish his sentence; as if suddenly he couldn't or didn't want to work out why, if the message was from Marina, she had left it for Stefan and not for him.

'It's from Alan. He says to come to his room immediately. He's got something important to tell us.'

'Michael's broken his neck,' Al smiled, visibly relieved.

'They've thought of a different ending, more likely. What's Alan's room number?'

'307, I think.'

307 it was, and Alan was waiting for them.

'You're never going to believe this,' he said. 'You know where Marina's gone?'

Neither Stefan nor Al returned the grin Alan was giving them. Stefan simply frowned; Al said: 'Where?'

'To the country with the witch.'

'With Nora!'

'Yes.'

'Why? I mean – '

'How do you know?'

'She called me. She was looking for you. But you were out.'

'What did she want?'

'Just to tell you not to worry. I guess.' Alan himself frowned now, though he was still unable to conceal his glee at this latest development. 'On the other hand, she sounded sort of – I dunno. Guilty? Uneasy? She said she hadn't told you where she was going.'

'She didn't. But – '

'Oh, shit' said Al. 'Oh, *shit*.'

The three men looked at one another; though Al and Alan ended up, as if recognizing that for some reason he had the most authority, looking at Stefan.

Stefan stood at the end of Alan's bed for a while, contemplating the dresser in front of him, the television that was on but had the sound turned down, a shirt of Alan's that was thrown over the seat of a chair.

'Do you know where she is?' he asked at length, his voice sounding as grave as he felt.

Alan shook his head. 'No. No idea.'

Al said: 'Nora spoke the other week about having some place near Siena. But I guess – '

'D'you think her parents know?'

'They might.' Stefan looked at his watch. 'It's late, but – ' He felt in his pocket, took out a small brown address book, and flicked through it. Then he went over to the side of the bed, sat down, and dialled a number on the telephone.

'Pronto,' he said. 'Buona sera – ' he closed his eyes for a second. 'Bon soir. Vous parlez français? Je suis Stefan, un ami de Marina. Nous nous sommes rencontrés la semaine dernière. Je suis désolé de vous téléfoner à cette heure – '

'What's he saying,' Al muttered to Alan.

'That he's sorry to be calling at this time.'

Al nodded, listening to Stefan.

'Mais je voulais savoir si vous savez où se trouve Marina. C'est très important . . . Non, il n'y a rien de sérieux. C'est une chose du film. L'acteur ne trouve pas des mots, il est hystérique – '

Al gave a twitch of impatience, as Stefan gestured for a pen. Alan took one off the dresser, and handed it to him.

'Elle habite tout près de Siena, non?' Stefan said, writing something on the back of an envelope.

'Bon, oui, d'accord. Non, je suis sûr . . . Je vous remercie. Et je m'excuse encore. Bonne nuit.'

Stefan replaced the reveiver for a second, then dialled again. He let the number ring for a long time.

'You got a number?' said Al.

Stefan nodded.

'There's no reply. How long ago did she call?'

'A couple of hours at least,' Alan said. 'Right after you went out. She sounded as if she was calling from outside. A bar or someplace. It was kind of noisy.' He paused. 'Maybe the phone isn't working in the house.'

'Maybe she didn't want Nora to hear who she was calling, or what – '

'They'd be back by now if they had gone out to eat, wouldn't they?' Stefan murmured.

'In the country? I guess. You never know though.'

'Maybe if we try again in half an hour – '

'I have a car,' Alan said, doubtfully.

'You do?'

'Yeah, I rented one. I was planning to drive to the sea someplace tomorrow. Away from the crowds.'

'That's sort of extreme, isn't it?' Stefan said. 'I mean driving up . . . Did she really sound worried?'

'I dunno about worried. Just – I dunno. Embarrassed, I guess, at what she was doing.'

'Why did she call at all though?' Al said. 'If she wasn't worried. I mean she could have just told us when she got back tomorrow where she'd been.' He cleared his throat, and adopted a more aggressive stance. 'I think we should go up tonight.'

'You don't seriously think the witch – ?' Alan stopped, and couldn't help, once again, looking gleeful. 'Well, I guess if she pushed poor Sergio – '

'What possessed her?' Al said.

'She probably felt sorry for her.'

'Yes, I know, but – '

'Do we know where the place is?'

'Near somewhere called Sinalunga, her father said. Near Siena. I guess if we call the phone company.' Stefan glanced at the envelope on which he had written. 'The house belongs to someone called Franca Cavallone.'

'Maybe she's there too,' Alan smiled. 'We can't suddenly turn up at two in the morning and wake a whole houseful of people.'

'Did Marina say she was?'

'No, I must say from the way she spoke it sounded as if there were just the two of 'em. Poor old Marina.'

Stefan thought for a moment. 'Alan, would you mind – I mean would you lend us your car? You're probably right. We're being ridiculous. And we'll turn up there in the middle of the night and – but as Al said. She wouldn't have called us if she wasn't feeling uneasy.'

'I'm not going to lend you the car. I'll drive. You don't think you're going without me, do you? I wouldn't miss this for the world. But why don't you call the phone company first. Or look in the book and see if what's her name – '

'Cavallone.'

'She might be in Rome for the weekend. Call her. She might give you the address. That'll be easier. And while you're doing that I'll get my cameras ready. What d'you think I should take? Black and white? Colour? I prefer black and white. But under the circumstances – '

Stefan himself couldn't help smiling at last, as he picked up the phone once more, to call down to the desk to ask them to look up Franca Cavallone's number in Rome. Al, however, continued to frown, and seemed if anything still more worried. He, his expression proclaimed, could see nothing amusing about this situation at all. Indeed, he could picture only too well the photographs that Alan seemed to be looking forward to taking. Marina, lying on the steps of some country house; Marina sprawled on a bed: her blood luminously red in the white light of the flash . . .

'Oh come on, Al,' Alan said, patting him on the back, and deciding now to look at least sympathetic, if he couldn't yet manage frantic. 'It'll be all right. You see. I mean you don't *really* think, do you – ?'

Alan's unfinished question remained with them for the next two and a half hours. It remained with them as they found – at the third attempt – the right F. Cavallone's number and explained with some difficult to whoever answered that they were friends of Nora Mellon's who was a friend of signora Cavallone and they were working on the same film as signora Mellon and were leaving first thing tomorrow morning for Siena and they wanted to stop by signora Cavallone's house and say hello and they were terribly sorry to call at this hour but could they have the address and how exactly did one get there and oh by the way is there a phone there, there is, and it's working? Oh wonderful thank you very much and so sorry again to have disturbed you.

It remained with them as they once again wondered why, since there was a telephone, Marina hadn't used that to call them, and came to the conclusion this was a bad sign and added cause for concern.

And it remained with them as they went downstairs, said good night to the desk clerk, got into Alan's rented Ford, and set off north first through the city, and then onto the autostrada heading towards Florence.

'What did the woman say?' Al asked, when they had been on the road an hour. 'Turn off after where?'

But it was just something to say, because he knew quite well where the turn-off was.

They weren't sure what they really thought; that was the problem. And as they sped along Stefan could feel their mood shifting between a sense of absurdity at what they were doing, a sense of their being the cavalry riding to the rescue, and a small but quite solid sense of genuine concern. Yes, all right, it was eighty, eighty-five, ninety-five per cent probable that they had embarked on a wild goose chase, and that they would wake up tomorrow morning in some hotel near Nora's friend's house unable to believe that they could have been so foolish. Embarrassed for themselves, embarrassed for Marina, embarrassed for Nora. Even so, had there been just a one per cent possibility that Marina's phone call had been a cry for help, it was essential that they act on it. If they didn't, and something did happen, they would never forgive themselves. And if they did something, even by omission, unforgivable, you could be sure that aside from what might have happened to Marina herself – though that was of course the immediate and most important concern – not only would he be very soon saying goodbye to Al, but, he suspected, he would be saying goodbye to everything that bound his life together. To his love of films; to his commitment to America; to, even – and this occurred to him for the first time now – his eventual, maybe years and years hence, return home. Yes, he told himself: that was what Marina was; what Marina

· 229 ·

represented. As well as being the person who would tie him to Al, Marina was the person who would in a sense redeem the selfishness that had caused him not just to come to the States himself, but to drag his parents there too. And, having redeemed him, she might well enable him, at some stage, to go back to Russia.

It would be a long time hence, of course; he couldn't contemplate it while his parents were still alive. That would have been too cruel. And it was very possible that by the time his parents were dead he would dismiss the idea of returning to his homeland as sentimental nonsense; or that Russia would not welcome him if he did contemplate gracing her with his presence. Nevertheless, he knew he was Russian and would remain Russian for as long as he lived; he couldn't help feeling that one's native country, one's native culture, was, as Marina herself had said the other week, rather like one's own body; and he suspected that as he grew older he might feel an ever stronger temptation to return to his own body. Particularly if that body was less wracked with the ills that had afflicted it for much of this century. After all, to be realistic about it, even if all his plans for Al and Marina worked out, the chances were that he would eventually find himself drifting away from them, if not precisely finding himself alone. And while, at the age of thirty-two, or forty-two, or fifty-two, the role of outsider might suit him, he guessed by the age of sixty-two he might be wanting to be an insider again; to inhabit his own body, instead of wandering the earth merely observing, or merely, as was in his case perhaps more apt, listening. Eventually, he told himself, he might want to act, to take part. And while, again, it was possible that by the time he did he would feel that the States was his home, was his body, he suspected that somewhere in the back of his mind his true reality would always be Russian. The America that he had always loved, the America of the movies, was just a dream of reality. An exciting dream. A lovely dream. All the same, in the end – a dream. And dreams were perhaps not quite enough . . .

Marina, Stefan told himself, will take me back to myself.

As long as they were on the autostrada – and even when they turned off it, and took the highway towards Siena – the headlights of the other cars, and the lights of service stations, houses and distant towns, ensured that, if a sense of absurdity wasn't their dominant mood, it more than held its own against their sense of doing something adventurous, or necessary. Once they were off the highway however, and were travelling along a narrow unlit deserted country road, though it might still have been present in some measure, it shrank into the background; as did their riding-to-the-rescue mood, that had in any case largely emanated from Alan. It was the darkness that made them feel sombre; it was perhaps a certain physical tiredness; and it was certainly the knowledge that they were by now very near, and that soon, for better or worse, they were going to have to do something.

'God,' Alan said, instinctively lowering his voice, as if afraid someone might hear him, 'it really is like approaching the lair of the wicked witch, isn't it?'

He said it intending to lighten the atmosphere; but not even he smiled. That was what it was like. Driving through the hot night towards the unknown.

'There should be a turn-off up – up there,' Al said, pointing to a track that led off to the left. But there was a catch in his voice as he spoke; and somewhere inside him Alan was clearly so unwilling to follow Al's instructions that for a moment he made as if to drive straight on. Then he braked hard, said – as if there had been some doubt – 'Up there?' – and, having reversed a few yards, took the turn indicated.

'There should be,' Al said, peering at the piece of paper on which Stefan had written the instructions, 'a fork about a mile ahead, halfway up the hill. Then we make a right, go another couple of hundred yards, and – '

The headlights picked out vines and cypresses on either

side of the rutted track; and, though they would have crashed had they turned the lights out, Stefan wanted to tell Alan to do just that. They must be visible for miles around, he thought; as he wondered if even now Nora were sitting up in her castle watching them approach. Nora, dressed in a long black dress. Nora, with a crazed expression on her face. Nora, thirsting for blood . . .

It isn't a castle, he told himself; and Nora isn't a witch.

The fork in the track was – alas, Stefan was aware of them all thinking – exactly where Franca Cavallone's friend had said it would be. Alan slowed the car right down; without anyone saying anything he dipped the headlights; but, even so, after those prescribed two hundred yards . . .

They stopped. Marina's car was parked in a bamboo-roofed shed. Now Alan did turn out the lights completely, and quietly, as quietly as possible, they opened the doors and got out.

Would a dog bark somewhere?

No. In the distance, the far distance, one was howling. But, other than that, there was only the sound of crickets chirping in unseen trees; and the occasional croak of a frog, or a toad.

They stood still; as slowly their eyes grew accustomed to the dark. The trees were no longer quite unseen; and over there, at the top of what appeared to be a few steps leading up through a garden, a large house loomed over them. A large silent house, that seemed entirely still.

Was Nora watching for them? Was Nora waiting for them?

Al started, in a whisper, 'Well, I guess – '; but by then Stefan had already begun to pick his way across the gravel patch on which they had parked the car, towards the garden path.

Crunch, crunch went their footsteps as, with the others following him, Stefan thought: someone must hear us. In this silence, we must sound like an army approaching.

He negotiated a step with his foot; moved forward; and

found another. There was a wooden railing running by the side of the steps. He put his hand out, and couldn't help giving a small gasp as his fingers touched something wet, and slimy.

'Uggh,' he said. 'A slug.'

There was a sharp crunch from behind him; and Alan whispered, 'And I just trod on a snail.'

Seven steps, eight steps, nine steps; and then they were on a sort of patio, outside what looked like the main door.

Across the garden, there was the glimmer of a swimming pool.

The door would presumably be locked. What would they have to do? Break it down, if no one answered? What would they say if someone did answer? If, that is, Nora answered. Oh hi, Nora, surprise, surprise!

'Let's just go round the house, see – ' Stefan whispered; as Alan, beside him now, breathed, 'Stefan, what the *fuck* are we doing here?'

Now, having come this far, it was Al's turn to take charge. It was Al, at any rate, who led the way round the side of the house; and Al who suddenly held out a hand as they turned a corner and whispered, 'Look, there's a light on.'

A dim lamp, it appeared; shining, not very brightly, through the almost closed shutters and the open windows of a downstairs room.

'You wait here,' Al hissed. 'I'll go take a look. It's probably only a corridor or something, but maybe – '

He didn't believe that, Stefan knew. He expected to see a room in which – what? A body was lying? Nevertheless, he nodded; touched Al on the shoulder; and whispered, 'We'll wait here.'

It was like a horror film, he told himself as Al crept forwards; making, oh God, such an incredible noise. At any moment now a figure with a knife was going to leap out uttering banshee screams. At any moment Nora was going to come flying towards them, her nightdress dripping with blood. At any moment –

As Stefan stood there, he felt Alan grip his arm.

But this was not a horror film, and no one did leap out. Instead Al got to the lighted windows and peered through the shutters; then summoned the others with a wave that, if it didn't seem tragic, didn't, either, express relief. It was rather, Stefan felt as he walked forwards, a chill of apprehension in his stomach now, an unwilling, weary wave.

Stefan didn't know what Al had been expecting to see when he had first peered through the shutters. What he himself saw was a large under-furnished bedroom, with a shiny wooden curly-footed wardrobe, a mirror with an unvarnished frame, a large expanse of shiny blue tiles, a worn grubby-looking rug that seemed vaguely Navajo in origin, a chest-of-drawers with spindly legs, a bedside cabinet of a type one expected to see in an old-fashioned run-down boarding house, containing perhaps a bible and a chamber pot, an overhead light with a grey Japanese shade covering it, a wrought-iron bedside lamp whose thirty-watt bulb was responsible for the faded yellowish glow coming through the window, a double bed covered with a sheet that had been repaired several times, and indeed – and it was this that accounted for the nature of Al's wave – a body lying stretched out on that bed.

It was not however a dead body, though it was breathing with difficulty, was clutching a whisky bottle that had spilled and stained the sheets, and had, on the pillow by its head, a grey tube that looked as if it had once contained pills. Nor, which for Al and Stefan was more to the point, was it Marina's body.

'Oh shit,' Al said, as Alan, behind Stefan, hissed, 'Let me see,' pushed forward, stared, and gave a low whistle.

'My God,' he said, 'the witch has tried to kill herself.'

Had she? That was something Al, Stefan and Marina, at least, were never to be sure of. Certainly to begin with they assumed she had; and they acted accordingly. Stefan, standing outside, said first softly, then more loudly, 'Nora?

Nora?' There being no answer, Al then bellowed, his voice now raising a whole chorus of dogs, that brayed and barked across valley and hill, 'Marina!' And a few seconds later Marina called from somewhere inside, 'Al? Stefan?', peered out through a window, let them into the house looking as if she were still sleeping and thought she was dreaming, and led them, utterly confused, into Nora's room. Where they shook the Englishwoman, lifted her off the bed, dragged her to the bathroom, and, letting Alan at this stage take charge – 'Here, let me,' he sighed, handing Marina the camera he had brought from the car: 'I'm used to this sort of thing, my mother's constantly killing herself' – watched as the young photographer held Nora's head over the lavatory bowl, stuck his fingers into the back of her throat, and observed with a combination of satisfaction and distaste as she vomited. Then he held out his hand for a towel, which Al passed him, and, patting Nora on the back, flushing the lavatory, and letting go of her head so that her neck rested on the rim of the bowl, he said with such an air of world-weariness, 'There we go, up it comes, all over now,' that Stefan found himself grinning and Marina, in a state of shock at this extraordinary interruption of her sleep, started laughing so much she had to sit on the edge of the bath, tears running down her face.

Encouragement that only made Alan put on a still more languid and sophisticated show – 'I'd take a photograph,' he said, 'except it's been done *so* many times before, and besides, the light's all wrong' – which he spoiled at the end by being unable to conceal a grin of his own, and by being unable not to treat Nora with genuine feeling, however much he tried to conceal it. 'Come on,' he said, standing behind her, putting his hands under her arms, and hauling her to her feet. 'Let's get you back to bed. You can have a nice long sleep, and in the morning you won't remember a thing.' He gestured to Stefan and Al to help him, and between them they steered Nora back to her room, and stretched her out on her bed again.

'Shouldn't we change the sheets?' Stefan murmured, nodding at the whisky stain, brown and Africa-shaped by Nora's side.

'No,' Alan said. 'Otherwise she really might not remember anything in the morning. You know what she's like. "Oh good morning, boys, how nice to see you here." In fact, just to be on the safe side, I *may* take a photograph. You must admit, this room does have a certain authentic squalor, doesn't it? I mean maybe they'll publish an Italian edition of *Hollywood Babylon* one day, and there'll be a chapter on the English ex-actress who came to grief in Tuscany. And there'll be old Nora, all laid out.'

'You sure she'll be all right?' Al murmured, not sure whether Alan was joking, and nervous in case he wasn't.

'Oh, of course she will.'

'And if we hadn't come?'

'She'd have been all right anyway.'

'How d'you know?'

'Oh, you can tell. From her colour. From her breathing. I guess Marina was meant to find her in the morning. I mean she'd have been sick, sure, and groggy for a day or two. She probably will be anyway. But – naaa – it was just a poor-me gesture.' He shrugged. 'Oh, I guess if she had a weak heart or anything, or if Marina hadn't bothered to come in in the morning and had just gone back to Rome without her – sure. But those are the risks of the game, aren't they? Nothing ventured, nothing gained.'

'Poor Nora,' Marina, who had come into the room behind them, and was quite awake and quite serious now, whispered. Then with a glance at Stefan she rested her head on Al's shoulder as he put his arm around her, and murmured, 'How did you all come? I mean why – I'm so glad you did.'

'We called, and there was no reply.'

'I heard the phone ringing and ringing. I thought it might be you. Then I thought you didn't have the number, and –'

'I called your parents. Why didn't you answer?'

'It's not my house. It's not my phone. And I thought if Nora doesn't want to – I suppose by then she'd already knocked herself out.'

'Did you phone from here when you called?'

'No. I didn't want to. I thought Nora might be listening. Or she might not – I don't know – *let* me. Silly, I know, but – I felt safer calling from the restaurant.'

'Thank God you did.'

'Yes,' Marina whispered, putting both her arms around Al now. 'I was frightened.'

'Thank God you left the number with your parents, too.'

'Yes, I suppose in the back of my mind – but I was too ashamed to leave it with you. To tell you – ' she smiled sheepishly, and lowered her eyes.

'And now?' Alan said.

'I guess we should all go to bed,' Al said. 'I know we weren't invited, but – '

'You're sure she'll be all right?' Marina asked, looking at her hostess. 'You don't think we should call a doctor?'

'Oh no,' Alan said. 'For God's sake. No one would come, for a start, and for another – I mean Jesus, in the old days they used to burn witches. She should be thankful we're so nice.'

'Poor Nora,' Marina repeated. 'And I was thinking – I suppose she must have been depressed. I suppose she is depressed.'

If, however, despite Alan's smooth dismissal, they went to bed that night – at four o'clock – still thinking that Nora had tried to kill herself, and woke around ten with their minds unchanged, by five o'clock on that Sunday afternoon they had begun to have their doubts. Not, even now, because of Alan's insistence that there had been no real danger – 'She might have *thought* she was killing herself,' Marina murmured – but because Nora herself told them she hadn't.

They had let her sleep undisturbed all day, just occasionally peering round her door to make sure she was all right;

when at four o'clock Marina went in to wake her, and see if she was feeling fit enough to return to Rome, Nora greeted her as if she wasn't sure what she was talking about.

'I *told* you we did right not to change the sheets,' Alan said, quite loudly, to Stefan and Al, as they stood in the corridor listening to the scene. 'She *would* have pretended not to remember anything.'

She couldn't quite pull it off, obviously; apart from the spilled whisky, and the empty tube of pills – and despite the fact that she had plainly been awake for a little while when Marina went in, and had changed her shirt, and combed her hair, and was doing her best to appear as plain and simple as ever – she didn't look well: her normally white face grey, her normally periwinkle blue eyes dull, and faded.

'Oh, how good of them,' she said when Marina told her that she had heard the phone ringing last night, had been surprised when Nora hadn't answered, had got up to see if she was all right, had seen her lying on her bed with the whisky bottle, hadn't been sure if – 'well, you know, if you were all right,' – and had thought she had better call 'the boys', and ask them to come up. 'How good of *you*, Marina. But they really shouldn't have bothered. I mean I'm terribly sorry about this' – she was presumably indicating the bottle and the empty tube – 'but really – it was very stupid of me. I was feeling a bit edgy, and I found those pills in the bathroom and I remembered one of Franca's friends a couple of weeks ago showing me them and telling me how good they were just to help you relax. So I decided to take one. But I wasn't sure if the water here is all right to drink, so I – as I say, it was terribly stupid of me. I knocked it back with some scotch. But that didn't seem to work, and – I'm not sure. I suppose I must have taken another one or two. And on top of everything we drank at dinner . . . I don't really remember. Are the boys still here?'

'Yes, of course,' Marina said; before, slightly too hurriedly, calling, 'Stefan, Al, Alan.'

They trooped in, the three of them, and smiled at Nora, stretched out on her bed.

'Hi, Nora,' they all said; though Alan, naturally, couldn't resist adding, 'How's the throat?'

'The throat?' Nora asked, as if she couldn't imagine what in the world he was talking about.

Perhaps she couldn't, Stefan thought.

'It's not sore?' Alan ground mercilessly on. 'You know sometimes after you throw up like that – '

'Oh, I didn't!' Nora said, in mock or genuine horror.

'You sure did,' Alan said. 'Don't you remember? Well, better that way.'

'Not in here?' Nora asked, gazing round wide-eyed as if she expected to see a pool of vomit she had till now overlooked.

'No, don't worry,' Alan smiled. 'I put your head down the toilet.'

'Oh, how embarrassing,' Nora said, her discomfiture at this point looking quite genuine. 'Oh, I'm so sorry, Alan. All of you. And really there was no need – but it was so good of you. Oh, really, I feel so ashamed – '

'Yes, well it's all over now,' Alan continued. 'You feeling okay?'

'Yes. I mean I feel a bit groggy. But – oh dear, really – I don't know what to say. I mean I'm just not the type to – '

'It's all right, Nora,' Stefan said, hoping to shut Alan up. 'It happens to all of us.'

'No, I know, but – ' she put a hand to her head. 'Really. I'd hate you to think – I mean honestly. I – '

'It's okay,' Al chimed in. 'Really.'

'But I didn't, honestly – I mean it was a mistake. I swear. I'd hate anyone to think – '

'It's all *right*,' Marina said. 'Truly, Nora. We won't tell anyone.'

'And if you're really good I won't even show the photograph I took of you to anyone,' Alan smiled.

'Oh, you *didn't*, Alan!'

'I sure did.'

'Oh, I – '

'It's okay,' Stefan said. 'He's only joking. Now – do you want to stay here, and rest, or are you feeling well enough to come with us? If you want to stay here we could come back in a couple of days and pick you up. Or maybe your friend – '

'Oh no,' Nora said, already starting to swing her legs off the bed, and get, cautiously, to her feet. 'Really. Of course I'll come back. I mean tomorrow – I've got to be there. Tomorrow's the start of the big scene, isn't it? And I know Judy doesn't like me, but if I'm not there – '

'I'm sure they could find someone else,' Stefan said, kindly.

'Oh no, really,' Nora said. 'Honestly, I'm so grateful to you all. But if you could all just give me a hand in changing these sheets – if we could just put them in the kitchen. There's a woman who comes in from the village to clean and take care of the washing.'

'It's okay,' Marina said. 'You keep still, Nora. We'll do it.'

'Oh thank you, Marina. Really I can't thank you enough. But – you didn't really take a photograph, did you, Alan?'

'I'll let you know at the end of the movie,' Alan grinned. 'At the wrap party. If you're good – I'll give you the negative. But if you're bad . . . '

'Oh stop it, Alan, please. *Tell* me.'

'Like hell I'll tell her,' Alan said an hour later, as he and Stefan and Al drove behind Marina's car, heading for the highway to Siena, and Rome. 'Keep her on her toes.'

'I don't know what to think,' Al murmured, more to himself than anyone else, gazing at the car ahead and clearly wishing he were in it. But Marina had insisted that she and Nora drive back alone together. 'Poor thing,' she had whispered. 'She feels humiliated enough. You go back with Stefan and Alan.'

'Well, I do,' Alan said. 'I've been telling you all along.' He paused, waiting for some comment from the back seat. When none came, he asked, 'What you think, Stef?'

'I'm like Al,' Stefan said, wishing that he didn't have to speak. He wanted to be quiet for a while. 'I don't know what to think. Last night I would have said yes, she did intend to do – something. Even if she didn't do it right. But today – I don't know. She put on a good performance, didn't she? If she did mean to kill herself.'

'She's always claimed she's a great actress,' Alan turned his head again briefly. 'But I swear to you, Stefan, she did not do it. For God's sake, why should she kill herself?'

'I should have thought she had a hundred reasons,' Al murmured.

'We've all got a hundred reasons.'

'Have we? I haven't,' Al said. 'I'm very happy.'

'And you, Stef?'

'Yes,' Stefan said. 'I think I'm happy.'

'Oh shit,' Alan said. 'Well, in that case I guess I am too. But even so, I don't see why – '

'If she did do it on purpose,' Marina said over dinner that night, back in the safety of her apartment, 'she did it for the sake of the film.'

'Oh Marina, please,' Alan said. 'We might not like her, and she might be a pest. She might be a danger. Even so – '

'I'm serious,' Marina smiled. 'I – ' she bowed her head over the candlelit table for a second. 'Do you know the real reason I called last night? This is ridiculous, and I'm ashamed of myself for saying it, but – I was afraid Nora was going to kill me. When we were having dinner together – and before – I could feel great waves of hatred emanating from her. I don't think she was really aware of them herself. And – oh, I don't know. It sounds absurd now. But last night – at the time – ' she looked up, straight at Stefan, as if he alone would be able to understand, 'and I wasn't really wrong. Only when it came to it, she either couldn't do it, or – I imagined that those waves of hatred were directed at me. Perhaps they were really directed at – '

'Herself,' Alan completed the sentence. 'Oh please, Marina, stop it. Really. And anyway, even if she did want to kill you, or herself, or anyone – I don't see what that's got to do with the film.'

'I think she was trying to make it good,' Marina said softly, reaching out to take Al's hand on her left, and Stefan's on her right. 'I think it was supposed to be a sort of sacrifice for – oh, I don't know.' She stopped, glanced at her lover, and at the man she loved, and then went on, to Alan: 'To art. Life. Civilization. Something like that.'

'Oh Marina,' Alan said a third time. '*Please*.'

After a little while he added, seeing that no one else seemed to find Marina's remarks strange, or ridiculous: 'And now that she's goofed it what's going to happen? The movie's going to be no good?'

'I don't know,' Marina smiled. 'But I suppose it's possible.'

CHAPTER 13

ANYTHING was possible. Perhaps Kostas's vision, that had so unexpectedly seemed to clear, had all at once clouded over again, and become obscured. Perhaps the continuing indecision over what ending to use had infected the spirit of the cast and crew – of the film itself – and that coming together that had been so apparent in the days following Sergio's fall became, in the week and weeks following Nora's failed or staged suicide attempt, a drifting apart again; a drifting apart that nothing now could check. Or perhaps it was simply that with the exception of Michael Toscanini, whom everyone ended up admiring, if grudgingly, for his seriousness, the principal actors were not, when it most mattered, up to their tasks: Jimmy proving incapable of playing a character that was too much like himself, and Judy of playing a character that was too dissimilar. Whatever the reason, way before the film was finished it became clear to one and all that *The Storyteller* was not destined to go down in history as one of the great movies. It would be, as long as the editor did a good job, all right: be deemed interesting, worthy of note, an honourable failure. But it would never really split the ice, as Alan Miller put it to Stefan; it would never really ring some bell in the public mind that would make everyone sit up and listen.

It wasn't a tragedy, it wasn't a matter for mourning. It was just one of those things. Every film is a gamble, however carefully it is prepared; this was one that didn't come off. 'Oh well, it's only a movie, and maybe next time –

in any case, we've had fun, haven't we? I mean it wasn't an absolute turkey. And I bet if Kostas sticks to adventure films, or makes something where he doesn't get involved in intellectual arguments with his star, sooner or later he'll have a big hit.' (He did; with his very next film.)

Nevertheless, for all this philosophical attitude taken by the majority of people working on *The Storyteller*, and for all that the blame was variously apportioned to Judy and Jimmy, to Kostas, and to the writer for not having decided right at the start how his story should end, for Stefan, Al and Marina – and, they were almost certain, for Nora – there was only one real reason for the ultimate failure of the film. Nora, the witch, in the end had lost her nerve. She hadn't dared cast her spell – bring down her curse – entirely. She had renounced her power, her talent, her magic. With the result that she had condemned the film – her film – to being merely interesting; and had condemned herself to spending the rest of her days within the confines of a ground floor flat in a mansion block just off Kensington High Street.

'I bet if she had killed me it would have gone better,' Marina said with a smile one night in the last week of shooting, as she and the boys were having dinner together.

'Or if she had killed herself,' Stefan murmured.

Although they all agreed that at least as far as Marina was concerned – 'Oh, and what the hell, as far as Nora is, too' – they were sort of glad the film hadn't turned out to be a great success.

As they agreed that when you came down to it Nora's sentence wasn't so awful, and that indeed her failure of nerve had occurred years ago, and all that had happened this summer was that she had come to terms with it.

'Poor Nora,' they told one another – off the set. 'Poor Nora.'

They told each other this off the set in case, in those last days of filming, Nora should still be listening to them. But in fact Stefan suspected that since her weekend in the country Nora listened to nothing except what Nora had to listen to – Judy's lines. She knew when she was beaten; and she no longer had to keep herself fit on a diet of humiliation. Her small room at the back of the set was demolished, as the church gave way to Michael's New York apartment and other places. In a sense though it was empty before it was pulled down. There was a space now behind the flaps or wherever it was that Nora chose to set herself up in business; and where formerly there had been a queen bee, or a monstrous spider who studied the death throes of her victims, now there was only a white-haired Englishwoman.

Judy and the others didn't know about Nora's 'suicide'; amazingly, even Alan Miller was reasonably discreet about that. At least until the final day and the wrap party; when he went round telling everyone. All the same, both she and the rest of the crew seemed to sense the passing of some malignancy, the ending of some fearful reign; and while, there again, it might just have been because everyone had become bored with sniping at Nora – or in Judy's case Jimmy might have had further words on the subject – Stefan couldn't help feeling that that wasn't the explanation, and the reason for this, too, had to be sought in that blue-tiled room in that ugly damp house on the wrong side of a hill in Tuscany. It was, for everyone, as if Nora had been erased; and just as when Stefan passed on to Judy some comment about a word or a vowel she had mispronounced she acted as if the advice were coming directly from him, so when people mentioned Sergio, who was making good prgress in hospital, it no longer seemed to occur to them to think of let alone mention Nora in relation to his accident.

Yet, despite his obvious relief that Nora had failed, and despite, in retrospect, Marina's having run a terrible risk in going away for the weekend with the woman, with part of himself Stefan was glad that Nora had at least tried to cast her spell in the way she had; or that she had done whatever she had done. For, although Nora wasn't certain whether Alan had taken a photograph of her lying unconscious on her bed, she did know that Stefan now had a certain hold over her, as she had formerly had a certain hold over him. And as long as he forbore to spread the word that she had tried to kill herself, she would forbear to tell Al that it wasn't really for him that Marina was contemplating leaving Italy, at least for a while, and moving to the States. Of course, had Alan not been as discreet as he was, Nora might well have decided that one final curse was in order. But perhaps even Alan, for all his scepticism, realized that a wounded witch, an unwanded witch, might be dangerous – though he might not have been able to guess in what way – and that was why he did hold his tongue.

By the final day and the wrap party he had probably decided he didn't care if there was one last dose of poison in Nora's cup.

But by then Nora was definitively unplugged, cut off; so she didn't hear what he was saying.

She attended the party like a distant relative whom everyone has almost forgotten; the elderly aunt who helps with the drinks, with whom one can exchange a few words if one finds oneself face to face with her, but to whom one doesn't have to say goodbye before one leaves.

A pale, smiling presence, she hovered on the fringes of the set not so much trumpeting her non-existence, as she had when she had first arrived, as silently assenting to it. Though even she didn't seem to think this final defeat of hers was any great tragedy; and displayed a grace in her fall she had rarely if ever displayed when in the ascendant.

To Al she said: 'Well, Al, what are your plans?'

'We're going down to Sicily for a couple of weeks, Nora. And then we're all going back to the States.'

To Marina she said: 'So you've decided then, have you?'

'Yes,' Marina smiled; looking, Stefan thought, more radiant, more beautiful than he had ever seen her. 'I'll see how it goes there. See whether I'm happy and whether I can get work. If not – ' she glanced at Al, 'I suppose I'll drag them all back here.'

'Will you be able to work over in the States?' Nora asked earnestly. 'You know, work permits and all that?'

'Yes, if I'm married I suppose I can.'

'You're getting married?'

For a moment Stefan felt apprehensive; but he need not have worried. Marina's glow was such today she could have softened Nora at her stoniest.

'Not only,' Marina said. 'I'm expecting a baby.'

'Good heavens,' Nora said. 'Congratulations.'

She turned at last to Stefan. 'And you, Stefan? What are *you* going to do?'

'We're all going to Sicily together,' Stefan told her. 'All three of us. And then, as Marina said – it's back to the States. We're starting another movie at the end of September.'

'My – our – eventual aim – I mean I don't know whether it's an aim, or a dream,' Al said, 'is to buy some land somewhere – somewhere in Tuscany probably, and grow grapes, make wine, make olive oil – raise chickens and goats – and children. I mean I don't know if it'll ever happen, but – '

Stefan noted that Nora did not ask who Al meant by 'our'.

'Well, I hope you'll all be very happy,' Nora said.

'You're going back to London?'

'Yes, tomorrow. Thank God. I must say – ' she looked around. 'I feel I should say something to Judy. But on the other hand – '

'I wouldn't bother, if I were you,' Al said.

'No. Maybe you're right. I would like to have a word with Kostas and Jimmy though. But perhaps I'll just slip away and – anyway, it's been very nice meeting you all, and, as I say, I do hope you'll all be very happy.'

'And you too,' said Al.

'Goodbye, my dear,' Nora said to Marina, leaning

forward and kissing her on the cheek. 'And God bless you.'

'Thank you,' Marina whispered.

'Goodbye, Al,' Nora said, and leaned forward to kiss him, too. 'You take care of Marina now. She's a very nice girl.'

'I will,' Al said, smiling, just slightly sadly maybe, at his future wife. 'Don't worry.'

To Stefan, however, Nora only gave her hand. 'And you, Stefan,' she said, looking him in the eye. 'My go-between. My sound man. You take care of yourself. And look after these two for me. You're the strongest and the oldest. It's up to you – '

She didn't finish; but she had, Stefan felt, said enough.

He watched her go, as he stood between Marina and Al, with one hand on Al's shoulder, and the other round Marina's waist.

'Oh well,' he said. 'I suppose in the end she wasn't so bad.'

Then he turned, as if to face the future; and to begin, though he might not ever get there, the long, slow drift home.